"I have asked for her hand in marriage..."

Mr. Harding raised his eyebrows. "Whose hand, your lordship?"

"Miss Adele Fairfax," Lord Ault answered. "She doesn't know it yet, but I spoke to Lady Fairfax about the matter...and now, Harding, I sincerely wish I had done no such thing!"

Mr. Harding frowned. "But why sir? She is so beautiful – "

"That's not the problem!" Lord Ault snapped. "You see, I won't be marrying just Miss Fairfax; I will be acquiring the entire lot of them – Miss Milsap, Lady Fairfax..."

His voice grew more bleak as he hoarsely ground out the last name "...and Miss Clairice! Damme! I would give anything to be able to retract that offer!"

THE FAIRFAX BREW

SARA ORWIG

Harlequin Books

TORONTO • NEW YORK • LONDON
AMSTERDAM • PARIS • SYDNEY • HAMBURG
STOCKHOLM • ATHENS • TOKYO • MILAN

Published July 1983
ISBN 0-373-31002-1

CHAPTER ONE

WATER SPLASHED on carriages; their black tops shimmered with wetness while their wheels splattered through puddles along the cobbles. High above the street the Prince of Wales gazed out the window at the incessant rain. "Confounded weather! Spoils everything!"

Behind an oak writing desk his companion raised a gloomy countenance. "Yes, Your Royal Highness," he answered abstractedly, idly scratching his thin cheek. "I am concerned with this matter still."

"Confound it! You are as nagging as the weather, Barthwell! I discussed this with Lord Ault only hours ago, and I know what I am doing. I am cognizant of the dangers involved, and heaven knows I desire the utmost secrecy and have given deep consideration to the most likely man to perform this delicate errand."

The prince shifted and leaned forward, his attention riveted on something outside. He continued, "Lord Ault is a credit to the kingdom. He has served his regiment with distinction and can be trusted implicitly. His friends are a superior sort, and I am aware of and approve his growing interest in the Fairfax family. You know he has Addington's approval."

He turned from the window and cast a disdainful eye on the elderly statesman seated across the room.

Sir Barthwell moved the portfolio lying open on the desk. A frown creased his brow; his long thin fingers riffled papers. He spoke in a high-pitched rasp. "We must be certain of Ault. We have already been dealt a treacherous blow in this matter by a traitor." He rubbed his chin thoughtfully and continued, "While I have not met his aide, Mr. Harding, the man's record is impeccable. Mr. Crenshawe concurs fully with me on this; we have no doubts whatsoever about Harding."

The prince's rotund shape was silhouetted against the gray window. "To be certain," he snapped testily, "since Harding is your selection. You are too worrisome, Barthwell!"

A peal of thunder rumbled, then died away as Sir Barthwell replied, "Perhaps. But it is imperative that the French do not discover what we are undertaking. It has been a little more than a year since Addington's agents signed the Amiens peace agreement with Napoleon, yet every second we grow more insecure. Britain teeters on the brink of a renewal of war with France, and this mission must be expedited in haste and achieved with ultimate success."

The prince rocked on his heels and raised his eyebrows. "Have no fear, Sir Barthwell. I give you my solemn promise that the man I have chosen is a paragon of secrecy and capability. Without question I would trust him with my own life. He is a confidant of both Pitt and Addington. I am certain that under torture he could not be coerced into revealing the merest hint of our project."

He faced the minister squarely and sternly. "End all of your qualms immediately, sir! The man drinks only in moderation, he does not gamble excessively, he is not a womanizer, he is inordinately intelligent—in short, he is a paragon of virtue and dependability and a nonpareil at holding his tongue!"

THE PARAGON, unaware of such commendable praise, was on a mission of his own personal interest. His broad shoulders rested comfortably in a wing chair in a pleasant drawing room. He stretched long legs before the fire, gazed with alert gray eyes at the white-haired woman across from him, and waited patiently while a servant placed a large silver tray bearing an ornate tea service on a low table between them.

Lady Fairfax reached forward to pour from an oversize teapot, then extended a large china cup and saucer to Lord Ault, which he accepted politely.

While the rain drummed against the panes, Lady Fairfax poured herself a cup of the steaming brew, sat back and placed slippered feet on the table beside the sterling tea service.

Any man less able to hide his emotions might have viewed the lady's feet beside the silver tray with slight apprehension, but Lord Ault was far above such uncontrolled slips. The feet received the merest flicker of a glance from his pale eyes.

"Well, Lord Ault, what's this about?"

He replied calmly, "I wish to discuss some matters of a private nature with you." He raised the cup of tea politely, drank, then blinked.

He leaned forward to place the saucer on a side table and coughed discreetly behind his hand. With open curiosity he gazed down at the brown liquid contained within the white china cup.

"Isn't the tea good?" Lady Fairfax inquired.

He swallowed and lifted the cup and saucer, once again leaning against the chair cushions while the fiery liquid burned his throat. His voice was quizzical and a fraction higher-pitched than before. "Quite a different flavor, ma'am. Is this a new type of tea?"

"My own brew. It's good for the blood," she replied enigmatically, then settled in the chair and sipped.

With a leisurely movement he placed his feet closer to the cozy fire and eyed the room appreciatively. Hand-tooled books, many with favorite titles, lined the walls; the furniture was comfortable and inviting, yet it was a mute testimony to the wealth of the woman clad in emerald silk who faced him.

His gaze met hers, and he saw clearly that her dark eyes were alive with curiosity. Lord Ault chanced another sip and this time blinked only twice. He coughed slightly, took a breath and spoke in low tones.

"Ma'am, I have come to offer for one of your granddaughters, namely, Adele."

"Good enough! Glad to get the girl off my hands. She needs a steady hand and you are well suited. Clairice is too young perhaps—"

He relaxed slightly and sipped once more. She inquired, "When will it be announced?"

His eyes darkened and he lowered the saucer. "That is precisely what I desire to discuss with you. My present course does not allow me to relate this to Adele."

"Going to have a difficult time without notifying her of the event!" she interrupted.

Lord Ault's jaw tightened. He spoke patiently. "I fully intend to inform her—later. This is highly secretive, which is why I preferred to speak with you alone."

"I can understand that." She moved a black cane beside her knee, poured more tea and offered him replenishment.

He declined politely and she squinted at him. "Nonsense! A big man like you cannot be fortified on such a cold day by one cup of tea. Hold that cup down here, please!"

Lord Ault was unaccustomed to arguing with his hostess. He lowered the tea cup and watched warily as she refilled it. She straightened. "I like to see a man enjoy his tea. Drink it down, my lord. Now, as you were saying, you have a worthy matter to discuss."

"Yes," he replied, "the cause for my delay in asking Adele for her hand in marriage." He lapsed into silence, unaware of a distant rumble of thunder. The orange flames flickered and danced in the grate, taking the chill off the dismal afternoon. Lord Ault's feet were warming at the hearth with almost the same speed as his fortified insides.

Both sat in an easy silence while the fire crackled. Lord Ault sipped his tea, then spoke. "I cannot go into details, but I have to leave London for a brief time. It is an errand for someone in government. I can neither reveal the nature of it nor disclose who is sending me. For that matter, I trust you will not divulge to any person what I am telling you. I have already stepped beyond my word of honor not to convey a hint of this to anyone.''

She nodded and gulped down her tea to pour herself another cup. She waved the teapot at him ''Place that cup on the table.''

He observed with mild surprise that he had consumed the second cup of the peculiar brew. He leaned forward and extended the cup while his mind rested on his dilemma. ''I will ask Adele immediately upon my return, but due to the, ah, nature of this mission I feel I must not do so until I have completed it. The less attention I draw to my absence from London, the more chances of success I shall have.''

She nodded sagely. ''Sounds dangerous to me. Must be going to France.''

It was not to Lord Ault's discredit that he flushed at her shrewd analysis, for seldom in his experience had anyone guessed with such casual ease what had been barely touched upon. He drank deeply of the tea.

Lady Fairfax sat up and poured another portion for herself, and without thought he extended his for a refill. ''Delicious brew,'' he murmured. ''Must have the recipe.''

Her eyes sparkled. ''I have never imparted it to another living soul, but for you, Lord Ault, I might relent and do so.''

''Obliged to you, ma'am.'' He settled in the chair and regarded her fondly. She tugged the bellpull. In a moment a servant appeared and was instructed to fetch more hot tea.

Outside, the rain continued to fall in a steady patter while inside the glowing coals warmed the room. They waited until the ornate teapot was replaced on the silver tray. Finally Lady Fairfax broke the silence. "Adele is a good girl; she will make you an excellent wife." She paused, then inquired, "How dangerous is this French venture?"

He waved a hand. "Merely tolerable. It shall not take long—I expect about three weeks—then I shall return and ask Adele for her hand."

"Hope you ask for the rest of her, too!" Lady Fairfax snapped and chortled at her own wit. Lord Ault smiled affably.

"Time for more tea. Here...." She refilled his cup and her own, then sat back and propped up her feet. He shifted his legs and she waved her hand. "There's room. Place your feet up on the other side of the tray. Unbelievably comfortable."

Lord Ault eyed her and yielded to temptation, settling his feet comfortably on the other side of the silver service. "Best tea I ever tasted," he said, continuing to sip it contentedly.

She narrowed her eyes and cocked her head. "So you are trying to slip past Boney on some dark mission. Will you have any aid in this endeavor?"

To his amazement, his answer came forth without hesitation, as if he had lost all control of his own speech. "Yes," he replied, "a splendid fellow, absolutely splendid!"

"Good! Would hate to see you on this venture without assistance." She grasped the ebony cane, moving it against her knee.

He waved his hand as if compelled to reassure her fully. "This chap has fought the French and has been decorated for heroism. Magnificent record for one so young... I would trust him with my life."

"Londoner?" she asked.

Lord Ault gazed at her, bemused, then answered, "Indeed. He has a country estate also. Marding Hister, er, Mr. Harding, I mean." He straightened in embarrassment. "Don't know what ails me, ma'am." He squinted at her. "What is in this tea?"

She shook her finger at him and scolded, "I shall divulge it in due time. Do not rush me, Lord Ault. It is not easy to part with a secret one has guarded zealously for over twenty years. Here, have another cup."

He shook his head, suffering a slight difficulty in focusing his eyes. "No, ma'am. Mustn't do so, I'm sure!"

"Nonsense! Not like you to be rude. Here!" She leaned forward and filled his cup. He blinked at it, then decided that as long as it was there he might as well drink it.

"What are you proposing to do in France?"

"Can't tell a soul," he mumbled, "not a soul."

"I do not count since I am almost your relative. That is a different kettle of fish, so to speak. I need to know if I am giving my granddaughter to a man about to be thrown into a French prison."

"Have no intention of such, I can assure you! No, indeed. No French prison for me!"

"What are you up to, going to France on a quick trip like that?" She scratched her head violently, stirring the mass of white curls into greater disarray.

"Ma'am, highly secret! Highly. Prinny himself is sending me."

"Do tell!"

"Yes, ma'am." He nodded solemnly. "Prinny. His minister, Sir Barthwell, may go part of the way, and Mr. Harding will accompany me for the entire mission."

She leaned forward and refilled both cups. Lord Ault drank his and set the cup down forcefully. "Thank you, ma'am. I think I have consumed suf'shent tea for one afternoon. Perhaps for one lifetime." He squinted at her and grinned, which gave him a much younger appearance. "Lady Fairfax, I suspect I am thoroughly bosky on your tea!"

She chortled. "Takes the kinks out of one, it does. Nothing finer for a rainy afternoon."

He smiled. "Damme, if I haven't let you get me foxed! Could lose my job and my reputation over this!"

"Come, come, Lord Ault. No one shall ever know, and I can keep a secret, I assure you. I need to know—you still have not informed me—what do you intend to do when you get to France?"

His grin widened. "Steal Bonaparte's invasion plans!"

CHAPTER TWO

LADY FAIRFAX'S POINTED CHIN dropped. She snapped shut her jaw, recovering quickly. She lifted the teapot to pour herself more tea and refilled Lord Ault's in spite of his mild protest.

"You actually think he plans to invade Britain?"

Lord Ault nodded solemnly.

"But we have the peace treaty. It has been a year since Amiens."

"'Deed. A year he has used to his 'vantage—gathering troops, men and materials into arsenals at Calais, Dunkirk, Boulogne, and building vessels to cross the Channel."

Her eyes narrowed. "You sound rather certain."

"'Tis certain," he replied soberly. "An Englishman, Henry Tayburn, spy for Addington, secured copy of plans. He was on way home to England—murdered—"

"How dreadful!"

He gazed at her mournfully. "God's truth! Murdered before he reached ship—plans dis'peared." He waved his teacup at her to emphasize his theory. "Spy in our midst, too, you know!"

"But if the plans disappeared, how can you steal them?"

"Lady Fairfax—" Lord Ault closed his eyes and swayed slightly in the chair "—the French minister of war has the plans. We have many spies, just as they do. They have someone high in office here." He opened his eyes and regarded her. "But we know with certainty that the plans are there."

"My lord—" she fixed him with a steady eye "—I hate to see you undertake such an endeavor."

Lord Ault crossed his ankles on the table; his white teeth flashed in a broad smile. "Ma'am, won't be so bad. Have the best help in the world. Mr. Harding is abs'lutely top branch. 'Cellent marksman, peerless whip, superior soldier. Couldn't do better, ma'am. Have all faith in him." He gazed at her over the teacup, amused at the turn of events, and raised the cup to her in salute.

"P'mit me to give you a toast, Lady Fairfax. You've 'complished what innumerable gentlemen have failed to do—here's to you and your tea!"

He gulped down the remains of the cup while she took a sip of hers. A flurry of raindrops spattered against the glass, driven by a rising wind. The noise went unheeded by the room's occupants.

She studied him speculatively. "Lord Ault, how soon do you leave for France?"

He laughed. "With all due respect, Lady Fairfax, do you recall that sometime this afternoon I informed you this was mission of abs'lute secrecy?"

"Bosh! Too late now! It shall never go beyond the two of us. Now answer my question."

He grinned with a set smile that was unusual in a man who spent most of his waking moments concerned with matters sufficiently weighty to cause a sober regard of life. "Dear lady, I depart at one o'clock tomorrow afternoon, to be precise. I shall be joined at Chatham by Mr. Harding. What other 'formashun would you care to hear 'bout my confidential errand?"

"Marvelous!" she replied firmly. "We had planned on leaving for Fairfax Hall within the week. If we go tomorrow we can have your escort to the coast. Would that be satisfactory?"

He nodded ponderously and blinked at her as if having difficulty focusing his eyes. "'Deed it would. Be delightful to have dear Adele along on the journey.

No harm—would give me a good cover—excellent...."
He gazed into space, bemused. "Adele, so quiet. Would
make a man a good wife...no trouble...good family...."

"You have not known Adele long, my lord." Lady
Fairfax looked at him intently. "You are not in love
with her?"

"Love?" He gazed at her. "Never expected to marry
for love, Lady Fairfax."

A gentle rap sounded and the dark oak door opened.
Miss Lavinia Milsap faced them. "Good afternoon,
Lord Ault, Aunt Cornelia." Behind rimless spectacles
she raised a dark eyebrow. "Tea?" she questioned
speculatively.

Lord Ault gazed at the figure dressed in black silk
from her scrawny neck to her long, narrow feet. He was
fully aware a lady had entered the room, but he was
having difficulty getting his legs to respond to the news
imparted by his brain.

Finally he succeeded in swaying to his feet from the
depths of the chair. Fortunately his blurred vision did
not see clearly the expression of horror on Miss
Lavinia's face as her eyes fastened on him.

"Lord Ault!" she exclaimed in tones of pure shock.

He could not banish his damnable grin, much as he
desired to. He bowed slightly. "Ma'am, I hope you will
forgive me, but Lady Fairfax—"

He was not given an opportunity to finish. Miss
Lavinia whirled and closed the door with a decided
click.

Lord Ault swayed and regarded Lady Fairfax.
"Ma'am, now I've done it. There goes a future rela-
tive." He blinked at the words and muttered sadly,
"Shame...shameful...."

"Bosh!" uttered the eldest member of the family.
"Sit down, Lord Ault. Lavinia will survive."

The door flew open unceremoniously and another
person burst upon the scene.

Clairice Fairfax entered in a flurry of white organdy. Her cheeks were pink with a healthy glow, a mass of red curls bounced with each step, and her wide green eyes took in the situation at a glance.

Lord Ault did not have to struggle to his feet because he was already on them. Wisely he kept his mouth shut and merely bowed in greeting.

Clairice halted and exclaimed, "Good heavens, grandmother, have you been serving Lord Ault your tea?"

Grandmother observed Clairice and snapped, "Child, either come in and close that dratted door or be on your way. Do not stand there staring, it isn't polite."

Clairice laughed and closed the door, then crossed to Lady Fairfax to kiss her cheek. Her eyes danced with mischief as she raised her head and viewed Lord Ault. "Pray be seated, my lord."

He swayed and smiled. "Miss Fairfax, I am fearful to move in any direction. I collect I may be on the verge of passing out before your very eyes. You shall have to forgive me, but your grandmother—"

"The tea!" Clairice bubbled mirthfully. "Sir, you are a victim of my grandmother's wicked wiles." She glanced at the culprit.

"Gammon! Enough of this business about my brew! Sit down, Lord Ault, before you fall into the tea service."

"Ma'am, I think I shall 'tempt to get to my carriage. With all due respect, I shall never again partake of your tea."

She squinted at him. "Thought you wanted the recipe!" she snapped.

He nodded. "Could be that I did. All I desire at the moment is to get into my own carriage, but I do not perceive 'xactly how I shall accomplish such a feat."

A giggle sounded and he turned to regard Clairice. She faced him solemnly except for her dancing green eyes. With an easy grace she rose from the divan and crossed to take his arm. "Come, Lord Ault, I shall rescue you from grandmother. After this you should be on your guard."

"Upstart!" Lady Fairfax exclaimed, but there was no bite to the word.

Clairice led Lord Ault into the coolness of the hall. He stumbled and caught himself, throwing his weight fully on her for a moment. "Oops—dreadful! Please forgive me."

She laughed. "Do not apologize. We should have warned you about grandmother's tea, but she rarely shares it with anyone. Usually she will not let a soul touch it. It is raining in torrents, Lord Ault. Do you have a cape?"

He nodded. "Perhaps I should forget the cape. Just fetch my coachman; he will take charge."

"Nonsense! Come into the front parlor. I shall fetch your cape and assist you into it before we summon the coachman."

She opened double doors into a drafty room furnished with a degree of elegance that belied so cozy a description as front parlor. She led him to a silk sofa and helped him down. "Now, wait here and I shall return in an instant."

She was gone in a flurry. Lord Ault closed his eyes, then opened them, deciding it was easier to view a blurry world than suffer whirling blackness.

Clairice returned within minutes. She draped the multilayered garment around his broad shoulders. He stared up at her and took her hand. "I am rooted to this couch, I cannot get up. Get my coachman...."

"Here, let me help you."

"What does your grandmother put...in the tea?"

Clairice laughed. "When you are sober I shall reveal it to you. It is a deep secret, but you deserve to know." She gazed down at him. "You are remarkably strong, Lord Ault. It is a wonder you are conscious."

"I am not in the least certain that I am."

"How many cups did you consume?"

"I could not possibly answer you. I have no idea... lost count after five...."

"Five!" She arched her eyebrows. "No doubt you went up enormously in grandmother's esteem if you consumed that many and can still talk. Come on now, I shall help."

She leaned down and his arms closed around her neck. Suddenly his intentions of rising vanished.

He was aware only of an armful of soft sweet-smelling girl, big green eyes and lovely red lips. He pulled her to his knee, placed his mouth on hers and slid his arm securely around her tiny waist.

Clairice's eyes flew open wide. A cry of surprise was halted abruptly by his mouth on hers. She locked her arms around his neck and surrendered to him.

After a moment Lord Ault released her and gazed at her affectionately. "You are 'dorable!"

She laughed and jumped to her feet, her cheeks flushed. "Come, sir, you will feel differently tomorrow."

He rose unsteadily, and she let him put his arm around her shoulders. Together they crossed to the door and into the hallway.

A red-faced coachman, his eyes boggling, stepped forward. "M'lord—ah—I will assist, ma'am." He gazed up at his master in profound shock. "Here, m'lord, lean on me," he whispered and hurried for the door.

An impassive butler held wide the door, and master and servant staggered into the rain.

CHAPTER THREE

CLAIRICE TURNED for the drawing room to meet her grandmother at the precise moment that dinner was announced. Lady Fairfax leaned on her cane and waved a hand at Clairice. "Now do not bedevil me! All I did was ask Lord Ault if he would care to join me in a cup of tea."

"Grandmother!" Clairice accused, "you know what a dignified man he is. He shall be mortified tomorrow. I have never heard it rumored that he has ever become foxed at any club. To the contrary, he has a reputation for not doing so, and you were abominably sneaky to ply him with your tea."

The little lady chuckled wickedly. "Do him good to let down a little. That boy takes life too seriously entirely. He needs some fun...." She hiccuped softly and ordered, "Come here, girl, and take my arm."

"'Tis a good thing Adele did not encounter him. It would be the end of any hope of romance between them."

"Bosh! Your sister is not that namby-pamby!"

They entered an enormous dining room with a long gleaming table set for four. The remaining members of the family were standing at their chairs, waiting.

Seated facing each other were Lady Fairfax's two granddaughters. An unacquainted person would have had a difficult time matching them as sisters. Clairice's red curls were a contrast to Adele's straight black hair; her green eyes were vastly different from Adele's clear blue ones, and while Adele was short and demure, gazing at the world with soft timidity, Clairice was tall, incessantly active, and viewed her surroundings with the same curious expectation of a child with a wrapped gift.

When the four ladies were seated, Edgars, the butler, moved quietly from one to another, serving from covered dishes, with the exception of Miss Milsap's plate, which was placed before her fully served. It contained a mound of bean sprouts, three carefully measured spoonfuls of curds, a thin wafer of brown toast and a serving of goat's whey in a teacup.

Lady Fairfax belched mildly; Miss Milsap blanched and frowned at the pale sprouts lying limply on her plate. After a moment she raised her head and inquired of Adele, "Did you have an enjoyable afternoon at your cousin's?"

The girl smiled sweetly. "Yes, we enjoyed playing checkers, and they served lovely tea cakes."

"Cakes are not good for your skin or teeth, Adele," Miss Milsap commented.

"Yes, ma'am." She continued, "The ride home in the carriage was dreadfully cold."

"Speaking of carriages," Lady Fairfax announced, "tomorrow we are leaving for Fairfax Hall."

Had the old lady opened a bag of caterpillars on the table she would not have stirred greater dismay. The others began talking at once.

"Grandmother! How awful to leave London now. I am invited to Amy Whitworth's ball...." Clairice broke in over Adele's softly murmured protests.

At the same time Miss Milsap exclaimed, "Impossible, Aunt Cornelia! This ghastly weather, too inclement to venture out of doors. We would catch our deaths of the ague!"

"Fiddlesticks!" Lady Fairfax snapped loudly enough to overcome the protests of all three. "We go tomorrow afternoon. Lord Ault has to travel to the coast, and we can go in his company if we leave tomorrow at noon."

"His presence can do nothing to protect us from the chill," Miss Milsap argued.

"I do not think I can get ready so soon," Adele stated, then took a deep breath and inquired, "May I please take the terriers along?"

"Of course," Lady Fairfax replied, then plunked a large bite of steaming pigeon in her mouth.

"Aunt Cornelia!" Miss Milsap raised her voice. "You know I cannot bear to have those hairy creatures near! How could I endure a journey in a closed carriage with them?"

"Perhaps Lord Ault would take them," Clairice suggested with a twinkle of amusement at the thought.

Miss Milsap laid her fork on her plate. "Aunt, I feel it is my duty to speak with you about a private matter after dinner."

"Bosh! Speak up now, Lavinia. These girls are old enough to hear anything you might have to say."

Miss Milsap paled, then braved the subject. "Henceforth, you must not serve that concoction you call tea to any guest of this family!"

Lady Fairfax cocked her head to one side and glanced briefly at her niece, then plopped another forkful of pigeon into her mouth and chewed vigorously before answering. "Think he enjoyed it, Lavinia. Why don't you let the man speak for himself? He even requested the recipe."

Adele glanced back and forth during this exchange, then her voice quivered, "Grandmother, you didn't! Your tea...and Lord Ault?"

Her grandmother viewed her calmly. "Be quiet, child. Lord Ault enjoyed it immensely."

"He certainly did!" Clairice could not resist adding mischievously and received an aggravated glance from her grandmother that she serenely ignored.

"Oh, grandmother! How mortifying! How could you?" Adele cried and lowered her head too late to hide the tears of embarrassment that rose to her eyes.

Miss Milsap glanced sharply at her niece and snapped, "Aunt, you will ruin the girl's chances with the man!"

Adele quickly raised her head and protested quietly, "I do not want to marry him, but grandmother's tea—"

"I am certain," Miss Milsap declared staunchly, "that he intends to offer for you, Adele. Otherwise, why would the man continue to call?"

"Perhaps he likes my company," Lady Fairfax murmured happily and waved a fork. "Lord Ault is traveling to Paris. As long as we are going to the coast anyway, I think it is time that we pay a visit to my sister Hyacinth and her husband. The girls would have an opportunity to see Paris, and heaven knows what that dreadful Bonaparte will do in the future. Such a ragtag government."

"At least, grandmother," Clairice remarked, "he welcomed the *emigrés*. They say he allowed more than fifty thousand to return three years ago. He cannot be all bad."

"Bah! The French still fume that we are in Malta, yet if we leave, Boney will only spread his power farther. The Corsican is crazy with ambition. It may be our last chance for a long time to take such a trip."

Adele regarded her grandmother with a knot of worry. "I would like...may I please take Tick and Tack? I do hate to leave them."

"Bring them if you must!" snapped Lady Fairfax.

Lavinia exclaimed, "Taking those dogs to Fairfax Hall is appalling enough. Crossing the Channel and suffering through a journey to Paris, much less descending upon relatives with two hairy animals is utterly impossible. You know how they irritate my nose!"

"The relatives or the dogs?" Lady Fairfax quizzed amusedly.

When no answer was forthcoming, Adele said softly, "Aunt Lavinia, I would not cause you discomfort. I shall leave them here. Edgars can care for them."

Miss Milsap responded quickly, "Perhaps that would be best, Adele." She glanced pointedly at Lady Fairfax. "And I am grateful to see that you are kind enough to have some regard for the feelings of others."

As soon as the meal was concluded the family departed the dining room, each with her thoughts on the prospective journey.

Lady Fairfax was escorted to her room by Clairice, and the maid, Betsy, was summoned to start the arduous job of packing.

WHILE THE LADIES WORKED diligently, another London household prepared for the same event. While the head of the house was sprawled on his bed, soundly sleeping off the effects of a hearty consumption of home-brewed "tea," the staff tiptoed about their tasks.

When he finally aroused, Lord Ault summoned his valet. While he waited, he sat on the edge of the bed with his stockinged feet propped on the high step stool and his hands on his head as if attempting to hold it on his neck.

"Good evening, my lord," the valet said impassively.

Lord Ault lifted his head—no small feat—and faced his faithful retainer. "Gammon, Dudley, I am dying!"

"Sorry to hear that, sir."

"I wonder if there is an antidote...." He squinted at Dudley. "Fetch a bath—perhaps that will aid this malady."

Dudley, a man given to even greater temperance than his master, could only gaze with sympathetic eyes and remark, before he turned to see to the bath, "M'lord, I have packed everything you requested."

Lord Ault raised his head. "Packed?" he inquired. Unaware of the look of dismay on his valet's face, he turned the prospect over in his foggy brain and finally remembered. "Oh, yes, Dudley. I am certain you have thought of everything. Help me to my feet."

Dudley moved to do as directed and steadied his master as he traversed the two steps down to the floor in one.

"Thank you," Lord Ault replied with a dignity he

was far from feeling. He clung to the furniture in lieu of his servant as Dudley departed to see to the bath.

Lord Ault was soon sunk into a tub of hot water, which did little to ease his throbbing temples. He stepped out of the water with just a slightly steadier movement and a fraction-clearer brain. As he donned his clothes with the aid of a silent Dudley, he turned and his gaze rested on the trunk.

"I trust everything will be ready to depart at noon," he commented, then halted as if transformed by some unearthly power. A thought so horrendous as to transfix him into immobility had arisen in his muddled mind.

"Sir?" Dudley blinked rapidly, aware that the arm he was attempting to slip into an elegant dark blue sleeve had become rigid at what would be considered an uncomfortable angle. "Sir?" he repeated.

"Good God!" Lord Ault muttered. "I promised Lady Fairfax to take them with—" He stopped as if a spell were broken. He lowered his arm rapidly, swearing in a stream of words that shook the valet's iron composure. Dudley blanched and hurried to continue the dressing.

Lord Ault spun about, causing Dudley to drop the coat. He hastily retrieved it with a mumbled apology, which was ignored and drowned out by forceful instructions.

"Dudley, hurry! I must see Lady Fairfax tonight on a matter of utmost urgency! Lord, what have I done! Send word and insist on a brief call."

"Tonight, m'lord?" Dudley inquired.

Lord Ault replied in such a manner that Dudley hurried from the room to accomplish the task as speedily as possible, while Lord Ault's befogged brain cleared with amazing speed.

LADY FAIRFAX CHUCKLED when faced by Edgars announcing Lord Ault's request to pay a call. Miss Milsap, in the room to present her list of health foods for the trip, turned shocked eyes upon the servant. When he had departed, she whirled with compressed lips to face her aunt.

"How mortifying! The poor man has sobered and is coming to apologize for an occurrence that was actually no fault of his own. I am certain the poor soul never suspected for a moment what you were plying him with. How excruciatingly embarrassing for him."

"Bosh!" Lady Fairfax mumbled mildly.

The remark sent Lavinia into greater agony. "I suppose there is nothing I can say to stop you from these antics. Kindly be civil to the man and do not remind him of this afternoon." She hurried to leave the room, then turned. "And, Aunt Cornelia, I beseech you in all earnestness, for the sake of your granddaughters—do not offer the man any more tea!"

Within the hour Lord Ault was once again ushered into the presence of Lady Fairfax in a small upstairs drawing room, and the door closed discreetly behind him.

Under her solemn scrutiny Lord Ault's compressed lips twitched. He crossed to where she was seated and bent over her hand, then raised his head to meet her eyes.

"Lady Fairfax, I never before have been tempted to wring such an aristocratic neck!"

"Sit down, Lord Ault," she urged with a smile.

He faced her. "I refuse to apologize for my ungentlemanly conduct this afternoon."

"And I refuse to apologize for my own actions," she replied.

"I deserve an apology, but be that as it may, I came to discover what took place here today. I have a vague recollection of imparting information of a highly confidential nature to you."

She confirmed his fear. "Indeed you did. Your mission to France for Prinny."

He paled. "I was afraid I remembered correctly. Lady Fairfax—" he began.

She waved a hand at him. "Hush! I can keep a secret, so waste no breath exhorting me to something I have already made up my mind to do."

His lips twitched again, then he gazed at her with narrowed eyes. "I also have a dim remembrance of consenting to allow companions on my journey."

She nodded. When he shook his head she said hastily, "Sir, you pointed out yourself this afternoon that your mission would garner less suspicion with us along."

"That may have been my view this afternoon, but with a clearer head I can discern certain ramifications I am convinced would justify me not to undertake this mission accompanied by four females."

"Rubbish!" She waved her cane at him. "Sit down, sir," she urged again and noticed the ease with which he moved in spite of his height and wide shoulders. He was quite handsome even in anger; his flashing gray eyes darkened with controlled fury. She met them calmly. He sat on a blue velvet love seat facing her.

Just as in the afternoon, a fire crackled in the grate, but the rain had changed to mist, the hour had grown late, and the two were coldly sober. To press her argument, Lady Fairfax thumped her cane and stated, "We shall provide an excellent screen for your true activities. The French will pay you little heed when you arrive with four females in tow."

He tilted his head; the barest flicker in his eyes revealed the shock he had just received. "The French? As I recall there was only mention made of the coast and Fairfax Hall."

She shook her head positively. "No, my lord. My dear sister and her husband reside in Paris. Why she ever married a Frenchman I shall never understand, but she did, and you promised to escort us there."

His humor vanished entirely. "Lady Fairfax, I may have been in my cups, but I cannot apprehend any condition that would cause me to commit such a folly! It would make my arrival in Paris of monumental notice."

He spoke sharply and viewed her with a grim countenance. "I cannot remember a hint of a promise like that."

She turned her cane carefully as if viewing it for the first time. "Well, my lord, you did. And I have informed the household of the event and have sent word to my sister to expect us."

He swore, then apologized hastily to her in halfhearted tones. "Under the circumstances, Lady Fairfax, I fear I shall have to beg off. You had me at a distinct disadvantage this afternoon. I will have to throw myself on your mercy and request that you free me from this promise. It may be ungentlemanly to do so, but I can only plead your forgiveness, for common sense tells me I must do so."

"Common sense will inform you of the wiser course of action in taking us along, instead of leaving us behind to inform the world of your mission."

His eyebrows raised. "Lady Fairfax, you cannot mean you would resort to such a threat to force your company upon me?" he inquired incredulously.

She merely nodded and brushed her sleeve, gazing up at him from under shaggy white brows. "It is difficult, my lord, to raise two granddaughters without their parents. A spinster niece in the household merely adds to the burden. Four ladies can hardly travel across the continent without escort in such troubled times."

"There will be men to go with you, your driver, your butler—" His eyes narrowed. "Madam, why do you want me along? I suspect there is more to this than you say. You must have some particular reason for wanting me to accompany you; I demand you speak up!"

"We shall not be that much trouble to you." She smiled.

He rose to his feet and paced back and forth in agitation, then stopped and stared down at her. "I may go to Prinny and ask to be freed of the mission."

"Then you would certainly be available to fulfill your promise to travel with us to Paris."

"Confound it!" He glared at her as she faced him calmly. "Madam, this is highly unconventional!"

"Perhaps, but I ceased concerning myself with convention several years ago."

He uttered through clenched teeth, "I made an excessive slip this afternoon. I let down my guard in your presence, and you are taking abhorrent advantage of the fact. What is worse, you are possibly jeopardizing the security of England, and the success of a venture that is of the utmost importance to the prince!"

She tilted her head and viewed him composedly. "If I considered this to be a hazard to you or your mission, I would not make such a request. In all due honesty, Lord Ault, I think it will catch two fish in one fell swoop, so to speak. It will provide an excellent cover for you, and it will accomplish our purpose.

"Your arrival in Paris will be noted whether you accompany us or not. There is no way a man of your distinction can arrive in Paris unnoticed and unheeded. Also, if such a personage as yourself arrives with a gentleman of the background and accomplishments that you mentioned this afternoon, it will be doubly noticed."

She stopped momentarily at his furious look, then went on. "But should two such gentlemen arrive in the company of two young misses and their adequate chaperones, an aunt and a grandmother, you will have a far more logical reason to explain your presence and attract far less attention. I think you have the wisdom to see this yourself."

He regarded her with a steely eye. "Perhaps that is so, but since we are speaking in a forthright manner, I do not relish the company of four females for such an extended trip."

"Lavinia is the only tiresome person in the entourage, Lord Ault, and I promise faithfully to keep her out of your presence as much as possible."

"Perhaps Miss Milsap is not the only tiresome presence!" he snapped.

Her eyes twinkled with amusement. "Come now, Lord Ault, I know my granddaughters are not that tiring."

"You surmise full well of whom I speak!"

She chuckled. "Give in, my lord. I have the upper hand!"

"So you do, and I have learned a bitter lesson this day."

They studied each other and Lady Fairfax asked, "Then you will take us along?"

"I perceive I have no choice."

She beamed and thumped her cane on the floor. "Capital! Now sit down and forget the matter."

Strong men had been known to quail at the icy tones delivered by Lord Ault. He leaned forward slightly. "Madam, I shall not sit down again in your presence for a cozy chat as long as I have breath in my body. You have taken foul advantage of my unsuspecting nature!"

"Bosh! You will thank me someday."

"I cannot imagine such an event," he replied stiffly. "I shall arrive at noon tomorrow, and I hope to depart promptly!"

"We shall be ready," she answered politely, and little could Lord Ault guess what feverish activity finally achieved this accomplishment.

THE ENTIRE STAFF was roused at dawn, though some of them had had only two or three hours' sleep during a night devoted to packing, pressing and folding a voluminous mound of dresses.

A trunk full of health foods for Lavinia—camomile tea, dried prunes, carrot juice, bean sprouts and camphor drops—was carefully packed and locked.

The traveling coach was prepared and ready, trunks lashed and horses eager; the town carriage also was put to use. Promptly at noon a shiny black carriage halted in front of the house, and Lord Ault descended to have his presence announced.

He was ushered inside to meet four ladies waiting patiently, ready to travel. The expression on his face was sufficient to cause the younger Fairfax females to make the barest greeting and lapse into silence. Its effect on their Aunt Lavinia was a smile of grim satisfaction indicating that she had been correct in predicting Lord Ault would despise their company. The eldest member of the family met him in the best of humor. She said, "Good afternoon, my lord. We have not waited long at all for your arrival. You are quite prompt, as a matter of fact."

Clairice's green eyes twinkled at her grandmother's impertinence.

Lord Ault took a deep breath and replied, "In that case, shall we go? My coach will lead and yours may follow." He turned abruptly on his heel, then halted to let them pass through the door before him.

With various sections of her body heaving in opposite directions, Lady Fairfax nonetheless moved with surprising agility, leaning on her cane and stepping along ahead of the others. She paused and pointed the cane, directing the flow of traffic.

The long, ebony stick waved toward their own vehicle. "Lavinia, you and Adele will join me in our carriage. The servants—Betsy, Ginnie and Edgars—travel in the last carriage. Clairice, you are to accompany Lord Ault."

"Aunt! We cannot send Clairice to ride alone with him; they will be unchaperoned!" Lavinia protested.

"Bosh! She is a mere girl, and it will give us all more room."

Without waiting for rebuttal, she propelled the two girls in opposite directions. "Get in, Lavinia, I promised we would depart on time."

Miss Milsap cast a lingering, doubtful look toward Clairice, who was ascending into Lord Ault's carriage, then followed Adele into theirs. Lady Fairfax had accepted the groom's arm to step up, when Lord Ault's voice sounded.

"What the devil?" His angry gray eyes flashed at Lady Fairfax. "Madam, did I see a skirt disappear into my carriage?" he snapped.

She nodded. "It will allow us more room and you a more entertaining journey. Good day, sir. It's time to be off." She sat down and closed the door.

WHILE LORD AULT GAZED in consternation at the closed carriage door, Clairice was accepting two more passengers for the ride.

"Hurry, Ginnie!" she urged in a whisper. "Quick—before Lord Ault comes." With deft hands Clairice leaned down and placed both terriers beside her ankles, then dropped her green silk skirt over them.

"Down Tick!" she urged one frolicsome dog. Clairice settled against the cushions as the door opened and Lord Ault entered.

He sat down without a word and faced her grimly. One of the dogs emitted a faint growl.

Clairice nudged the dog quickly with her toe and covered her mouth. Her cheeks flushed with warmth as Lord Ault looked politely away.

The carriage rolled forward and they were under way. He faced her. "I owe you an apology for my behavior," he said quietly.

Her flush heightened. "Do not mention it, Lord Ault. I understand fully."

His eyes searched hers a moment, and he remarked, "I expect you do. I would hate," he said solemnly, "to challenge a little grandmother to a duel, but the possibility has crossed my mind."

Clairice laughed and relaxed. "You have every right to be miffed. Grandmother's tea is potent, and I presume you were an unwary victim."

He cocked his head to one side. "Do you know what is in that tea?"

"Not exactly. Adele and I have been instructed never to sample it. I have watched them mix it, though. It is a highly complicated procedure done in the cellars of Fairfax Hall. It is an immense brew that is bottled and stored in the cellar, then the contents of a bottle are added to the brewed tea.''

"What goes into a bottle?"

"Several ingredients I am not familiar with. Grandmother demands that the process remain a secret. I know they use oil of almonds and sulfuric acid—"

"Oh, Lord!" he exclaimed.

Clairice continued, "It is brewed, fermented in the cellar and finally placed in bottles to be stored for later use.''

Lord Ault's brows raised. "I think I am to be excused for my behavior. How much of the bottled mixture goes into the tea?"

She tilted her head and considered gravely. "I would guess it is two parts tea—strong tea—to one part bottled whatever.''

"Gammon!"

The dogs began to fidget, and Clairice wriggled on the seat, scooting forward to view the familiar scenery with sudden interest. The day was gray and chill with clouds obscuring the sun. In her nervousness over the dogs, Clairice declared, "Lovely day, is it not?" She studied her own neighborhood, the familiar elegant houses set back from the cobbled street, as if it were a novel view.

He regarded her curiously and remarked with a shrug, "Slightly chilly.''

A soft furry body moved against her ankle. Clairice slipped her one foot free of her shoe, raised her toes and gently pushed one of the dogs to the floor. She patted his head lightly with her foot and caught Lord Ault openly studying her. She smiled and hummed a tune in time to her tapping knee.

He smiled politely and glanced toward the window. but within seconds she felt his eyes on her once more.

The dog wiggled again, and to her horror, she saw a brown furry paw extend beneath the hem of her skirt.

She flounced her skirts, smiling at Lord Ault. The paw disappeared.

Clairice blushed and gazed out the window, scratching one dog with her toes while keeping a foot securely on the other's back.

"Is this a new style in ladies' slippers?" Lord Ault inquired politely.

Clairice looked down. The brown paw was once again extended into view. She stammered, "Lord Ault—Adele...."

He ignored her and leaned down, deliberately whistling softly.

Tick poked a shiny nose from under the hem and gazed up in rapture at Lord Ault.

Lord Ault patted his knee, and the dog crawled out and jumped up amidst Clairice's embarrassed explanations. Another black shiny nose poked out from under her skirts. Lord Ault's brows raised. He gave her a startled glance and his smile vanished.

She blinked. "You see, Lord Ault, Aunt Lavinia is bothered by dog hair, and Adele did not want to leave London without her precious pets, and so...."

"Lady Fairfax resolved this arrangement no doubt," he said wryly.

"Yes, my lord."

Lord Ault patted his knee, and Tick was joined by Tack. Lord Ault scratched the two heads, and the dogs settled on each side of him. He glanced at Clairice. "Their names?" When Clairice answered Lord Ault looked slightly pained, but he made no comment and merely continued to scratch their ears. Clairice did not offer further explanation or apology, as it seemed unnecessary. Lord Ault appeared perfectly pleased to share his coach with two dogs. He regarded her with amusement and looked pointedly at her skirt. "Any more?" he inquired.

She jumped. "Oh, no, my lord! Only two. I am sorry to have hidden them in such a manner."

"I know—grandmother," he remarked dryly. "What else does she have in store for me?"

Clairice smiled. "I do not know, your lordship. Grandmother has a way of arranging people's lives," she added defensively, "but usually she does quite satisfactorily."

"I can imagine to whose satisfaction," he remarked.

They lapsed into silence, and Clairice withdrew a small book from her reticule. She glanced at him. "Do you mind if I read?"

He smiled. "Of course not."

She settled comfortably into the seat and read, occasionally glancing at him out of the corner of her eye. She could not understand Adele's aversion to Lord Ault. He was certainly handsome, and his dark blue coat fitted across his broad shoulders to perfection. He was tall and commanding, and Clairice suspected his presence was too overpowering for her shy sister.

He idly scratched Tick's ears; Tack slept with his head on Lord Ault's knee. They rode in such manner until the carriage halted in the middle of the afternoon for refreshment at a coaching inn.

LATER, WHEN THEY STROLLED toward the carriages to resume the journey, Lady Fairfax told Clairice, "It is time for Lavinia and your sister to ride with Lord Ault; you come with me."

Clairice gathered the terriers and climbed inside the Fairfax traveling coach. Lady Fairfax directed Lavinia and Adele, then climbed in beside Clairice and called to Harkens, their driver, that they were ready.

Lady Fairfax placed her portmanteau carefully beside her feet, cast an eye at the dogs and raised her nose. "Keep those little devils on your side of the carriage! Can't abide that hair myself, but I wouldn't give Lavinia the satisfaction of knowing it."

"Yes, grandmother," Clairice replied with twinkling

eyes. She scooped the dogs up on the seat beside her.

"Did Lord Ault mind them?"

"No, he liked them quite well. As a matter of fact they rode in his lap."

Lady Fairfax nodded in satisfaction. "Good. He can have them in his carriage for the rest of the journey. We shall leave them at Fairfax Hall. Have no business taking dogs across the Channel." She reconsidered thoughtfully. "Of course, the little devils might fall in and we'd be rid of them."

"Grandmother! How dreadful!" Clairice cried in mock horror. "You know Adele would suffer."

"Bosh! Girl needs a husband, she does. That would get her mind off dogs."

"Maybe after this trip she will like Lord Ault better," Clairice mused aloud, then promptly forgot her sister in viewing the countryside.

It was a chill April day; the sun was shining and the wind was brisk. The gentle rolling hills were not yet greening, but a few scattered fruit trees were budding. A low stone wall bordered the lane, and Clairice looked at the open field beyond with longing for her horse and a good gallop.

In a short time the rocking carriage lulled Lady Fairfax to sleep. She slumped into a corner, and a gentle snore erupted with each exhalation.

The road curved gradually on a level stretch of land. In sudden curiosity Clairice leaned out the window and was surprised that Lord Ault's carriage was no longer in view. She sat back against the cushions and once again drew the dogs into her lap and got out her book to continue reading.

By the time Lady Fairfax aroused, Clairice had covered another chapter. She laid the book on her knee. "Did you have a good nap?"

"Good enough to have to suffer doing so in a stuffy coach."

Clairice curled Tick's soft ear in her finger and asked

thoughtfully, "Grandmother, is Lord Ault traveling to France to visit friends?"

"Perhaps." Lady Fairfax regarded the view with rapt attention.

Clairice studied her grandmother. "Why is he on this journey? I suspect you know. He appeared less than happy to have us along."

Lady Fairfax fixed her with a penetrating glance. "Child, keep your questions to yourself. I know the curiosity you have. He is on an errand of secrecy for the government. It is dangerous, Clairice, and he does not want anyone to know about it."

"Grandmother!" Her eyes grew wide and she exclaimed, "The tea!"

"Exactly. He revealed his plans after he'd had a fair consumption of my brew. It is galling him to know he revealed such information, so do not inquire anything about his destination. I feel I can trust you as well as I can myself; you know I would not reveal this to Lavinia or Adele. Adele could be trusted, but she would worry constantly."

"You perceive it is dangerous."

"Yes," Lady Fairfax replied forthrightly. "A man will meet him in Chatham, and he will aid Lord Ault in the venture. Lord Ault assured me this man bears in abundance the qualities necessary to assist competently in the endeavor. He is said to be an excellent shot, a superior horseman and military man— all the necessary traits—so perhaps it will not be too difficult a task." Lady Fairfax paused and looked intently at Clairice. "I have made a revelation to you of something told to me when the man was not himself. I took unfair advantage of him and have placed him in a precarious position with the prince." Her voice grew stern. "Clairice, we must never reveal a word of this. Lord Ault's life will be at stake, so do not whisper a hint of the matter to another soul on this earth."

"I promise, grandmother; I would not think of it. You have not been too kind to Lord Ault."

"Perhaps not, but I shall make it up to him."

Clairice tilted her head. "Grandmother, why did you insist that he accompany us to France? You know we could get there without him."

"It is safer than four women traveling alone, Clairice, and it is vastly more entertaining, among other reasons."

"Grandmother, you sound as if you are up to something you do not want known yet."

"Bosh! I wonder how they are faring."

"I could not venture a guess, but they have left us quite far behind."

"Confound that Harkens! The doddering old fool could not drive a baby carriage, and he may be on the sauce again. I am getting a new driver. In all the rush to get away, I did not consider his driving."

"They will wait at the next inn for us, I am certain."

Lady Fairfax snorted. "Lord Ault is not going to ride a great length of time with Lavinia in his charge. Another hour and I am certain he shall have reached the limits of his endurance."

Clairice laughed at the suggestion.

Suddenly they were jolted as the coach halted abruptly.

"What in thunderation....?" Lady Fairfax exploded.

CHAPTER FOUR

CLAIRICE SCOOPED UP one of the dogs, which had fallen to the floor at the abrupt halt. Shouts reached them and Clairice exclaimed, "Highwaymen, grandmother!"

"How dare they!"

"Stand and deliver!" a hoarse voice bellowed.

"I shall deliver, all right!" Lady Fairfax grumbled and retrieved the portmanteau from the floor. "Confound that Harkens for falling behind and losing Lord Ault."

"Grandmother!" Clairice's eyes widened at the sight of the long pistol produced from the traveling bag.

"I shall not permit such effrontery by scoundrels who belong in the graveyard for their impudence!"

"Is it primed?" Clairice whispered.

"Certainly, girl! High time you learned how to use one. When we return home, I shall see that the matter is remedied."

"I know how, grandmother."

For a fleeting second Lady Fairfax looked with surprise at her granddaughter.

"Ladies, come out!" a man ordered roughly.

Lady Fairfax's brows flew together. "Damn that Harkens! No doubt he told them there are only two female passengers. Man is not worth a sixpence!" She scooted along the seat to the window. "Get down, child. I shall resolve this quickly."

In an unfamiliar high voice Lady Fairfax gazed out the window and cried, "Spare us!" She withdrew her head and snapped, "Spineless creatures—the men are all off the coach...."

With a sweeping motion she thrust the snout of the long pistol out of the window just as a masked highwayman strode into view. Wasting no breath in warning, Lady Fairfax pulled the trigger and gunned the man down.

In retaliation, an explosion sounded and a shot tore through the top of the coach with a dull thunk. At the noise the horses bolted.

Lady Fairfax fell into the corner with unladylike swearing as she struggled to reload the pistol. The dogs tumbled to the floor, barking wildly at the tumult. Clairice was thrown against the cushions, then raised herself up to gaze out the rear window with dismay.

"Grandmother, there is no one outside to control the horses!" Even as she watched, a highwayman moved to his crumpled companion and lifted him to a saddle, then mounted his own horse and turned for the woods. The staff ran uselessly after the runaway coach.

The coach careened around a bend onto a straight downhill stretch of road, gaining speed and causing Clairice to lose sight of the trailing servants. She clutched her grandmother's arm. "What shall we do?"

"Fool horses! They will wear down in a minute," Lady Fairfax muttered tightly.

The carriage rocked violently from side to side. "If we are not killed first!" Clairice exclaimed, clutching the sides to prevent being tossed about. "Grandmother, put away the pistol."

For once, her grandmother obeyed. "I—damme!" Lady Fairfax clung to the window frame and to the edge of the seat as the ride grew rougher.

Clairice gazed in horror at the trees flashing by them. They rounded a bend and swung in a sickening roll, then straightened out and continued down the lane. Something caught Clairice's eye and she cried, "Grandmother—a rider!" She leaned forward to gaze out the window at the man galloping toward them.

Lady Fairfax clung to the coach with one hand and

reached for the portmanteau with the other. "The confounded villain!"

Clairice glanced quickly at her. "Grandmother, I do not think so. He does not wear a mask. I think he is coming to rescue us!"

Lady Fairfax released the portmanteau and clutched the seat grimly.

Clairice's voice rose excitedly. "Here he comes! He will stop the horses!"

Lady Fairfax did not reply. Her entire concentration was on holding on to the seat of the violently swaying coach. They thundered along the lane, swaying dangerously and stirring a great cloud of dust behind. The dogs yapped in a frenzy, unable to stand but tossed about on the floor.

Clairice's heart pounded with hope as she watched the man riding like the wind, leaning low over his horse as it raced directly for them. The man's hat was gone, his long blond hair blowing in the wind; he whipped the horse to its utmost.

The big sorrel lengthened his stride and the distance between rider and carriage narrowed; the man's dark coattails flapped violently as his steed pounded closer.

Clairice watched in breathless hope. "Grandmother, here he comes!"

"Thank the Lord, child. We are saved!"

Hooves thudded with dull chunks against the earth; the man raced alongside the coach, determined to halt the runaways. Side by side along the narrow lane they sped while he readied himself to reach across the space and shift to the coach.

Clairice watched in silence as the slender man edged ever closer.

The hero made his move finally. Both ladies watched breathlessly as he stretched a hand for the coach, grasped the side and leaped from his saddle. He clung to the side of the rocking vehicle, struggled frantically— and fell to the ground.

Clairice screamed while Lady Fairfax swore heartily. "The damn fool!"

"Grandmother!" Clairice shrieked. She twisted to peer out the narrow oval rear window at the inert figure lying face down in the dusty lane. "I think the fall killed him!"

"I pray to the Almighty it did!" Lady Fairfax snapped from the corner of the coach.

The coach lurched violently. Clairice glanced around, then moved to the door and thrust her head out the window. Instantly Lady Fairfax snatched at her dress and tugged on the material. The dogs yapped, and Lady Fairfax thumped Tick soundly with her cane. "Hush, you little beast! Get in here, child! You'll be killed!"

Clairice ignored the admonition and faced the interior, then moved her head and shoulders outside and grasped the top of the window frame and moved to sit in the window.

All the while her grandmother screeched in fright. "What do you think you are doing? Girl, come back in here immediately!"

Clairice ignored the frenzied exhortations and clung determinedly. The wind tore her curls loose, and her bonnet fell behind her head, secured by the tight bow under her chin.

Inching her way carefully, Clairice reached for a secure grip, higher and higher until she was standing on the window frame and clinging to the roof of the coach. She heaved and tugged herself onto the roof, oblivious to the dusty coach or the wind. Her whole concentration was on gaining the top of the carriage.

With each bump and sway she felt she would fly off into space, but she clung tightly. Finally she reached the driver's seat, then gazed in dismay at the reins trailing in the dust. Two had been caught loosely on the coach within her grasp.

The others trailed out of sight in the dust stirred up by the horses' pounding hooves. Clairice unwrapped the ones in reach, clambered onto the seat and turned, bracing her feet. She pulled tightly.

The coach left the road and bounced against the rolling earth. Lady Fairfax's screams became hoarse, but Clairice paid no heed.

The coach slowed, then rolled to a halt near a copse of trees. Dust swirled and billowed, then settled to earth. Clairice leaned forward and laid her head on her shaking knees while everything swam before her eyes. A sudden silence enveloped them.

The coach door opened with a click, and Lady Fairfax called her name.

"I'm all right, grandmother," Clairice answered.

Within seconds the woman appeared and gazed up at her granddaughter. "That was a fool thing to do!"

Clairice smiled weakly and began to climb down. A gentle breeze tugged at the curls that had come loose. Her red hair shone with coppery glints in the sunlight. She smiled at her grandmother. "I have to get the reins...." She patted a horse's lathered neck and reached down to retrieve the fallen reins. The big animal quivered at her touch and shook his head with a jingle of harness.

Lady Fairfax watched and snapped, "Think you can drive this thing?"

"I suspect the horses will be sufficiently worn down from their flight and will not give me any difficulty," Clairice answered with more assurance than she felt.

Lady Fairfax climbed inside and slammed the door. Clairice gained the seat once more and flicked the reins. The coach turned as she pulled on the reins, and they headed in the direction from whence they had just come.

It was a country lane, quiet, remote, with oaks lending a stately grace to the gently sloping land, all of which belied the violent activities they had just encountered.

The moment the carriage turned to retrace its path,

Lady Fairfax's head was thrust through the open window and she screeched at her granddaughter, "Clairice, we are traveling in the wrong direction!"

"No, we must go back, grandmother, and pick up that poor man in the lane."

A violent thumping followed this announcement. Clairice glanced over her shoulder and saw the end of the cane striking the top of the carriage. "Stop this carriage at once!" Lady Fairfax shouted.

"Grandmother, we can discuss it later," Clairice called.

"Mind your manners, chit! Stop at once, I say!"

Reluctantly Clairice tugged on the reins and the horses obeyed. The door swung open, and Lady Fairfax exited to squint up against the sun at her errant granddaughter.

"Young lady! Turn this thing around immediately. Lord Ault can send for our driver. I shall not permit Harkens to touch this vehicle again. I shall not let the man near it."

"Grandmother, I intend to return to aid that poor fellow who tried to save us," Clairice replied calmly.

"I shall have none of that! Do you want to find a dead body, child?" her grandmother yelled in agitation. "We cannot be looking to strange men!"

"Get in, grandmother, or I shall leave you standing in the road."

Lady Fairfax's mouth opened, then suddenly snapped shut. A great deal of incoherent mumbling came to Clairice's ear, but she ignored it.

The door slammed, Clairice flicked the reins, and once again they moved leisurely down the lane. They rounded a turn, and Clairice saw the inert form of their well-intentioned rescuer.

She halted the coach and climbed down carefully. Her grandmother exited, holding the pistol. "You are an impertinent chit!" she directed at Clairice.

"Grandmother, I do apologize, but we could not remain in such a manner all day.'' She looked at the man stretched out in the lane. Nearby, his horse grazed quietly, reins trailing. It raised its head and eyed them.

Clairice knelt and felt the man's throat, relieved to find the flesh warm and a throbbing pulse.

She tugged his shoulder to roll him over. He was slender, quite tall, and young-looking, his face fair and his shock of blond hair in disarray over a handsome forehead. His long lashes rested against his cheeks. A large dark knot was forming on his forehead under the blond locks.

The sound of male voices was heard, and Lady Fairfax swore. ''The devil! Here comes that simpleton, Harkens.'' The driver, a groom and a lackey appeared, hastening their steps at the sight of their mistress. Harkens strode forward in apology and stopped short to gaze in wonder at the body on the ground.

''Run him down, ma'am?'' he inquired.

''No, you simpleton!'' Lady Fairfax snapped. ''He fell off the coach.'' Harkens knew better than to make further inquiries, Clairice thought, looking up. The terriers trotted close and sat down to gaze at the stranger.

Clairice rose, saying, ''Harkens, will you and Ogden get him into the coach and fetch his horse, please. We shall convey him to the nearest coaching inn.''

''Perhaps we should not, Clairice. We do not know him,'' Lady Fairfax protested.

''Grandmother, we cannot abandon him unconscious in the lane. The least we can do is take him to an inn.''

''Very well.'' Lady Fairfax motioned with her cane, lowering the long pistol, to Harkens's obvious relief. ''Inside the coach with him and tether his horse to our coach, then let us be on our way. Harkens, you should never have lost sight of Lord Ault's carriage!''

''No, ma'am. No indeed! But he drives a fast rig, ma'am.''

''Harkens, our horses are as fine as Lord Ault's, and we should not lose sight of him again.''

"Yes, ma'am," he replied with a weary sigh. While the men lifted the inert body into the coach, Clairice gathered the terriers and climbed inside to sit next to her grandmother.

Harkens placed the man in the corner and tried to fold his long legs in such a manner as to give the ladies sufficient room, but with the terriers it was crowded.

The coach commenced rolling, and within minutes the man's eyelids fluttered and deep blue eyes gazed into Clairice's. He straightened and mumbled, "Where am I?"

"Inside the coach you failed to halt!" Lady Fairfax snapped, receiving a dark look from Clairice.

He groaned and held his head, sitting straighter and placing his feet squarely on the floor. "My apologies," he muttered. "Terrible job I did." He lifted his head from his hands and looked at them. "How did you get it halted?" Before they could reply, he glanced about and inquired, "Who is driving now?"

Clairice related briefly what had occurred.

"Highwaymen? Terrible! Allow me to introduce myself; I'm Anthony Harding." He nodded slightly.

Clairice introduced her grandmother, then herself. "We do appreciate what you attempted. I hope you are not hurt badly."

"No," he grinned, "knocked the wind out of me mostly. I shall ride with you to Chatham, which is the next village, then bid you adieu."

Clairice nodded agreeably while Lady Fairfax lifted the portmanteau to return the pistol, primed and ready, to its resting place. Mr. Harding watched the proceedings amusedly.

"Do you always travel with a loaded pistol?"

"Certainly!" Lady Fairfax declared.

"Singular!" he remarked in admiration. He reached down idly and scratched one of the terrier's ears. "Cute little fellows."

Lady Fairfax sifted through the portmanteau and

withdrew a dark green bottle containing an even darker liquid. She reached in and produced a bundle wrapped in clean linen. Removing the cloth carefully, she placed two glasses on the seat and instructed Clairice to hold them while she poured. Then she extended one to Mr. Harding. "This may help your aching head."

"Thank you kindly," he murmured, gazing at the drink thoughtfully. "Brandy?" he inquired.

"Grandmother—" Clairice began.

Lady Fairfax waved a hand at her granddaughter and answered, "Tea, sir, my own brew. Have a sip."

"Think I shall. Just the thing." He smiled politely and drank. He lowered his glass swiftly, given to a sudden fit of coughing. His face was suffused with color and Clairice looked darkly at Lady Fairfax.

"Grandmother. . ." she remarked in a warning voice.

"It will do the man good, Clairice. Do not be a nuisance like Lavinia." She smiled at the gentleman. "Drink up, sir, there is an abundant supply."

He did as she urged and settled against the cushions, looking considerably improved. Within a short time his color had returned. Lady Fairfax produced the second bottle of tea from the portmanteau. Suddenly there was a commotion outside, and the carriage lurched to an abrupt halt, throwing Clairice forward. The gentleman caught her quickly and gazed down into her wide green eyes.

"Lord God Almighty! What now?" burst from Lady Fairfax, chagrined that she had spilled a dopple of tea on her skirt.

"Stand and deliver!" a voice cried.

"Again!" Lady Fairfax exploded. "I cannot believe this."

"Ladies, come out at once, and no firearms!"

The three passengers looked at one another. The gentleman flattened against the cushions. While the dogs barked wildly, Lady Fairfax glanced out and hissed, "It is indeed the same ruffians!"

"Get out," the gentleman urged. "They do not know I am in the coach. I shall take your pistol and surprise them."

Clairice opened the coach door; the terriers burst forth, barking their loud protests at the masked men. Clairice emerged into the sunlight and turned to assist her grandmother to alight.

Clutching the side of the carriage with one hand, cane hooked over her wrist, and holding the uncorked bottle of tea in the other, Lady Fairfax slowly descended, placed the cane in her hand and strode forward to face the highwayman. Clairice closed the door and followed.

Wearing muddy top boots, a battered tricorn, rumpled black breeches and coat, one ruffian sat astride his horse, a flintlock held on Harkens and the other men.

The second highwayman was as disreputably dressed and sported a ragged bandage around one arm. A stain of blood darkened the cloth, which bore out Lady Fairfax's conclusion that they were the same two brigands who had accosted them earlier.

Lady Fairfax, with Clairice steadying her, had moved about ten steps from the coach when the man waved his pistol and ordered them to come no farther. The dogs barked constantly, and the highwayman snarled, "Shut them bloomin' little beasts up or us 'll kill 'em."

Clairice swept both wriggling terriers into her arms. She thrust one into her grandmother's grasp. Lady Fairfax blinked at it, far more dismayed to have it foisted upon her than the brigands she faced. She clutched the neck of the bottle with her arm wrapped around the dog. Her other hand rested on the cane, upon which she leaned slightly. She eyed the wounded man. "I see I did not have good aim."

"Shut up," he growled.

Lady Fairfax drew herself up and raised her chin in distaste. For an instant, all was still except the noises of the countryside. Then the silence was broken by a command for Harkens and the men to climb down from the coach.

Clairice had halted and stood with her left side to the coach. She studiously ignored glancing at it, but waited tensely for the shot that would soon be forthcoming.

Both thieves were toward the front of the coach and, Clairice judged, at an excellent angle for Mr. Harding to fire at them. The one standing before her eyed Lady Fairfax's bottle.

"Wot 'ave ye there? Brandy? 'And it over 'ere."

Lady Fairfax clutched it closer to her bosom. "I shall do no such thing!" she declared with indignation. "It is tea, and damme if I shall give it to such riffraff."

The man had taken a step forward at her refusal, but the minute he heard the word "tea," he halted and studied the bottle, then shrugged.

"Get on with it!" the mounted highwayman commanded his partner. He glanced at the ladies and ordered sternly, " 'And over your valuables!"

Clairice and Lady Fairfax exchanged a glance; Clairice lifted the reticule that hung from her wrist and worked the drawstring slowly. Harkens and the men began to paw through their pockets. Suddenly the coach door flew open.

"Drop your weapons!" Mr. Harding shouted, and shot the pistol from the injured highwayman's grasp. The mounted man swung about and fired the flintlock in return.

Mr. Harding's boot caught in the coach step and he pitched forward, sprawling on his face as the bullet whizzed harmlessly over his head.

For the second time within the hour, Mr. Harding had hit the ground forcefully enough to render him unconscious.

Clairice screamed, unaware that he had merely stumbled, or that the shot had passed harmlessly overhead. Convinced that it had gained its mark, she flung herself down beside his inert body. The horses, recovered from the earlier run and standing driverless and uncontrolled, once again bolted.

Lady Fairfax viewed the lurching coach calmly and declared, "There go the real valuables."

The highwayman overheard the remark. He dashed for his horse and yelled to his companion to follow. The two robbers galloped after the vanishing coach.

LADY FAIRFAX LOST NO TIME. "Flee the place at once!" she cried, gathering her skirts and dropping Tick unceremoniously to the ground.

Clairice was horrified. "Grandmother! We cannot abandon Mr. Harding!"

Lady Fairfax halted and looked over her shoulder. "Isn't he dead?" she inquired.

"No!"

As if in answer, the gentleman stirred and blinked, raising himself slightly. Clairice tugged at his shoulder. "Quickly, sir, we should hide."

Without a word he staggered to his feet and put his arm about Clairice's shoulders to steady himself. All three headed for the dense trees with Lady Fairfax leading the way, hobbling at a rapid pace on her cane, the bottle of tea still held securely in her grip. A few yards into the woods they stopped, and she said, "Now, we shall wait awhile and see if they return."

She sat down on a log and motioned to the others to do likewise. The staff remained politely to one side and sat on the ground, engaged in their own quiet discussion. While Clairice whistled the terriers to her side, Lady Fairfax uncorked the bottle, took a long drink of tea, then handed it to Mr. Harding, who accepted it gratefully. He drank deeply, then extended it to her.

Clairice looked down at the frisky dogs. "Grandmother, if those men return, the dogs will bark. Should I take them deeper into the forest?"

Lady Fairfax contemplated the terriers. "If there was

something for them to drink from, we could give them some tea.''

"Tea? For the dogs?'' Mr. Harding murmured.

Clairice gazed about. ''There is nothing here we can use.''

With a baffled expression on his countenance, Mr. Harding rose to the occasion and scrambled to his feet. He produced a piece of curved bark. Lady Fairfax poured carefully while he held it under the dogs' noses.

"Pitiful waste,'' Lady Fairfax declared.

The dogs, hot and thirsty after all the running and barking, drank eagerly. Lady Fairfax poured again.

Mr. Harding gazed at her. ''Madam, that is an unusual brew.''

Lady Fairfax smiled sweetly. After one more serving to the dogs, she sat back on the log and lifted the bottle to her lips. ''That should be sufficient, Clairice. Put them down and let us see. . . .''

Clairice did as instructed, and Lady Fairfax passed the bottle once again to Mr. Harding. He watched the dogs and remarked, ''Perhaps I shouldn't. . . .''

The terriers stretched out at Clairice's feet and closed their eyes in contentment while Mr. Harding drank more tea.

Within moments hoofbeats sounded. Everybody stiffened and peered through the trees at the lane. The highwaymen rode into view, reined and gazed about.

Clairice studied the sleeping dogs and decided there was no danger of being exposed by their barks. The ruffians faced each other as if engaged in discussion; one waved a hand in the air and looked directly at the woods. Then they wheeled their horses and cantered out of sight down the lane.

Everyone in the small group remained silent until all sound of horses had faded and the only noise was a gentle rustle of the dry leaves of oaks and an occasional birdcall. Lady Fairfax urged Mr. Harding to drink more tea. He grinned at her and accepted.

Clairice frowned at the wide smile on his face. "Grandmother," she whispered, "perhaps Mr. Harding has had sufficient tea."

"Nonsense, girl! The man has two terrible bruises on his head." She glanced at the staff. "Harkens, try to find the coach. I do not care to sit on this log all through the night."

"Yes, your ladyship." All three men rose and moved cautiously toward the lane, eventually emerging into the sunlight and disappearing around the bend in the lane.

By the time they returned, the tea had been consumed, and Mr. Harding looked beyond the point of suffering from his mishaps. The terriers had awakened and were gazing peacefully at the trees.

"Come here, you two, and help me up off this confounded log. I am not certain my bones will ever straighten," Lady Fairfax moaned.

Anthony Harding rose and steadied himself against a tree trunk.

Clairice asked, "Are you all right?"

He blinked. "I think I am. . . ." he replied slowly with a degree of uncertainty. The dogs rose and stretched. Clairice and Mr. Harding moved to each side of Lady Fairfax and assisted her to her feet. The task accomplished, Mr. Harding released his hold on her arm immediately and clutched at the nearest tree.

Clairice leaned down to whisper, "Grandmother, see what you have done!" Lady Fairfax waved a hand impatiently and moved slowly, leaning on her cane.

Clairice called the dogs. Tick trotted ahead happily, his gray ears flopping, but Tack was still suffering the effects of the libation and moved in a weaving path to bump gently into a tree trunk and sit down. Mr. Harding was not managing much more successfully than the terrier. He moved slowly, clinging to each tree he passed.

"Here, can I help?" Clairice moved beside him.

He placed an arm about her shoulders. "Thank you. I

do not know what is wrong; must be the knock on the head I received, but I am having diff—difficulty. . . ."

Lady Fairfax led the way, and together they all walked slowly toward the waiting coach. Lady Fairfax reached it ahead of the other two, but Tick bounded in front of her with no respect for age or person, almost causing her to fall. She waved her cane at him and thumped on the carriage step, making the little dog leap frantically inside.

As Clairice and Mr. Harding approached, hoofbeats sounded again, and everyone gazed down the lane with concern.

CHAPTER FIVE

ASTRIDE A BLACK HORSE Lord Ault rode into view. His immaculate dark clothing did not have a wrinkle, and he looked quite dashing. Suddenly Clairice was aware of her own disheveled appearance. He reined and dismounted, remarking, "I became concerned that you'd had an accident, or that the coach had broken down."

Lady Fairfax thrust her head through the coach window and greeted Lord Ault. "We encountered highwaymen," she explained.

Lord Ault's eyes rested curiously on the stranger, and Lady Fairfax said cryptically, "He attempted to save us."

"Mis'rable bungle...." Mr. Harding mumbled and swayed slightly. He steadied himself by gripping Clairice's arm. "Missed and fell—"

"Gammon!" Lord Ault glanced at his forehead. "I presume that is what caused the bruises."

Mr. Harding nodded solemnly. "'Deed. Caused one bump. Got the other later."

"Extraordinary!" Lord Ault pronounced. Clairice remembered her manners and spoke up.

"Lord Ault, may I present—" she began, as Lord Ault studied the gentleman before him with a wary eye "—Mr. Harding."

"Good God!" burst from Lord Ault. He peered at Mr. Harding with the same intense curiosity he would have given to a creature that had dropped out of the sky.

"Lord Ault..." Clairice remarked to Mr. Harding, concluding the introduction. Her voice trailed off in the realization that there was something occurring that she did not understand. Lady Fairfax's sharp eyes were on the two men.

Mr. Harding, in turn, swayed slightly and exclaimed, "Lord Ault! Splendid!" He lurched forward, hand extended, and nearly fell; Lord Ault reached out and steadied him.

Clairice grasped Mr. Harding's arm and explained, "While we waited, grandmother and Mr. Harding shared...."

Lord Ault glanced sharply at Lady Fairfax who smiled sweetly. "Tea!" he finished for Clairice, and she nodded. He gazed at Mr. Harding and swore softly under his breath, then he turned to Lady Fairfax and snapped, "They need to lock you up as a menace to the public!"

She gazed at him intently. "Is this the man you were to meet at Chatham?"

In a tight voice he replied, "Madam, you shall make an absolute lifelong teetotaler out of me."

Lady Fairfax observed Mr. Harding and spoke softly. "You cannot take this man with you, my lord. Someone has handed you a plate of bubbles."

"That is my concern," Lord Ault replied icily. He looked down at Clairice. "You say he fell?"

She nodded. Mr. Harding grinned amiably at no one in particular.

Lord Ault took a deep breath and shook his head. "Well, so be it. I can do nothing about such matters now. I shall help Mr. Harding into...." His voice trailed away.

At that moment Tack lurched out of the woods and trotted in a stumbling, weaving course to them, bumping into Clairice's skirts head-on. Lord Ault's countenance reflected a murderous anger. His gray eyes bored into Clairice's like ice. "Even the dog!"

Clairice's eyes widened at the look of suppressed fury; she scooped the besotted animal into her arms and climbed into the coach hurriedly.

"I shall assist you into the coach, Mr. Harding," Lord Ault stated.

"No, indeed, Lord Ault. I shall ride beside you. Merely aid me into the saddle."

Lord Ault motioned for a groom and instructed the man to fetch Mr. Harding's mount and help him into the saddle. Then he turned on his heel and walked away with a slight shake of his head.

Clairice watched the proceedings from the window. Lord Ault mounted and rode close beside Mr. Harding. She observed them for a long stretch, then shifted with troubled eyes to study her elder. "Grandmother, Mr. Harding is the man who is going to accompany Lord Ault to France, isn't he?"

Lady Fairfax's eyes narrowed. "Now, Clairice, I specifically said that you must not divulge even a whisper of that business."

"Tush! I am not divulging anything if I discuss it with you. You are the one who informed me of the affair." She glanced out the window and her brows drew together. "Grandmother, he cannot undertake such a dangerous task. The poor soul will be killed!"

Lady Fairfax snorted. "Hmpf! You best be concerned with the survival of Lord Ault. He was counting on a steady hand and an agile brain to aid him, not a bumbling fool who cannot untangle his own two feet!"

Clairice tossed her an impatient glance. "Do not be so unkind to a man who attempted valiantly to rescue us."

Her grandmother paused in adjusting the lap rug and narrowed her eyes at her granddaughter. "Clairice! Do not become taken with the likes of that young man."

Clairice blushed. "There are moments it would be nice if you did not speak quite so plainly."

"Bosh! Plain speaking gets the task accomplished. Now you mind me, child. Get away from that window." She nudged Clairice with her cane.

Clairice slid back in the seat and allowed the dogs to climb into her lap. The ride to the coaching inn was

short. When they arrived, Lord Ault dispensed all to
their quarters and disappeared from sight, taking Mr.
Harding in tow.

DINNER WAS SERVED in a private room reserved by Lord
Ault. Clairice felt none the worse for her adventure, and
her mirror told her she looked presentable in a deep
green silk gown trimmed in lace and ribbon, which ac-
cented her tiny waist. Adele wore a pale rose velvet
adorned with a necklace of pearls. Both girls brought
bright color into the room, their gay dresses contrasting
with the dark blue and dark green clothing of the men,
and with Miss Milsap's usual black.

The late April night had a nip in the air, but a fire
roaring in the mammoth hearth filled the parlor with
warmth, and bayberry candles gave off a delectable
scent.

Lady Fairfax sank into a large chintz wing chair until
they moved to the private dining table where she sat as
hostess at one end of the long table, facing Lord Ault.
While the roast duck and lark pie were served, Miss
Milsap received the regular portion of her own health
food. Lord Ault asked politely, "A doctor's prescrip-
tion, ma'am?"

"Indeed not!" Lavinia answered stoutly. "Wouldn't
let one of the creatures near! Sir Weltham Twiligar."

Lord Ault inquired, "Sir Twiligar, ma'am?"

"Blithering idiot!" came a rumble from the end of
the table.

"Aunt Cornelia!" Lavinia gave her a dark look, then
continued forcefully. "Sir Twiligar is a brilliant man.
He has studied in the Orient and throughout Europe
and written lengthy discourses on his findings. The body
should be kept pure, the veins unclogged and the system
regular."

Both girls blushed at this; Mr. Harding missed the
remark altogether, and Lord Ault suddenly found it
necessary to place his hand before his mouth. For once,

Lady Fairfax remained silent, her attention given to the steaming duck on her plate.

Lavinia continued, casting a pointed glance at Lord Ault's plate. "Meat of any kind is the worst offender. It thickens the skin, puts on inordinate fat and poisons the system."

"You don't say," Lord Ault commented dryly.

"Indeed! You are consuming a large serving of poison, my lord!"

"Most amazing, ma'am. I was under the delusion that the only poisonous concoction I had consumed lately was hot tea."

Lady Fairfax's dark eyes snapped in his direction, and he met them squarely.

Lavinia, not to be put off, continued, "That is certainly true, also." She scowled at her aunt. "Dreadful mixture, even worse than meat. Alcohol affects the brain, you know."

"I surmised as much, ma'am," Lord Ault replied under his breath, and Lady Fairfax chuckled.

At the mention of tea, Mr. Harding turned to Lady Fairfax. "I have never consumed such a brew. It does not have the tang of Congue, nor the mildness of Pekoe...." He pondered the matter. "Usually I can tell. Is it Chinese tea?"

"Secret recipe, sir."

"Certainly stout. Not that it wasn't delicious," he added hastily as if in fear he had sounded unkind.

Bored by a conversation she had heard all her years, Clairice inquired of Mr. Harding about his birthplace.

"Norfolk." he replied.

"Do you live there now, sir?"

"When I can. I have been away, first at Oxford, then with my regiment."

"Did you fight the French?"

"Yes, Miss Fairfax."

"Quite honorably," Lord Ault said. "He has earned several decorations." Both girls murmured politely over such accomplishments while Mr. Harding waved them away modestly. "I was fortunate."

"Were you wounded?" Adele inquired.

He rubbed his chin idly and remarked, "Yes, during the battle at Malta. Shot in the leg, as a matter of fact, but not a serious wound."

Lord Ault did not hear their conversation, for he had turned to Adele. Her eyes were downcast as she ate with dainty bites. He said politely, "I trust your dogs traveled well?"

She glanced quickly at him and blushed, then looked down at her plate. "Oh, yes, they enjoy a ride."

"They are charming little fellows. Have you had them long?"

"No, my lord."

Lord Ault studied her. He inquired, "Do you enjoy traveling?"

"Yes, Lord Ault."

Half-listening, Clairice sighed in exasperation at her sister. "Have you ever been away from England?" Lord Ault inquired easily as if his casual conversation was being reciprocated.

"Yes, grandmother took us to France once before when we were quite small." She smiled briefly. "I do not recall much about it except a terrifying boat ride."

He smiled at her and turned his attention to Mr. Harding, who was relating the names of his brothers and sisters to Clairice.

"How many are there?" Lord Ault inquired.

Mr. Harding smiled broadly. "Six of us, as a matter of fact."

"That is hard to envision," Lord Ault commented, "since I was an only child." He listened politely while Mr. Harding related the whereabouts of each offspring.

When he finished Lord Ault said, "I never have heard the full details of the attempted robbery this afternoon What occurred?"

Clairice glanced at her grandmother. Lady Fairfax

swallowed a mouthful of peas and commenced to relate the events, beginning with a disgruntled mention of the fact that Lord Ault went off ahead and left them alone on the road.

"Lady Fairfax, I am sincerely sorry about that. I had no idea we had gained such a distance on your coach. I was thunderstruck when I discovered it, but never suspected you would be stopped by brigands in the daylight hours."

"Well, we certainly were!" she snapped querulously.

"They made Harkens and the other men get off the carriage," Clairice added. "Grandmother shot one of them."

Lord Ault had been in the process of lifting a glass of wine to his lips. His hand halted in midair while Mr. Harding exclaimed, "Superior!"

"You shot one of the highwaymen, Lady Fairfax?" Lord Ault questioned, then added wickedly, "I expected fully that you had plied him with your tea."

She smiled at his remark while Clairice continued, "One of them fired at us and the horses bolted. There was no one to drive them, and we were in a runaway coach. Mr. Harding attempted to halt it, but he was knocked unconscious in his efforts."

Mr Harding smiled and stated happily, "Fell off the coach, as a matter of fact. Just didn't get a good grip on the thing."

Lord Ault remained impassive at this bit of news. His eyes rested briefly on Mr. Harding. "How did you get the carriage stopped? Did the horses wear down?"

Lady Fairfax studied her wine. Clairice glanced at her grandmother. When no answer was forthcoming, she replied quietly, "I halted it."

Lord Ault's eyes widened slightly. "You?"

Lavinia's fork clattered to her plate. "Aunt Cornelia! Did you permit such a thing?"

"Permit it? Good God, Lavinia. The child saved both our lives!"

Lord Ault once again had to place his hand over his mouth; Mr. Harding's eyes danced. He stared at Clairice in open admiration. "Magnificent! You accomplished what I failed to do!" he said without hesitation.

Clairice blushed under the praise. "I did not stop to consider the possibilities. It seemed like the necessary thing to do."

"Remarkable feat! How ever did you do it?" Mr. Harding inquired, gazing in unrestrained admiration at the younger Miss Fairfax.

Her color heightened; a delicate glow suffused her with embarrassment from the neck of the green silk dress to her auburn curls.

"I climbed up onto the seat and pulled them to a stop."

"Superior!" Mr. Harding exclaimed once again.

Lord Ault gazed at her in surprise. "How did you get to the driver's seat?" he inquired.

Clairice's green eyes met his. "I had to climb out and get up there, as a matter of fact."

Lavinia's eyes closed and she swayed in the seat. "Merciful heavens!" She opened them and regarded her aunt. "Aunt Cornelia—" she started sternly, to be nipped immediately.

Aunt Cornelia waved a forkful of duck in the air "Lavinia! Had you been in that coach, you would have been thankful to have it stopped. Our necks were about to be broken!"

"Dreadful! Absolutely dreadful!"

Adele had already been informed of the event by Clairice when they'd been alone before dinner, so she ate quietly while the conversation ebbed and flowed around her.

Lord Ault inquired, "After you gained control of the coach, what occurred?"

Lady Fairfax began eating again with gusto, forcing Clairice to answer.

"We returned for Mr. Harding."

"So glad you did," that gentleman said.

"We put him into the coach and had once again proceeded on our way when the highwaymen returned to hold us up. I am certain Harkens informed them there were only females, for they demanded that the ladies exit. Of course, they knew nothing of Mr. Harding. He hid, and we descended from the coach.

"They forced the men off the carriage, and while we were held at gunpoint, Mr. Harding attempted to save us. When the guns discharged, the horses once again bolted."

Lord Ault inquired, "You were in the coach, sir?"

Mr. Harding flushed and replied forthrightly, "No, Lord Ault, I fell out of it."

Lord Ault's brows flew together. "You *what*?"

Clairice spoke quickly. "He saved us from those terrible men. The coach was gone, and grandmother said our valuables were in it. So the highwaymen rode off after it, and we hid in the woods."

Lord Ault's pleasant composure was gone. His jaw tightened, and he stared fixedly at Mr. Harding, who was beginning for the first time in the evening to look slightly uncomfortable.

Lady Fairfax looked at Lord Ault and at Mr. Harding, then applied herself to dinner with renewed enthusiasm.

With a slight frown on her fair brow, Clairice continued directing her conversation to Lord Ault. "We hid in the wood and the highwaymen returned, but did not discover us. Shortly afterward you arrived. You know the rest," she concluded lamely, discouraged that Lord Ault's grim countenance had not changed.

A silence ensued during which Mr. Harding studiously regarded his wineglass and Lord Ault's gaze rested with a disconcerting steadiness on Mr. Harding.

Lady Fairfax drank heartily of the wine and plopped her glass on the table. "Excellent repast, Lord Ault. Good place to stay. Fine lodgings."

He acknowledged the compliment frostily, as if his mind were on other matters. "Thank you, Lady Fairfax."

The meal was speedily ended, to the relief of several of the participants. When the ladies rose to depart, Lord Ault stepped quickly to Lady Fairfax's side and spoke. "If I may, Lady Fairfax, I would like a brief visit with you later this evening."

"Certainly. Due to my aching joints, I would prefer that you come to our quarters, my lord."

He nodded. "Within the hour, ma'am." He glanced at Clairice, who was supporting her grandmother, and nodded in her direction also, as the ladies left the room. The instant Clairice closed the door, she whispered, "Grandmother, Lord Ault is so vexed with Mr. Harding. Do you think he will send him home?"

Lady Fairfax chuckled. "Don't blame him. I'd throttle the boy if I were in Lord Ault's shoes. Just like old Barthwell to foist an incompetent off on Lord Ault."

"Grandmother, do not call anyone as nice as Mr. Harding an 'incompetent.'"

Her Ladyship wheezed as they mounted the stairs. "Damnable steps! Why don't they furnish rooms below stairs. I need a chair. Stop a minute, girl, and let me get my breath." She rested a gnarled hand on Clairice's arm.

"Clairice," she puffed, "do not...let your affections...get entangled with...Mr. Harding. The boy is not...the type to make you happy."

Clairice laughed. "Grandmother, I suspect he just heard every word! Lower your voice. I have no intention of getting 'entangled' with Mr. Harding. I merely feel he is in terrible danger."

"Certainly is. Lord Ault may do him in within the next few moments."

Clairice looked mildly provoked. "That is not what I was referring to and you know it!"

"Come, child, I am ready to ascend a few more of

these wretched planks. When I get up I am not coming down until we depart. The next meal they can serve in my room. I should have had them do so for dinner.''

They strolled to their rooms. Lord Ault had made arrangements for them to have two bedrooms, one for Clairice and Adele, the other for Lavinia and Lady Fairfax, with a small sitting room between the two.

Promptly upon arrival, Lady Fairfax amended the arrangements, placing Adele with Lavinia and Clairice with herself. She reached her door, telling Clairice, ''Send Adele in to see me. Tick and Tack are to be sent back to Fairfax Hall. We cannot carry two dogs to France.''

''I suspect Adele has already decided that herself. If you will send word to James to fetch them, I am certain she will be content.''

''I am well aware of that, miss. When I dispatched Harkens for Fairfax Hall earlier, I sent word for James to come get the dogs. I would not even leave the dogs with Harkens.''

They reached the room and Clairice helped Lady Fairfax to a chair, then left to find Adele.

The dog situation was speedily disposed of once Adele discussed it with her grandmother. Both girls sat facing Lady Fairfax, who had her feet propped on a stool and a soft quilt thrown over her legs.

''I would most heartily like to retire. I do wish Lord Ault would get himself up here and be done with it,'' she grumbled.

Adele raised her head at the words. ''Lord Ault is coming up to see you?'' Without waiting for an answer, she rose to her feet. ''I think I shall retire to bed now, grandmother.''

Clairice smiled. ''Addie, sit down. Why do you run from the man? One would think he is a monster!''

Adele blushed. ''I . . . I just feel nervous in his presence, Clairice.''

Clairice laughed. ''He is far too handsome, Addie, to

cause anyone to suffer from his presence. You are being ridiculous!''

Adele's color heightened. "Clairice! Really!"

"Well, it is true. Don't you think Lord Ault is handsome, grandmother?"

Before Lady Fairfax could reply, Adele announced firmly, "I am going to bed." She hurried from the room.

Clairice stared into space with a smile hovering on her lips. "And isn't Mr. Harding handsome?" Her gaze rested on Lady Fairfax, who was poking through her portmanteau.

"Grandmother, don't you think so?" Clairice asked insistently.

"Eh, child? Oh, Clairice, you think every male you have encountered since you were twelve years old is handsome! Where is my snuff?"

Clairice jumped to her feet. "I will fetch it. I saw it before dinner." She departed into the bedroom and crossed to a small marble-topped table to retrieve the gold-enameled box. When she reentered the sitting room, Lord Ault was there.

He stood just inside the door; his expression was grim as he nodded in her direction. Clairice handed Lady Fairfax the snuffbox and hurriedly excused herself. She returned to the bedroom, quietly closed the door, then knelt to peer through the keyhole. She shifted, with green skirt and petticoats billowing, first to one side, then a fraction to the other, until she gained a view of Lord Ault's knee. He spoke in soft tones, but sufficiently loud to carry to Clairice's straining ears.

"Lady Fairfax, we have a matter to discuss."

"Sit down, Lord Ault, sit down."

"I think I shall stand if you do not mind. I shall be brief, for the hour is late and I know you are weary from travel. I cannot take you to Paris. I shall convey you to Fairfax Hall tomorrow morning at whatever time you wish. The carr—"

"Bosh!" she interrupted him. "We shall accompany you to Paris. Or, you shall accompany us, however you wish to state it, but we shall arrive together. Now I have you on that score, and you might as well yield to the fact."

"Then I throw myself on your better judgement and your mercy. Today has been tedious. I cannot undertake what I have to accomplish and guard four females at the same time. I have enough to worry about as it is."

"Decidedly poor choice," she stated obliquely. "I would guess old Barthwell picked the boy."

Lord Ault's voice held a weary note. "I wish he had your mind; I would certainly be relieved."

She chuckled. "Thank you for such a compliment. Sit down, Lord Ault. You look as if you are on the verge of collapse. Are you certain that this boy has done all the things you were told?"

Clairice shifted as Lord Ault's legs moved. Suddenly his face loomed in sight as he sat down in a wing chair facing her door. She jumped away from the keyhole, startled that he might notice her. Within a second, curiosity overcame caution, and she knelt at the hole once again and listened.

"Mr. Harding has done them, all right," Lord Ault sighed, "though God knows how he did. Perhaps today was an off day. I shall hope so." He leaned forward. "Lady Fairfax, I beg you, do not go on tomorrow. France is not a safe place. There are spies everywhere—even one in our midst. War with Bonaparte could break out at any second; that is part of the urgency of what I have to accomplish. If it does, your niece and granddaughters, as well as yourself, could be in a precarious position." He spoke emphatically. "Napoleon hates the British. We are the force blocking his path to conquering the world."

"I understand thoroughly, Lord Ault. That is part of the reason I must insist on having my way in this matter. I have relatives in France, and I intend to convince them to return to England with me. I will have to go in person to do so."

"God help me!" he ejaculated and fell back in the chair. "How many do I have to bring back to England?" Without waiting for her answer, he snapped, "I shall not do this!"

"You have no choice," she replied. "Now look here, Lord Ault, we shall be no trouble to you. I will not place Lavinia in your carriage again. You cannot tell me that you mind the company of my granddaughters, for I know better than that."

Suddenly he leaped to his feet and crossed the room in long strides.

He yanked the door open violently, and Clairice fell forward with a shriek, gazing up at him in fright, her eyes wide.

His eyes flashed in anger, and his face mirrored his fury. When he spoke it was in a tightly controlled tone. He leaned down and grasped Clairice's arm to raise her to her feet, glaring into her eyes.

Her cheeks flamed. "I . . . I am sorry."

"Did you do that for your own amusement?" he lashed out.

She nodded and he snapped, "I could have you placed under arrest for spying! You could use a good thrashing. Do not ever do that again, do you hear?"

"Clairice! Of all things!" Lady Fairfax interrupted in exasperation.

"I am sorry," she whispered.

"Terrible child! Lord Ault, you will have to forgive the girl, but I can assure you she does not tell tales. Your secrets are safe; now come sit down."

Lady Fairfax retrieved a bottle of tea from her portmanteau. "Clairice, fetch some glasses. Lord Ault has earned a cup of tea tonight."

"The devil!" he exploded. "This confounded family is going to drive me wild!" He whirled and stomped from the room, slamming the door with such force that the windowpanes rattled.

Lady Fairfax looked at her granddaughter and her lips curled in amusement. "You little scamp! Got caught that time!"

Clairice blushed. "Oh, grandmother, I have made him so angry!"

The other interior door flew open; Adele stood in the doorway, clad in a gown and robe. "What was that terrible bang?" she asked in wonder.

Lady Fairfax uncorked the tea and took a swig. "Lord Ault," she said. "He caught Clairice listening at the keyhole to his conversation."

"Clairice!" Adele cried. "You didn't? How awful! I shall never be able to face him."

"I am sorry, Addie. How was I to know he would find out?" She blinked rapidly and glanced at Lady Fairfax. "How did he discover me, grandmother?"

"Deuced if I know." She lowered the bottle. "Summon that maid of mine; I am worn out. I do not want to hear any more about it. You will be able to face him, Addie, for you were not involved." Her gaze rested on Clairice. "As for you—I would step lightly around the man for a day or two. He has his troubles, girl. Don't add to them."

LORD AULT'S MOOD did not attain a degree of improvement with the passage of time. The women breakfasted without male companionship, dining on cold grouse, deviled kidneys, omelets, melon and hot porridge, none of which looked appetizing to Clairice, who was still suffering acute embarrassment from the night before.

After breakfast Lady Fairfax hurried her family, minus the canine duo, into one carriage to leave the men to themselves. Mr. Harding appeared, gracing them with a pleasant greeting, then turning away as though his mind was on other matters. A hint of a frown showed on his bruised forehead.

With the barest of nods to the Fairfax family, Lord Ault climbed into his own carriage to embark on the last lap of the journey to Dover.

The ride was uneventful, and by noon they halted at a large coaching inn to partake of a repast before boarding a waiting yacht.

The innkeeper greeted Lord Ault. Then in an undertone that carried clearly to Clairice and Lady Fairfax, he informed Lord Ault that two gentlemen awaited his company.

With a word to Mr. Harding, Lord Ault moved away from the rest and followed the innkeeper around the side of the inn. In the meantime, the ladies were shown rooms in which to rest and refresh.

When they joined Mr. Harding once again, Lord Ault was also in attendance. His gaze rested on Lady Fairfax, and with a steely glint in his eyes he bore down on her.

"Lady Fairfax, may I have a word with you?" He waved his hand in the direction of an adjoining room.

Lady Fairfax leaned on her cane and accompanied him. Once the door closed and they achieved privacy, he spoke. "Lady Fairfax, Sir Barthwell and Mr. Crenshawe have joined me to travel to France." His face flushed. "You have put me in a high pickle indeed! Do you realize what you are doing to my career?"

"Stuff and nonsense! We shall be out of your way once we reach Paris. We have been over this far too many times, Lord Ault, to accomplish any purpose in another discussion of the subject. The matter is closed."

Had Lady Fairfax not been made of strong stuff and fortified with an ample helping of her own brew, she might have withered under a look that had caused strong men to pale. Lord Ault stared at her in consternation, while she looked him directly in the eye.

His voice was a tight rasp as he spoke. "Madam, if Boney throws you into prison, for the first time in my career that strutting leader will have a grain of my sympathy. I will not be responsible for your safekeeping, or for that of your family! Once I have accomplished my purpose, you will have no weapon with which to exert your influence over me, and you had best beware that I do not abandon you in Paris, for I am sorely tempted to do so!''

Her ladyship considered this solemnly. "I can understand your feeling at the moment, for you have weighty matters on your mind, but we shall keep out of your way and cause you no trouble—" she regarded him with narrowed eyes "—and in all honesty we have not actually thrust a spoke in your wheels thus far. Once you have accomplished your purpose, my lord, you will view the whole matter in a vastly different light.''

His chest swelled with a deep inhalation. "Perhaps, Lady Fairfax, it is you who will soon view the matter in a vastly diverse manner. I simply cut my ties of any responsibility for the outcome of your deplorable actions!''

"I am prepared for such an event," she replied calmly.

His color deepened. "Do you realize what kind of fool you have made me appear?''

She gazed at him steadfastly. "Now, however could I have done that?''

"I am certain you know full well!" he snapped. "Sir Barthwell and Mr. Crenshawe both have joined me. I could not explain your presence to them by revealing that I have been so indiscreet as to allow you to control my activities through intimidation. The only course open to me—other than full revelation and ruin to my career—was to convince them that I think having you along will give me a ploy to hide my true reasons for a journey to France.''

"Gammon!" she chuckled. "I would like to have heard you present my own theories, for I know you could do so convincingly.''

His eyes blazed. "Lady Fairfax, I have never before encountered such odious behavior in a female. You have taken the worst sort of advantage of my unsuspecting nature, your granddaughter is a sneak and a busybody, listening at keyholes, and your niece would try the patience of a saint. To combine this with a jackanapes who cannot keep his own feet untangled is sufficient to drive the most patient soul to commit violence,'' he added darkly.

She shrugged. ''I will admit that Lavinia is all you say. Clairice meant no harm, though, and she will not reveal a word of what she heard. Mr. Harding must have some ability somewhere to have accomplished anything in his past career. As for me—'' her eyes settled on him in a hard look ''—I did not force the tea down your throat, sir. From your reputation, I feel that you are worldly and experienced to a sufficient degree to be responsible for your own actions.''

The last remark caused a fearful darkening of Lord Ault's countenance. He turned on his heel and departed from the room in long vigorous strides. He passed through the adjoining chamber without a word to its startled occupants.

Lady Fairfax emerged slowly in his wake. Clairice rushed to her side, and while polite conversation resumed, she leaned down to whisper, ''Grandmother, what did you do to Lord Ault? I have never seen such a fit of blue murder!''

''Lord Ault is steaming, Clairice, over events he cannot control. I do not think the man is used to such a turn, but he will come to no harm from it and will be the better man for having had to cope with such a knotty problem.''

Clairice blinked. ''What knotty problem?''

Lady Fairfax looked up serenely and smiled. ''Us, granddaughter, us.''

CHAPTER SIX

WITHIN THE HOUR they had boarded a trim yacht. It was a cool overcast afternoon with a brisk breeze that caused small whitecaps to roll across the gray sea. Lady Fairfax settled herself in a large deck chair, while Bessie piled pillows behind her back, then covered her with a lap robe.

Lavinia disappeared instantly for her cabin to prevent any ray of sun from ravishing her delicate skin, and the two girls paused at the rail near Lady Fairfax, excited over the prospects of crossing the Channel.

The next to board was Lord Ault, in the company of Sir Barthwell and Mr. Crenshawe. Introductions were performed, with the exception of Lady Fairfax and Sir Barthwell who were old acquaintances. Sir Barthwell excused himself to go to his cabin due to gout, while Mr. Crenshawe found it more entertaining to take a position at the rail beside Clairice.

Clairice's cheeks flamed at the sight of Lord Ault, for all too clearly could she recall their encounter at the keyhole. She turned away, but not before receiving an angry glance from him.

Her gaze fell on Mr. Harding, who stood on the quay giving instructions to a burly seaman about a large collection of trunks and baggage piled nearby. The wind caught a lock of his blond hair and blew it gently away from his forehead.

Finally Mr. Harding turned toward the yacht, then glanced over his shoulder to reply to a question from the sailor. As he conversed he continued to approach the ship.

At the sight of him striding directly on a course to collide with the railing of the gangplank, Clairice exclaimed, "Oh, no!"

Lord Ault ceased a conversation he was having with the captain and followed Clairice's gaze to view Mr. Harding a mere yard away from the flimsy post at the bottom of the gangplank.

"Harding!" Lord Ault snapped loudly.

Mr. Harding's head swiveled, and he discovered the post blocking his path. He sidestepped quickly, but unfortunately in the wrong direction.

His foot trod on a thick length of rope lying in wait on the quay, his arms flailed the air, he stumbled and snatched at empty space, then toppled from the quay into the water with a hearty splash.

Both girls shrieked; Lord Ault gave vent to vigorous swearing, which turned Adele's face a deep scarlet and caused her to edge away from him. Clairice's only concern was for the disappearing blond head in the murky waters below.

"He will drown!" she gasped.

"Pray for it!" Lord Ault ground out in a lowered breath, which carried only to Clairice's ears.

She flicked a horrified glance at him, then clutched the rail in fright and gazed at the widening ripples.

At the sound of the commotion Lady Fairfax sat up. "What in heaven's name . . . ?"

Between the cries of her progeny and Lord Ault's swearing, she sank back against the pillows, murmuring, "Harding, no doubt."

The object of concern bobbed into sight, his blond head emerging from the water. He swam the few strokes to the dock and was hauled up by two sailors. He climbed soggily out of the water and turned to face his audience with a dramatic shrug and a sheepish grin.

Lord Ault spun on his heel and disappeared into a cabin.

Within moments Mr. Harding gained the deck. Dripping and red-faced, he nodded to the girls and extended a wet hand to Mr. Crenshawe, who greeted him pleasantly but did not offer his own hand in return. Small puddles formed around his boots as the water dripped from his ruined clothing.

Clairice inquired breathlessly, "Are you hurt?"

He shook his head. "No, but I'd better change." He hurried out of sight. Clairice and Adele looked at each other.

"How awful for the poor man," Clairice murmured.

"Lord Ault is furious with him," Adele replied.

"Chuckle-headed nincompoop, if you ask me," Mr Crenshawe remarked casually.

"Oh, no, sir!" Clairice rose quickly to Harding's defense. "Anyone can stumble; it was not done deliberately."

Lady Fairfax, overhearing this exchange, glanced at her granddaughters. Both girls turned again to the rail and engaged in soft-voiced conversation with Mr. Crenshawe, which did not carry clearly to Lady Fairfax.

She studied them, noticing with satisfaction that their contrasting appearances complemented each other. Clairice's deep blue silk pelisse, trimmed with dark mink and a matching blue bonnet, was pleasant beside the soft rose of Adele's lovely spencer and gown. Adele's bonnet was graced with deep blue plumes that matched Clairice's pelisse.

Mr. Crenshawe's broad frame separated the two girls, but he moved smoothly to Clairice's right and lounged with his arm against the rail facing them, so he could converse more easily with both at the same time.

It also left his countenance open to Lady Fairfax's keen eyes. His splendid physique, as broad-shouldered and tall as Lord Ault's, was, in her judgment, offset by a heavy thrusting jaw and slightly small eyes set a fraction too close together. Her lips tightened in an awareness of which girl was entertaining him sufficiently to cause the man to continue standing at the rail. His gaze rested far more often and lingered a greater length of time on Clairice.

If Clairice had come to the same realization, she gave no notice of it, but chattered unselfconsciously with him.

At length Adele tired of standing and joined her grandmother, sitting alongside her in another deck chair.

THE CROSSING WAS UNEVENTFUL and no mishaps marred the journey to Paris, other than a dampening of everyone's spirits by Lord Ault's frosty disposition, Lavinia's grumbling and Sir Barthwell's gout.

After landing, their carriages rolled through small French villages, and everywhere there were signs of a military nation. The blue-and-white coats of uniformed men were abundant amid the simple country folk whose women were dressed in red camlet jackets and high white aprons. The older men were dressed in plain dark clothing, contrasting with the colorful uniforms of French cavalrymen, Hussars, Lancers and various regiments.

By the time they reached Paris, the passengers were weary of travel, but Clairice and Adele gazed out of the carriage with eagerness at the new sights.

"Look at all the construction. It looks as if the First Consul is creating a new city!" Clairice declared.

"They are wealthy enough to do so," Lady Fairfax commented dryly, "with the monies gained from conquered countries."

Lavinia shifted and frowned. "I wonder when this dreadful ride will end. I feel as if I have been traveling for a fortnight," she complained, pulling her heavy wool cape tighter about her neck.

"We shall soon be there," Lady Fairfax reassured her. "Ah, the Seine."

"Oh, isn't it pretty with the trees all along it!" Clairice exclaimed, leaning forward on the seat to press her nose against the edge of the window.

"Same dirty-looking river as the Thames," Lavinia stated. "Smells terribly of fish.'

The procession halted, and within seconds their door opened. Mr. Harding smiled at them. "We are stopping here for a moment to allow Lord Ault, Mr. Crenshawe and Sir Barthwell to alight. I shall accompany you to your destination, then return here to the Embassy. It will only be a moment."

He closed the door and was gone, but true to his word, they soon rolled along down the narrow cobbled street once again.

When the entourage rolled to a halt at the home of Hyacinth and Marcel Rollet, Lady Fairfax was the first to alight. She allowed Mr. Harding to escort her to the entrance.

The door was flung open by Madame Rollet herself. She threw her arms around Lady Fairfax, and the two sisters embraced. Then Madame Rollet stepped back to gaze down at her sister.

"I am so happy you are here!" She looked around. "And this must be little Clairice—my dear!" Clairice and Adele each dutifully kissed Madame Rollet's proffered cheek, and Lavinia extended a gloved hand for greeting.

Mr. Harding was introduced, then Madame Rollet took Lady Fairfax's arm. "Come with me. Marcel so regrets that he could not come down at the moment, but he shall dine with us. He is not well. It seems he has contracted a bad case of *démangeaison,* the itch."

"Oh, God help us!" Lavinia murmured, and steadied herself by gripping Adele's arm as she looked wildly around the hall.

"His nerves are in a deplorable condition, due to the suffering he has been subjected to by this miserable rash."

Lady Fairfax wavered from side to side as she proceeded to the salon on her cane. "I shall settle his nerves. I can do that quite ably—have just the thing."

They entered an elegant salon decorated in ornate gilt furniture upholstered in rose damask and velvet. A dainty footstool ensnared Mr. Harding's foot, but he recovered swiftly with only the slightest stumble.

"We shall have tea," Hyacinth announced pleasantly as a maid appeared with an elaborate tea service.

Lavinia perched on the edge of a chair and announced, "Aunt Hyacinth, I have brought my own tea, as well as my own food."

"Your own food! *Tiens!*" She laughed with a high tinkling sound. "Two diets! Marcel eats only certain things, you know. He thinks there are foods that contribute to his misery." She smiled and shrugged. "Even the First Consul eats beans and sometimes olives for breakfast." She gazed at them happily. "I am so pleased to see you. Cornelia, if I had had more notice of your coming I could have had more parties for you to attend while you are here."

"I am certain that we shall have sufficient entertainment. I am surprised to find that you will have any parties at all."

"Ah, the gloomy days of the Revolution are passing away; it is a new age for France. And spring is here—such a lovely time to visit Paris. The terrible winter—everyone had *la grippe*—is gone. And such fine gentlemen to escort you; I am certain you had a pleasant journey."

Lavinia leaned forward. "The grippe, you say?"

Hyacinth laughed as she poured tea. "Do not concern yourself, Lavinia dear, the English tourists withstood it remarkably well."

Tea was served while she continued talking. "I do hope the teacakes and jam are as you like them. I still have our old recipes, but Jacques is a thoroughly French cook and prefers his own style in the kitchen. One of the first parties, a dinner, will be held at the home of the archchancellor. His parties are given with regularity each Tuesday and Saturday, and he is an absolute dictator on promptness. Next week you will be presented to the First Consul at a reception in the Tuileries.

"The dinner at the home of Cambacérès will be tomorrow evening, so no time must be lost in visiting our marvelous dressmaker, Mlle Despeaux. We have two superb dressmakers—a new young man, Leroy, and Mlle Despeaux, whom I still prefer. The First Consul has banned her from the premises for persuading his wife to overspend. You will find her delightful."

Lady Fairfax closed her eyes momentarily, then said loudly, "Hyacinth, I do believe I had forgotten how much you enjoy talking."

Her sister giggled. "I hope I am not tiring you after your travel. Have—" Madame Rollet paused at the sight of a tall gaunt man appearing in the doorway.

"Marcel, here they are!" Madame Rollet called.

Her husband shuffled into the room; his sad droopy eyes, with permanent dark circles underneath, moved from relative to relative as he crossed to greet them. Lavinia sank back into her chair and merely nodded at him.

Marcel Rollet spoke slowly and scratched his shoulder idly while he talked. "Welcome to France. I am certain Hyacinth has informed you of the malady from which I am suffering, so you will have to excuse me from certain social amenities. We are so happy to have you." He looked sadly from one to another.

"Sit down, Marcel," his wife said. "Marcel cannot attend to his business affairs until he has recuperated."

"And what business is that, sir?" Mr. Harding inquired politely.

"A director of the Banque de France," he replied. Mr. Harding paled and fell silent.

Madame Rollet declared, "*Monnaie—monnaie, mon Dieu!* The all-consuming thing! Thank goodness Marcel has to be away from it for a time, and we can enjoy his company all day long. Have you been to Paris before, Mr. Harding?"

He smiled over his teacup. "Indeed after—"

"Good. But another visit is always welcome, and you must see the things the First Consul is doing to improve this city. He is rebuilding and changing countless sites. We shall have an even more beautiful city when he is finished. He has commenced a road between the Tuileries and the Louvre. And, of course, you must see the Venetian horses brought from the Church of St. Mark's, and the Elysium, and the Banque, which was established three years ago. The First Consul intended the Banque to be located in the Church de la Madeleine, but eventually they settled on the Hotel Toulouse, a mansion that had belonged to the Comte de Toulouse. Marcel shall have to give you a tour—there are one hundred and seventy rooms. You cannot miss the Louvre; the First Consul is making it the finest collection of art in the world. The director, Monsieur Denon, acquires paintings constantly. Some treaties of war have included stipulations that art treasures must come to France. We have the Apollo Belvedere and the Venus de Milo...."

Lady Fairfax sat forward and announced bluntly, "Hyacinth, I am weary and need a nap."

Immediately Mr. Harding rose and made his farewells, and the Fairfax ladies were shown to their rooms.

CLAIRICE LEFT HER BEDCHAMBER to join her grandmother and aid in supervising the unpacking. No sooner had they commenced than Lavinia appeared.

"Aunt Cornelia, we must depart this place instantly!"

"You will get accustomed to Hyacinth's constant chatter, Lavinia." Lady Fairfax sank into a chair and studied the articles of clothing removed from the trunk by Betsy.

"Bring a bottle of my tea, Clairice," she requested.

Lavinia persisted. "Aunt Hyacinth is pleasant company; that is not the matter to which I am referring."

Clairice handed an unopened bottle to Lady Fairfax.

"What is the problem, Lavinia? Sit down, you look on the verge of collapse."

"I do not want to sit down in this house—or eat here—or sleep under this roof. We must depart!"

Lady Fairfax uncorked the bottle and asked Betsy to fetch a cup. Clairice inquired politely, "Aunt Lavinia, what is the difficulty?"

"Uncle Marcel has an infectious disease, and we could all come down with it." She shuddered and scratched her elbow.

"Fiddlesticks!" Lady Fairfax snapped. "If it was infectious, Hyacinth would have it."

"That is not necessarily so. I shall fetch my medical book and read the information to you," Lavinia replied.

"Damme if I shall listen to any medical treatise!" Lady Fairfax pounded the floor with her cane. "Lavinia, pack your bags and stay in a hotel if you wish, but the rest of us are not moving from this house!"

"I could not possibly reside alone in a French hotel! An unmarried female in a hotel in a foreign city...." She closed her eyes.

Clairice turned away quickly and began to help with the unpacking. Lady Fairfax poured a cup of tea and drank, then remarked, "Lavinia, I suspect that you would be safe."

THE AMBASSADOR STROLLED IDLY in front of a wide oak desk at one end of the room. He spoke in solemn tones.

"As I was saying, gentlemen, I expect hostilities to break out at any moment." He gave each man a long hard look. "We must locate those invasion plans and convey them to the prince. The fate of our country may hang in the balance." He stopped pacing and locked his hands behind his back while he talked. "I have word from our agents that the camp of Boulogne has been reactivated and orders issued that soldiers be taught to swim in three-hour shifts around the clock."

"Damme! If that doesn't sound like preparations for an invasion!" Lord Ault exclaimed.

The ambassador nodded. "Word of this has been sent to the prince. The courier may have passed you on your journey."

Sir Barthwell shifted in his chair as he inquired, "What are your feelings on this?"

Lord Whitworth answered, "I am certain you have been apprised of the February meeting I had with Napoleon. He went into one of his towering rages. The man has an uncontrollable temper, stomping and screaming in front of the diplomatic corps, shouting at me, asking me if we want war."

"Colossal gall, I would say," Sir Barthwell murmured. "The man has instigated wars all over the continent!"

Lord Whitworth replied, "He threatened war, but he declared that we are forcing him into it. He was enraged about armaments along our coast and the fact that we have not respected the Amiens Treaty, but when I attempted to explain, he would not pause to listen or let me speak."

"Impossible!" Lord Ault declared. "We cannot abandon Malta. The French have not lived up to their agreement to evacuate Holland."

"Not to mention the annexation of Piedmont," Mr. Crenshawe added.

Lord Whitworth urged, "Gentlemen, you must locate and get those invasion plans to the prince. If war breaks out, I do not know if we can withstand the French."

Lord Ault spoke quietly. "We shall have two formidable weapons—" he looked at the others and finished "—Lord Nelson and Pitt."

"Indeed," Mr. Crenshawe agreed.

Sir Barthwell crossed his thin legs. "I wonder if it is a tempest in a teapot. I, for one, am still not convinced that all of this will lead to war. Boney may be pushing us to get what he wants, with no intention of carrying out his threats. I cannot believe he actually cares to pit his forces against our fleet. I even wonder if invasion plans exist, or are merely a hoax.''

Lord Ault interjected, ''Henry Tayburn was killed because of those plans.''

Sir Barthwell nodded. ''Yes, yes, I know. I concede that some papers exist, but perhaps Tayburn was tricked. Perhaps they are merely empty plans to worry us.''

Lord Whitworth replied, ''Make no mistake, Napoleon does not make idle threats. He will not hesitate to attack if he so chooses.''

''It would take everything we have to repel him,'' Lord Ault commented. ''He has performed miracles before, pulled together ragged armies, undisciplined men, then whipped them into a superior fighting force. His defeat of the Austrians with only fifteen cannons, as opposed to their two hundred, will go down in history as a remarkable feat.''

''We are dealing with a brilliant mind,'' Mr. Crenshawe remarked, ''which makes him one of the most dangerous opponents.''

Lord Whitworth turned toward the window and smiled. ''Well, gentlemen—'' he looked at them again ''—it is late in the day and I am certain you are weary from your journey. Shall we meet again early in the morning and go over the information I have received?''

There was a murmur of agreement and the men rose slowly, turning and moving down the length of the elegant room to the tall double doors. Lord Ault and Lord Whitworth fell into step. Behind them, Sir Barthwell spoke. ''You have not convinced me yet, Lord Whitworth, that we are not reading threats into every action of the man.''

Lord Whitworth paused at the closed doors, his hand folded over the knob, and looked at Sir Barthwell. ''I disagree. One of our agents has informed me where Napoleon plans to land—thirteen kilometers from Dover—where Julius Caesar disembarked.''

"Gammon!" Lord Ault looked at his superior. "That should be sufficient evidence of how cautious we should be!"

Sir Barthwell shrugged. "I suppose you are correct, but I cannot envision an actual invasion of England. It is unthinkable."

"We have not been invaded," Mr. Crenshawe added, "since the Battle of Hastings. The French cannot match our fleet."

"They shall not have to, if they attack on land," Mr. Harding spoke quietly.

Lord Whitworth opened the door, and they moved into the hall. The ambassador paused and faced them. "We are all invited to a dinner by the archchancellor tomorrow evening. The Rollets and their guests will also be present, which should please you, Lord Ault."

Lord Ault smiled frostily and made no comment.

Lord Whitworth continued, "We shall meet again in the morning and be finished around noon."

Sir Barthwell raised watery eyes to gaze at Lord Ault. "That should leave you some time to visit the young ladies."

"How nice," Lord Ault replied tightly.

"Perhaps I shall do the same myself," Mr. Crenshawe announced with a smile. "We could take them to view the sights of Paris."

"Splendid! I would enjoy spending the afternoon in such a manner." Mr. Harding smiled with enthusiasm, which increased the icy glint in Lord Ault's eyes.

Sir Barthwell's gaze moved across the men. "Very well, gentlemen, but do not forget—" his voice dropped "—your purpose for this trip."

After farewells were said, Lord Ault and Mr. Harding climbed into the coach for the short ride to their hotels, each staying at different ones for security reasons.

En route, Lord Ault muttered grimly, "Harding, I cannot reach the hotel too soon. This has been a tiring afternoon. Thank heavens we do not have to spend the evening with anyone.''

"Where are the others staying?'' Mr. Harding inquired.

"Barthwell is at another hotel, closer to the Embassy, and Crenshawe is in a hotel near ours.''

"Four hotels?''

"Sir Barthwell felt it would be prudent. There are too many eyes and ears watching everything, listening. You missed nothing this afternoon while you escorted the ladies to their lodgings. We shall get down to the important matters in the morning. Sir Barthwell was obviously quite weary from the journey, and we had little time.''

They lapsed into silence. Lord Ault gazed at the buildings and listened to the clatter of the carriage along the cobbles. He replied to a question from Mr. Harding and noticed a peculiar expression on the man's face. "Something wrong, Harding?''

"Er, no, your Lordship. I thought, ah, is anything troubling you, sir?''

"Troubling me? I suppose my mind is on the matter before us. I am sorry if I did not hear what you said to me.''

"That is nothing, your Lordship.''

Lord Ault gazed at the younger man. "Ever think of marriage, Harding?''

"Marriage, my lord? No, not particularly. I suppose there never has been the time. The day will come when I shall settle down and wed.'' He smiled. "Are you thinking of it, sir?''

"I wish to heaven I had not.'' He stared thoughtfully at Harding. "You think your life is orderly, and then something happens and everything is topsy-turvy.''

"I am dreadfully sorry.''

Lord Ault shrugged. "I have asked for Miss Fairfax's hand in marriage.''

Mr. Harding raised his eyebrows. "Miss Clairice Fairfax, your lordship?''

"My God, no! 'Tis bad enough as it is. . . Miss Adele Fairfax. Oh, she doesn't know it, but I spoke to Lady Fairfax about the matter."

Harding ran slender fingers through his blond hair in a quick nervous sweep. "Miss Adele, your Lordship? And she does not have knowledge of it?"

"No. But now, Harding, I sincerely wish I had done no such thing. When one marries, one marries not only the lady, but also her entire family. You cannot eliminate them."

"Oh, no, sir." Mr. Harding frowned. "Miss Adele Fairfax. And you don't want to marry her? She is so beautiful. . . ."

"But that's the thing. I won't be marrying just Miss Fairfax; I will be acquiring the entire lot of them: Miss Milsap, Lady Fairfax—" his voice grew more bleak until he ground out the last name hoarsely "—and Miss Clairice! Damme! I would give anything to be able to retract that offer!"

"Then I shouldn't think you would have a problem," Mr. Harding responded brightly. "Merely go to Lady Fairfax and retract the offer."

"Harding, men—honorable men—do not retract offers of marriage, and you know it."

"Then, my lord, ask the lady herself. If you do not love each other, Miss Adele Fairfax looks sufficiently independent to decline your offer."

Lord Ault gazed in surprise at Mr. Harding. "Harding, I don't think the lady has the least shred of independence."

"Oh, indeed she does. Perhaps it shall be much easier than you anticipate."

Lord Ault shook his head. "I don't know, Harding. I shall face that problem when we return to England. At the moment I feel more that it should be *if* we return to England." He sighed. "I do not know what is happening to me. I can never recall burdening another person with my problems. It seems I am suddenly doing all sorts of things I have not done before.''

"Think nothing of it," Mr. Harding said reassuringly.

"There is another pressing matter close at hand. Tomorrow night, Harding, we shall dine at the home of the archchancellor. If there is any opportunity for me to slip away from the crowd and discover any useful information, I shall do so.''

"Of course, your Lordship, I understand.''

Lord Ault said reflectively, "We must do something to discover who in our own ranks is disclosing information to the French. Henry Tayburn would be alive today if it were not for this man. We *must* discover his identity.''

"Indeed, sir. Our own lives are in danger from this traitor.''

The two men observed each other solemnly. "You are quite correct," Lord Ault stated. "Whoever he is, I am certain he knows of our mission. He may even know our every move, for he circulates in high circles both in England and France. And I do not agree with Sir Barthwell. I feel certain there are invasion plans and that they are not a hoax.'' His voice deepened with feeling. "I intend to deliver them home to the prince. Perhaps I can turn up something helpful tomorrow night.''

"We shall hope so, sir. We need to move quickly. I shall stay on the alert.''

Lord Ault looked at him keenly. "Try to be as unobtrusive as possible, Harding.''

"Right, sir. You can count on me.''

The two drifted into an easy silence. Cabriolets, gigs and barouches passed as Lord Ault's carriage moved through the traffic. Lord Ault glanced briefly at Mr. Harding, then his gaze returned to rest on him in speculation.

"Harding. . . .''

Mr. Harding's blue eyes returned to meet Lord Ault's gaze. "My lord?"

"I feel something is troubling you, too."

Mr. Harding smiled. "Ah, no, your Lordship. Merely lost in my thoughts about the Rollets."

"I see." Lord Ault dismissed his concern and turned to the window.

After a moment Mr. Harding spoke. "Monsieur Rollet is a director of the Bank of France. At the moment he is—"

"God in heaven! What did you say?" Lord Ault whipped about in the seat and stared in horror at his subordinate.

"Oh, dear me, you didn't know. Sir, he is a director of the bank—"

"And appointed by Napoleon, who created the bank!" Lord Ault roared. "That woman! That confounded woman! Blast!" He swore heartily.

Mr. Harding regarded Lord Ault a moment, then cleared his throat. "Er, your Lordship, is there anything I can do?"

"No, thank you, Harding."

"Sir, I do not intend to pry, but has some woman— that woman to whom you referred...."

"It is a long story, Harding, and not a pleasant one. I am astounded to find, while on the mission in which we are engaged, that I have escorted a young lady to Paris whose granduncle is one of Napoleon's hand-picked selections to manage the finances of the country."

"Oh, I see." replied Harding in a tone that conveyed no such clarity. After a moment of silence he added, "That should be of no concern where the ladies are involved, my lord. They know nothing of our plans, so what harm could there possibly be?"

Lord Ault's gray eyes shifted and rested on Mr. Harding. "What harm could there possibly be...?" he repeated.

BY THE FOLLOWING AFTERNOON Lord Ault's humor had shown little improvement as he waited in the front salon of the Rollet house along with Mr. Harding and Mr. Crenshawe.

When they were joined by the young ladies, even Lord Ault's commodious carriage was crowded with three large-shouldered men as well as the two girls.

Clairice, dressed in a demure white organdy that belied the lively curiosity of her impish green eyes, sat between Mr. Harding and Mr. Crenshawe, while Lord Ault and Adele, in pale blue dimity, shared the opposite seat. Both girls looked as fresh in their crisp dresses as the spring day.

Under a cloudless blue sky the carriage rolled along the Quai Des Tuileries toward the Tuileries Gardens. The passengers alighted at the enormous grounds to stroll among the majestic trees, early blooming flowers and cooing pigeons.

The five divided in the same manner as they had ridden in the carriage, until Mr. Crenshawe took Clairice's arm and pulled her back to look again at a statue they had just passed. Mr. Harding fell into step with Lord Ault and Adele, who remarked, "The gardens are magnificent."

Mr. Harding gazed about. "They were designed over an old brick yard centuries ago. Le Notre laid out the lake and the paths." His blue eyes rested on the wide walk. "During the Revolution the king's Swiss Guards were murdered here."

"How terrible! On such a beautiful day, in such a place, it is difficult to imagine." Adele drew near to a small pond. "Look at the children!"

Under the watchful supervision of nurses, two small boys were floating narrow short planks on the smooth surface of the shallow pond. Adele and Mr. Harding drew close, while Lord Ault paused a short distance away and gazed absentmindedly at the view. He turned and saw Clairice approaching, Mr. Crenshawe's dark head bent attentively to converse with her.

Shifting, Lord Ault lounged against the warm stone base of a tall statue and observed those around him. Clairice and Mr. Crenshawe strolled to stand at the edge of the pond alongside the others. Mr. Crenshawe retained hold of her arm and was far more interested in Clairice than the glittering pond. Soon the four moved along. Adele stopped and glanced over her shoulder at Lord Ault.

He smiled and sauntered after them, following at a short distance for the remainder of their visit to the gardens. Finally they climbed into the carriage and once again proceeded along the stone-parapeted Quai du Louvre until Mr. Crenshawe asked that the carriage be halted. He gazed down at Clairice. "Here is the oldest bridge in Paris. You must view it." He glanced at Lord Ault. "Do you mind if we stop?"

"Of course not," Lord Ault replied and climbed down from his carriage after the others. Once again he fell into step behind them. Mr. Harding's voice carried clearly, "Once you are on the bridge you have a fine view of the construction just commenced for a new bridge—the Pont-des-Arts, which will be built of iron."

They walked onto the wide stone Pont Neuf. Lord Ault paused at the foot of the bridge, and when Mr. Harding glanced at him, he waved a hand. "Go ahead, I shall wait."

He turned to stroll along the quai and was gazing into the water, his thoughts lost in the coming event of the evening, when a voice sounded at his elbow.

"You are very angry with us."

He turned to look down at Clairice's worried countenance. He glanced quickly at the bridge and spotted Mr. Crenshawe engaged in conversation with the others.

His eyes returned to rest on her. "How did you ever get away from Crenshawe?"

She answered, "I said I needed to speak with you a moment."

For the first time in the last hour a fleeting smile crossed his face. "And now you are speaking with me."

"Why are you so angry?"

He looked at the river. "I find this a tiring afternoon. This is not the way I planned to spend my time in Paris, but I must do so because of your grandmother."

"That is nothing new, your lordship. I feel something else has occurred."

He looked down at her and his jaw tightened. "I am provoked that your grandmother has caused me to reveal a diplomatic and political mission to a family who claims as one of its members a director of the bank of France."

"I do not see that it is of any impor—"

He cut short her words. "A group of men agreed to loan twelve million francs to Napoleon to finance the public treasury. Your uncle is a supporter of the First Consul in the highest sense, and his sister-in-law knows fully England's scheme to confiscate Bonaparte's invasion plans." He faced her and his eyes blazed. "All morning I have expected to be arrested at any moment."

"But you need have no fear of that," Clairice insisted. "Grandmother and I are the only ones who know. She will not hint to Uncle Marcel, and you know I would not."

"Is he a Royalist?"

"No. Nor does he support Napoleon Bonaparte as he once did. According to grandmother, Uncle Marcel is concerned only with France, and he feels that Boney is beginning to give indications of craving power for its own sake. My uncle would never give you away, even if he knew."

"Here they come." He spoke under his breath and gazed over her shoulder at the others who were approaching.

"Please do not be concerned," Clairice urged, then turned with a smile.

"It is time we get you home," Mr. Crenshawe said pleasantly to her, and once again he took Clairice's arm. "Have you enjoyed this?"

They moved away and her reply was lost to Lord Ault. He followed and entered the carriage to ride in silence, relieved when they finally parted company with the girls. They dropped Mr. Crenshawe off at the Embassy, then proceeded to their separate hotels.

Within a few hours they were once again together, seated with more than forty other guests at an elaborate dinner at the home of the Archchancellor Cambacérès.

Adele, a vision of loveliness in a rose-satin gown, was seated to Lord Ault's right. She leaned close to whisper, "Aunt Hyacinth has told me of the archchancellor, and that he always insists on eating promptly at five-thirty."

"Indeed. Watch and you will notice that they are closing the doors. Any latecomers will not be permitted to enter."

His gaze took in the length of the elaborate table, set with sparkling crystal and fine china on a white Brussels lace cloth with a ten-branch silver candelabra casting a warm glow. Farther down, Mr. Crenshawe was engaged in conversation with Clairice, his dark head bent attentively close to hers. She was dressed in pale russet velvet, an unusual color, which flattered her red tresses, but her beauty did nothing to stir Lord Ault, who suffered a flash of impatience at the mere sight of her. Mr. Harding was seated on her other side, and she soon turned to converse with him.

Adele remarked, "There are so many Britons present, I feel I am at home."

Lord Ault replied, "This dinner is especially for us. It is diplomacy to attempt to better relations between Cambacérès and Lord Whitworth."

"I have met so many people this evening, I hope I can keep them straight. Perhaps you can help me.

There is the Duchess of Gordon at the end of the table...."

"Indeed, and never a more tiresome person existed. They have placed her close to your grandmother," he noted with satisfaction, "which should take care of the duchess for some time to come."

Adele continued, "Next to her is a Monsieur Berthier...."

"Yes, the minister of war."

She forgot the people at the sight of the elaborate dishes being borne in by uniformed footmen. "Look at the food—how magnificent!"

"Chartreuse de perdreaux," Lord Ault declared as the first huge silver platter with ornately decorated partridges was placed before them. Quickly, other platters followed, according to the French custom of placing everything on the table at once and allowing the guests to freely serve themselves.

During the meal Adele remarked, "Such marvelous food! Poor Aunt Lavinia, she is not enjoying the delicious cooking." The object of her sympathy sat a dozen seats away, merely picking at her food and not touching most of the dishes.

Lord Ault commented, "You have not begun to taste the best of French cooking. You are to dine at the foreign minister's home next week; I know, for we are all invited. You will find the ultimate then in excellent French fare. It will be a small intimate dinner. Prince Talleyrand usually does not have enormous affairs, but he has the best chef in all of France and perhaps in the world. Antoine Carème cannot be surpassed."

Lord Ault continued to converse pleasantly with Adele throughout the meal, but a small portion of his attention was on the conversation of the men around him, in order not to miss any useful tidbit of information. At the first good chance after dinner he slipped down a deserted hallway, away from the noise of the crowd.

HE HURRIED ALONG opening door after door upon empty lighted rooms, dissastisfied until he found a library with a tall closed secrétaire. He crossed to it and found it securely locked.

He pulled a wire from his pocket and hurriedly unlocked the desk. With a glance at the door, he bent over and began a swift perusal of the contents of the pigeonholes, searching in vain for some clue to the invasion plans or to the French secret agents' identities.

A voice sounded behind him. He whirled, fists clenched, and froze at the sight of Clairice. His glanced flicked to the closed door and back to her.

"How did you get in here?" he snapped in a tight whisper.

Her eyes were wide. "I followed you. I felt you might be in danger."

"Not half as much as you are!" he hissed furiously "Get out of here!"

"Very well.... " She blinked and glanced at the papers on the desk, then at him.

"Go!" He struggled to control his anger and to keep his voice down.

She turned away and moved toward the door. A noise came from the hall.

Instantly he reached out and caught her by the arm. With one hand behind his back he swiftly closed the desk, while at the same time he pulled Clairice to him and bent to kiss her.

In fury, to teach her a lesson, he kissed her in a manner intended to intimidate her. His lips pressed against hers, hard and passionate.

His lean hard body bent over hers. Her lashes lay on her cheeks, long and thick against the creamy pink of her skin. He continued to kiss her while gazing over her head at the door. It opened slowly, without a sound, and the dark eyes and hawk nose of Cambacérès appeared.

The archchancellor smiled, stepped back, quietly closed the door and left them alone.

Lord Ault continued the searing kiss on the soft warm lips under his. Finally he released her. Clairice opened her eyes and gazed up at him dazedly, then took a step away.

Resisting an overwhelming urge to shout at her, Lord Ault struggled to keep his composure. "You are the most infuriating person—next to your grandmother—I have ever encountered!"

Clairice stared up at him with wide eyes, her lips red from his kisses and her cheeks flaming with embarrassment. "I was merely concerned about you—" she began.

He interrupted. "Spare me your precious consideration and do not come creeping up after me again! You are fortunate I did not turn around and hit you, thinking that you were someone who was about to attack me bodily."

Clairice's color heightened and her eyes flashed angrily. "I was merely being kind."

"Spare me your kindness, Miss Fairfax, before it kills me!"

Clairice stamped her foot. "Do not bully me, my lord! I am not afraid of you! Someone else followed you, and if you had not had me to foist your attentions on just then, you would have been caught in the act of searching another man's property."

"Miss Fairfax," he stated with chilling emphasis, "you had best depart this room in the greatest haste, for your precious self is in very grave danger of being bullied in a far more violent and painful form!" He added in a growl, "You are a busybody child and deserve being treated as such!"

Her eyes narrowed, "Oh!" she exclaimed; then suddenly her eyes widened. "Oh!" she muttered again, but in a different tone of voice. "Don't you touch me!"

He advanced a step. "I think you need a lesson to teach you not to meddle in other people's affairs!"

Her anger changed to a look of alarm. Suddenly she

turned and fled the room, leaving the door open in her haste.

Lord Ault hurried after her, gazing in both directions up and down the hall; then he stepped back into the room, closed the door and hastily continued his search of the contents of the desk for another few minutes. He finally closed it, crossed the room and left to rejoin the others.

The evening was a waste, and Lord Ault's disposition continued to suffer through the night and also through a good portion of the next few days.

Having been precipitated into a situation where he had to convince his aide as well as his superiors of the merits of escorting the Fairfax contingency to Paris, Lord Ault now had to stand by his guns and continue to pay heed to the ladies. Much to his gall, his vexation had to be hidden and to all the world he had to appear interested in them.

It was not difficult to center his attention on Adele, since she was the only member of the Fairfax family he did not actively detest at the moment.

Wherever he escorted them, they were also accompanied by Mr. Crenshawe and Mr. Harding, who stumbled blithely along with them. In the next few days they took in the sights of Paris during the day, watched the fireworks each evening and enjoyed the lights of the Elysium at night. Invitations arrived and were accepted to soirees, dinners and balls, with a reception at the Tuileries and presentation of the Fairfax sisters to the First Consul.

CHAPTER SEVEN

AN ELEGANTLY DRESSED THRONG milled around the large salon. The afternoon sun poured through high windows and caught the light in the glittering diamonds that adorned the ladies. Two men stood out for their simplicity of clothing—Lord Ault and the First Consul.

Clairice smoothed her skirt nervously, then smiled as she was presented to Napoleon Bonaparte.

"Welcome to France, *mademoiselle,*" he said with a warm smile.

She replied in French, as she observed the man about whom she had heard so much discussion for as long as she could remember.

She was surprised at his reddish brown hair, which hung in shaggy disarray to his shoulders, but his charm was instantly apparent, putting her at ease. In spite of his simple dark green uniform and short stature, he was commanding and impressive. Then all too quickly he moved on and was gone.

"You appear quite overcome by the First Consul," a voice sounded at her elbow. Clairice turned to face Lord Ault, accompanied by Adele.

"Indeed, I think I am."

Both sisters were wearing white Empire dresses that set off Lord Ault's dark handsomeness as he stood between them. His dark blue coat was unadorned and as plainly cut as the Consul's.

Adele leaned forward slightly. "I cannot believe we have met Napoleon Bonaparte." She glanced about and waved a slender hand. "Isn't this beautiful, Clairice? And all the ladies are dressed so elegantly!"

Lord Ault smiled in amusement. "You need not fear, Miss Fairfax. You and your sister are unsurpassed by any of the French ladies."

Adele blushed hotly and was saved from answering by the arrival of Mr. Harding and Mr. Crenshawe.

In a low tone Mr. Crenshawe spoke to Clairice. "I cannot take my eyes from you. How lovely you look!"

To Clairice's annoyance she looked up to find Lord Ault watching her with an amused gleam in his eyes. Mr. Crenshawe raised his voice and continued, "Have you been presented to the First Consul yet?"

"Yes, and I shall always remember this moment."

"You sound quite impressed," Mr. Crenshawe said.

"And why not?" Lord Ault rejoined. "She has just met one of the most brilliant men the world has ever produced."

Mr. Crenshawe's gaze left Clairice and shifted to Lord Ault. His voice dropped. "My, what admiration of the wiliest enemy England has ever known."

Lord Ault returned the stare. His voice was cold as he inquired, "Are you implying something, Crenshawe?"

Mr. Crenshawe smiled broadly. "Of course not, my lord, merely an observation of surprise that you should feel that way." He smiled at Clairice. "Come, Miss Fairfax, there is something I wish to show you." He took her arm and his gaze moved across the others. "If you will please excuse us."

Clairice allowed herself to be led along. "That was a dangerous remark to make."

He smiled down at her. "I have no concern about it. I was sincerely surprised at his admiration." He shook his large head.

"Grandmother has told me there are French spies both here and abroad."

"Your grandmother is correct. French and English."

Clairice frowned. "But you made it sound as if—" she hesitated, then plunged on "—as if you think Lord Ault is...." Her words trailed into silence as she could not bring herself to utter aloud her thoughts.

"A spy?" He finished with a small mirthless laugh. "It would not be impossible, you know."

"Of course it would! He—" Clairice stopped abruptly as she realized that she was about to reveal more than she should.

Mr. Crenshawe gazed down at her curiously. "He what?"

She attempted to cover her words. "Well, he...he simply does not appear to be one."

Mr. Crenshawe laughed loudly. "Do you think he would announce it? How do you do, I am England's spy?"

She blushed at his question. "Of course not! He seems quite dedicated to England."

They paused and she glanced across the room at Lord Ault. He remained talking to Adele, Mr. Harding and a French general who had just joined them. She studied his face as if she could read an answer to the question. His glance shifted and met hers. Clairice turned away quickly, but her thoughts remained on the question.

Mr. Crenshawe took her elbow again. "Come, I have something I would like you to see."

Clairice moved quietly beside him, contemplating the idea that Lord Ault could possibly be a spy for the French. It could account more fully for his anger in having them along.

"I want you to see a collection of art. The First Consul is gathering a magnificent group of paintings."

They strolled along a marble floor in a hall filled with master works. Mr. Crenshawe pointed first to one, then another until they had turned a corner and reached a sufficient distance from the salon that the noise of the guests was gone. They halted in front of a large Rubens.

"How lovely!" Clairice breathed.

"Do you like Paris?" he asked.

"Oh, yes! We have had such fun. It is dreadful to

think that we have fought with these people—'' her eyes clouded ''—or that we might again.''

"Politics," he replied. "Power and politics, that is what causes such events between people."

"It is terrible. I shall never understand."

"I hope you shall remain in Paris for a while longer."

She looked up into his brown eyes. "I do not know. We do as grandmother plans. I fear it shall not be much longer."

"Since I have to stay, I find that pronouncement a calamity." They paused in front of another picture and Clairice blushed at his statement. She studied the painting, all the while conscious of his eyes on her. "Look at the soft rose in this; it is beautiful!"

"Exquisite," he murmured softly, moving close against her and taking her hand.

"Mr. Crenshawe—" Clairice started, but he interrupted.

"You are lovely, Miss Fairfax."

"Sir, I think we had best return to the salon."

"I love you, Miss Fairfax."

"We do not know each other that well. Please, we must return."

"Very well. But I can assure you, you will soon feel just as I do." He smiled and dropped her hand, falling into step beside her and conversing easily. "Tomorrow I would like to show you the Louvre."

Clairice was torn between wanting to view the Louvre and the thought of spending many more hours with Mr. Crenshawe. She looked up and replied, "Adele and I would love to see it."

If he minded the inclusion of Adele, he gave no indication. "Splendid! You shall find it all you have ever heard and more."

They returned to the salon and shortly departed for the Rollet residence. A light mist fell, carrying a damp chill and becoming heavy enough to cause droplets of water to form and run in jagged thin courses down the carriage windows.

Adele rode quietly beside Lord Ault while Mr. Harding discussed farming.

"I am a firm advocate of the Tullian methods. Our old ways are antiquated," he said.

"Perhaps I have not kept up with the times," Lord Ault remarked.

"We have purchased new Rutland plows. Our soil is light, and I favor this type of plow for it. Norfolk is much given to dibbling, and few have converted to a more modern system."

Adele asked, "What is dibbling?"

He waved his hands. "A method of planting in which a light roller is passed over the soil. Then the farmer walks along a row with an iron dibble in each hand."

"A dibble sounds like a child's plaything," Adele said.

"It's a long pointed rod," Mr. Harding explained and stretched out his arms to demonstrate. "The man holds one in each hand and drives holes into the ground. Then someone drops a few grains into each hole. Later the holes are covered with a harrow or roller."

Lord Ault shifted and gazed attentively at Mr. Harding, then remarked, "On my land we are still using the broadcast method, unless it has changed without my knowledge."

"Your lordship, furrows are far superior. When we return, perhaps you can visit my home and I shall let you decide for yourself."

"I would like that. If we ever have war again, we shall have need of the most productive methods possible."

Clairice only half listened, growing bored with the talk of soil and plows. She studied Mr. Harding as he talked and her alarm for his well-being grew. His enthusiasm and love of farming showed in his conversation; clearly he expected to return to his country home and settle, as if no danger existed in his current occupation.

Her attention shifted to Lord Ault. She wrapped her fingers tightly together at the thought of his being a spy. Mr. Harding might be in a great deal of danger. She studied him obliquely, looking up at his profile while he engaged in conversation about potatoes and turnips.

If Mr. Harding were apprehended and thrown into a French prison, or worse.... Clairice shivered and tore her thoughts from such dreadful speculations.

Adele was studying him. "How you must miss your home, Mr. Harding."

"Eh? Yes, never want to be away long, you know. We added a new strain of cattle. I think they will do well. Far better than we had in the past. Prime beef. Farming in England is being revolutionized."

"The new Dishley longhorn cattle developed by Bakewell are a superior stock, I am told," Lord Ault commented.

"Indeed, sir. It will increase Britain's beef industry. Just talking about it makes me long for home. Would like to sink my teeth into one of my own roasts."

Clairice laughed. " 'Tis a good thing Aunt Lavinia is not present. She would give you a lecture on the evils of beef."

"By jove, when we are once again home I shall bring you some of our beef. It is superb quality. Let her try one of my roasts, and she will forget about bean sprouts and celery sticks."

Clairice and Adele both laughed. "Sir, you do not know our aunt!" Adele remarked mirthfully.

Mr. Crenshawe, who had ridden in silence throughout the discussion of agriculture, inquired, "How did you come to live with your aunt and grandmother?"

Adele replied, "Our parents were killed in a storm at sea so we were sent to live with grandmother."

"I am sorry," Mr. Harding said hastily.

Clairice smiled at him and added, "Aunt Lavinia's mother was grandmother's sister. Aunt Lavinia's father died when she was an infant. She lived with her mother until about six years ago when she died."

Mr. Crenshawe spoke. "I shall be happy to include your grandmother and Miss Milsap when we view the Louvre tomorrow."

Before either of the girls could reply, Mr. Harding exclaimed, "The Louvre! Excellent! I have been anxious to visit there once again."

A slight frown crossed Mr. Crenshawe's face, but was gone in an instant. Clairice spoke quickly to ensure Mr. Harding's welcome presence. "Is it all they say?"

"Yes, you shall see for yourself," Mr. Harding replied and turned to Lord Ault. "Are you joining us?"

"Thank you, no. I have matters to attend to." He added quietly, "You have an appointment in the afternoon."

Clairice grew alarmed at the solemn tone of Lord Ault's voice. Mr. Harding reassured him. "I have not forgotten, but there shall still be time earlier to take the tour."

Clairice glanced up at Lord Ault. She was squeezed between the broad shoulders of both Lord Ault and Mr. Crenshawe, but she was far more conscious of touching Lord Ault. He seemed displeased with Mr. Harding's plans. She stirred in misery because she did not know what was ahead. The carriage slowed to a halt at the Rollets, and Mr. Harding and Mr. Crenshawe assisted the girls down, then bid them farewell.

As soon as they entered the house, the sisters did as they had been instructed and rushed to Lady Fairfax's room to relate their afternoon adventure and the details of their meeting Bonaparte. Finally, after the conversation had covered the subject fully, Adele rose to go to her room for a nap. Clairice also excused herself, but once she had bathed and was dressed in a warm robe, she returned.

Lady Fairfax lay propped against a mound of pillows,

her snuffbox at her side and a mug of brandy on a side table.

"What is troubling you, child?"

Clairice sat on a chair close to the bed and leaned forward, speaking earnestly. "Grandmother, I am so concerned about Mr. Harding. I am afraid that something dreadful will happen to him."

Her grandmother looked at her in an intense scrutiny. "Do you love him, Clairice?" she asked bluntly.

Clairice blushed and looked down at her fingers twisted together in her lap. "I don't know—I am uncertain. I think I do. I don't know...about such feelings." She then exclaimed, "It is just the terrible danger I know he is in!" A tiny frown furrowed her brow. "I am scared he cannot do what he needs to."

"Clairice, the boy must be able to do more than one would judge on first meeting," Lady Fairfax said with a trace of impatience in her voice. "They would not have selected him for such a task if several capable men had not expected him to be able to perform."

"You know how he is!" Clairice cried.

"I certainly do!" Lady Fairfax snapped, then fell silent. When she spoke again her voice was normal. "Now, Clairice, you must not fret about a matter over which you have no control. None of that, child, for it is useless." She narrowed her eyes and studied her granddaughter with a piercing observation. "And, Clairice, do not let your heart be fooled and mistake concern for love."

Clairice's blush deepened. "Grandmother, I wish you would stop making remarks about love. Also, I am concerned with all the talk of a French spy." She bit her lip and then said, "Mr. Crenshawe all but accused Lord Ault of being one."

"Gammon!" Lady Fairfax choked on a swallow of brandy. She coughed and sputtered, then regained her composure and stared at Clairice in shock. "Is he still alive?"

"Who? Mr. Crenshawe?"

"Indeed."

"Yes. He did not actually say it, but do you think it is possible?"

"Of course not! Utterly ridiculous."

"I do hope so. If he is, then Mr. Harding is in a great deal of danger."

"Or the other way around," Lady Fairfax said. "If it were Harding, then Lord Ault would be in danger."

Clairice's frown was replaced with mirth. "Mr. Harding—a spy! Grandmother, that is as close to becoming bird-witted as I have ever known you to be!"

"Such disrespect!"

"He could never be a spy."

"Not unless he is far more clever than any of us give him credit for."

"I am certain he is not one." Clairice's worry returned. "I do fear for him. Can you get Lord Ault to tell you their plans?"

"Of course not. He is still angry over having to escort us to Paris, and I do not care to push him any further. What difference would it make if you knew? There is nothing you can do to prevent it."

Clairice sat back in the chair and stared at the foggy windows. Lady Fairfax spoke again. "If it is any consolation to you, I think it will be soon."

"What gives you cause to think so?"

"Because Lord Ault stopped beside my chair last night when no one else was near and asked if we wanted to return to England at the same time he does. I told him we most certainly do. He suggested that I be ready anytime after this coming week."

Clairice jumped to her feet and paced the room. "Oh, I wish I knew!"

Lady Fairfax glanced idly through a paper. "You are better off not knowing."

Clairice moved to the bed and kissed her grandmother's cheek, then departed for her own room. The

evening's entertainment and the following day's visit to
the Louvre did nothing to relieve her mind.

When they departed from the Louvre, Clairice
strolled toward Lord Ault's carriage, but Mr. Crenshawe took her arm and led her toward a different vehicle. He said easily, "This way, Miss Fairfax, we will ride
in this one."

Clairice glanced over her shoulder, but the others
were not in sight. She shrugged slightly and climbed inside. Mr. Crenshawe followed, and as soon as the door
was closed, the carriage began to move. She looked at
him in astonishment.

"We are leaving Adele and Mr. Harding."

He smiled broadly. "No, Mr. Harding has Lord
Ault's carriage and he will escort Adele home. I have a
surprise for you, something I wish to show you."

In rising consternation Clairice sat forward. "This is
quite unthinkable! You know I should not be riding
around Paris alone with you."

He laughed. "Come now, Miss Fairfax. Do not be
prudish. This will not be long. I have informed your
grandmother, your sister and Mr. Harding, and we shall
return soon. I promise I shall do you no harm."

Clairice studied him, then relaxed against the seat. "I
see I have little choice. What is it you are planning to
show me?"

"A surprise, Miss Fairfax."

The sun shone brightly and the day did not portend
any evil happening, but aggravated by the turn of
events, Clairice shifted on the seat to face him. "Mr.
Crenshawe, I think you should tell me what you are
about."

His smile remained fixed. "All females like pleasant
surprises, and I am certain this shall be one. If it is not
enjoyable, then I shall deserve such looks."

Clairice smiled slightly and attempted a light answer.
"Very well, but I do need to return home in time to
dress for the ball tonight.'

"I promise."

They rode in silence. Clairice gazed out the window, aware that the surroundings were changing to less congestion and elegant homes. Beggars disappeared and few soldiers were seen. Finally the carriage halted in front of a mansion of yellow-hued walls with wrought-iron balconies and a tile roof.

She looked at him questioningly. "What is this, Mr. Crenshawe?"

"Soon you will see," he replied, then alighted to assist her from the carriage. She followed in silence through a wide doorway held open by a butler in scarlet-and-green livery. He greeted Mr. Crenshawe with a pleasant, *"Bonjour,* Mister Crenshawe."

Again Clairice turned questioning eyes on Mr. Crenshawe. He smiled and led her along the marble hallway. In silence she gazed at the magnificence of the furnishings.

Alcoves held large marble statues, and the ceiling was arched and painted with a mural. Clairice glanced at Mr. Crenshawe and found him watching her closely. A footman stepped forward to open a door to a room off the hallway, and as soon as Clairice entered, Mr. Crenshawe closed it softly, leaving them alone.

The salon was as magnificent as the hall, with ornate Louis XV furniture in muted colors. She turned to face Mr. Crenshawe.

He stepped forward and took her hands. "Miss Fairfax, I wanted you to see this, for I am proud of it. This is my Paris home."

"Yours!" she cried. "You have said nothing about a home here."

While he answered, his gaze went over her features in such a manner as to make Clairice want to bolt and run. "I know. This is not the best of times for an Englishman to own a home in France—or for an Englishman to admit to his fellow countrymen that he has such a residence."

"It is beautiful."

"I would like to show you all of it." As she opened her mouth to protest he added hastily, "I know, you are unchaperoned and it would not be proper. I have no intention of doing so now; I merely said I would like to." His hands, feeling hot and clammy, tightened on hers in a crushing grasp. He leaned forward. "Miss Fairfax—" his voice deepened "—will you be my wife?"

Clairice gazed up into his burning dark eyes. "Mr. Crenshawe, this is not the place. I appreciate your offer, but I am not ready to wed."

"Miss Fairfax, I am not prepared to take no for an answer. I will persist. I wanted you to glimpse what I have to offer you. I can wait for an answer—" his eyes burned into hers "—but I do not give up when I want something." He pulled her roughly to him and his lips sought hers, but Clairice pushed against his chest and turned her head away.

"Please—"

He released her slightly, still holding her arms. His voice deepened. "I am in love with you, Miss Fairfax, and I intend to have you for my wife!"

He turned. "We shall get you home now, but sometime soon I want to bring you here again for a tour. There are many items of antiquity and historical significance; I think you would enjoy viewing them."

Clairice murmured politely while actually feeling no desire to return to his home ever again. Especially since it would most certainly further the conversation just terminated. She glanced at him as he walked beside her and merely wanted to be away from his presence.

As soon as they were seated in the carriage, she said, "Mr. Crenshawe, I cannot allow you to go on thinking I might accept. I do not feel that marriage is what I want now. I am flattered by your offer, but I . . . ."

He raised his hand and lightly touched her lips. "Say no more! You shall not stop me no matter what you say! Do not waste your breath with such talk. I intend to sweep you off your feet, my darling. I can be very persuasive, and I am patient. I do not want to hear another word from you about it until you are ready to say yes."

Clairice sighed and changed the subject. "I have not heard it mentioned that you had a home in Paris. I thought you were residing in a hotel."

"I am."

She looked up in surprise and he replied casually, "I find it far more convenient to keep the fact of my home as secret as possible, for it is a place I can escape to and not be disturbed by politics and politicians." He looked at her and smiled disarmingly. "Perhaps you cannot understand that."

Clairice recalled the longing in Mr. Harding's voice when he talked of farming and his home. She contradicted him, "No, I think I do understand." She viewed him intently. "If such is the case, you have just shared your secret with me, and I presume you would prefer I did not reveal it."

He gazed out the window, then back to her. "I would rather that you didn't." He shrugged, then said, "If you do, it is no great matter."

She recalled the rumors she had heard that Paris was not a safe place for Englishmen. She repeated this in a low voice and watched him laugh aloud.

"Ridiculous! Do you know how many Britons are in France now? Also, I am a politician. I know some of the most highly guarded secrets of our government, and I can assure you it is safe enough here in spite of the rumors."

The carriage halted. Mr. Crenshawe raised her hands to his lips and said, "*Au revoir, ma chérie.* I shall look forward to tonight."

She attempted politely to extricate her hands from his, dreading the kiss she felt certain was coming. When it did, a shiver of dislike ran through her. Before she could get free, he pulled her close and whispered, "For now, let us keep the knowledge of my Paris home a secret?''

She nodded mutely and he continued, ''I would like to think that only you and I know of it. That it is a secret place I can share with you where we can be away from the world. I adore you—''

Clairice interrupted him. ''Mr. Crenshawe, please! I must go in.''

He pulled her close for a quick kiss, then released her. His eyes swept over her. ''I must have you.''

CLAIRICE FLED THE CARRIAGE and ran into the house. She gave a perfunctory greeting to the butler and raced upstairs. In the hall she encountered Adele and Lady Fairfax. Lady Fairfax leaned heavily on her cane. ''Ah, Clairice! 'Bout to run me down, girl. You look like the demons of hell are at your heels.''

Clairice panted for breath. ''I feel like it.''

Lady Fairfax waved her cane. ''Come in here. I cannot stand out in this drafty hall. My legs ache and we have a long night ahead of us.''

''Oh, the ball at the Delesserts'. Now I no longer want to go!'' Clairice cried.

Lady Fairfax ambled into a sitting room and sank heavily into a small chair, while Adele took a window seat and Clairice perched on a low footstool facing her grandmother.

''You shall have to attend,'' Lady Fairfax said. ''Monsieur Delessert, as head of the *banque*, is Uncle Marcel's superior, and you cannot insult the family.''

''I know. . . .'' Her voice trailed off.

''Now what has occurred?''

Clairice looked at her grandmother. ''It is Mr. Crenshawe, grandmother. He is becoming quite tedious—he wants me to marry him!''

Lady Fairfax merely nodded. ''I know, Clairice.''

''You know! How could you? I didn't until this afternoon!''

Before she could reply, Adele spoke. "Clairice! Are you going to wed Mr. Crenshawe? Did he ask this afternoon?"

Lady Fairfax waved her cane. "One thing at a time, Adele." She turned to Clairice. "I know, because the man has talked to me. He has offered for your hand in marriage."

Clairice let out a wail. "Grandmother, how dreadful! I do not want to marry him! I loath the man! He is awful, just—"

"Clairice, calm yourself. I did not say that I had accepted."

Clairice blinked. "What did you tell him?" she asked quickly.

"I said the choice would be yours."

Adele reached down and gathered up her sewing to commence working quietly.

Clairice grasped her grandmother's hand in gratitude. Lady Fairfax continued, "The man does not have a title, and I feel I know little of him, but I feel also, with both of you, unless you do something utterly outrageous, that you should have a say in your own marriage partner."

Clairice jumped up and flung her arms around Lady Fairfax. "Thank you! You are the most wonderful grandmother anyone ever had!"

"Here, here." Lady Fairfax extricated herself and smiled at Clairice. "Now tell us about this proposal. I take it you do not choose to marry the man."

"Oh, heavens, no!" Clairice once more sank down on the footstool.

"I am so glad," Adele declared softly. "There is something about Mr. Crenshawe that makes me nervous any time he is near."

"I told him no, but he said he would not take no for an answer."

"Clairice, I am certain you shall be able to hold your own," Lady Fairfax said.

"Besides, I think I am in love with another," Clairice announced with an impish grin.

Adele looked up from her sewing. "Who, Clairice?"

Clairice blushed, but answered with a faraway look in her eyes, "Mr. Harding."

"Oh!" Adele sank against the window seat while Lady Fairfax thumped the floor with her cane. "Damme! Clairice, I may retract what I just declared, about letting each of you make your own choice!"

Clairice was not intimidated by the statement. She giggled and squeezed Lady Fairfax's hand. "Grandmother, I know you better than that!"

Lady Fairfax jerked her hand away. "That confounded boy has been nothing but trouble since the first moment he rode up beside our carriage."

"No one could dislike Mr. Harding," Clairice stated, then jumped up. "I must get ready for tonight. It will be our first ball in Paris."

CLAIRICE'S PROMPT DISMISSAL from her mind of the persistence of Mr. Crenshawe changed little until the evening wore on and he danced time and again with her.

Finally Mr. Harding achieved a dance. Clairice gazed up at him, enthralled, until they turned and she met Lady Fairfax's baleful stare. Clairice wrinkled her nose mischievously at her grandmother. Then, as she glanced away, she caught Lord Ault looking at her, his eyebrow raised in amusement. The instant the dance halted, Mr. Crenshawe returned to claim the next, but as soon as it ended, Clairice broke away with the excuse that she was needed by her grandmother.

Before he could follow, she rushed to join the matrons, who included Aunt Lavinia, seated next to Lady Fairfax. Clairice stepped close to them and said in low tones, "Grandmother, the man is driving me mad!"

"Sit down with us, Clairice," Lavinia urged, moving slightly to make room.

"No, thank you, I think I shall move elsewhere. Perhaps Mr. Crenshawe will find someone else if...." Her voice trailed off at the approach of her granduncle Marcel.

"Are you enjoying the ball?" he inquired, idly scratching first his wrist, then his ear.

"Indeed, Uncle Marcel," she replied politely.

He gazed at his other relatives and bowed low in front of Lavinia Milsap. "Miss Milsap, would you care to dance?"

Lavinia paled and replied quickly, "I am sorry, I do not dance."

He smiled and turned to Lady Fairfax. "Cornelia?"

She laughed and poked his shin lightly with her cane. "Marcel, what would I look like on the dance floor with a gentleman on one arm and a cane on the other? No, thank you."

He faced Clairice and threw up his hands. "I shall not ask you, *ma petite,* for you can find far more enjoyable companions than an itchy old man."

Clairice's denials ignored, he shambled away to join a cluster of gentlemen. Clairice slipped away into the hall, relief sweeping over her at escaping Mr. Crenshawe's attentions, even as she resented that he was also preventing her from dancing with Mr. Harding.

She descended the steps to a lower floor and stood aimlessly in the hall listening to the wafting strains of a reel. Then, on the gallery leading to the ballroom, Mr. Crenshawe wandered into sight and stopped with his back to her. She lifted her skirts a fraction and dashed into the nearest darkened room.

The cool interior carried a faint scent of roses. She stopped just inside the doorway, waiting and listening to her own heartbeat throb in her ears. In the dimness across the room her reflection was thrown back in a tall mirror. Her white silk dress glimmered in the glass, the heirloom diamonds sparkling in a dainty circle about her neck. Slowly her eyes adjusted to the darkness, and

she could see the heavy pieces of furniture splashed with
streaks of moonlight that poured through narrow windows.

After a few minutes the sound of men's voices came
to her, and in consternation, Clairice realized one of
them was Mr. Crenshawe.

She rushed across the room and stepped outside onto
the terrace. The night air was cool and fresh on her skin;
a cloud drifted across the moon, obscuring the bright-
ness. The end of April carried with it a promise of
flowers and leafing trees, but Clairice paid little heed.
She hurried along the rough flagstones to get farther
away from Mr. Crenshawe.

A low murmur of voices reached her, and she stopped
in surprise that she was not entirely alone. She listened,
in sudden fear that Mr. Crenshawe had in some way got
ahead of her. The voice was low, but distinguishable.

All thought of Mr. Crenshawe evaporated instantly at
the next words Clairice heard.

CHAPTER EIGHT

"IT MUST BE LATE TONIGHT, Harding. We have no time to lose. Kenning has been arrested in the last hours; they are getting too close!"

Clairice clutched the cold stone wall of the mansion and tiptoed a step closer, straining to hear the familiar voice of Lord Ault as he whispered, "Now that we have this information we must act immediately!"

"You are certain Marshal Berthier has the invasion plans?"

"That is the message Kenning sent—that the minister of war has the plans. We cannot both leave here soon; it would attract too much attention and is too early yet. We shall meet at St. Eustache, then travel together. Is that acceptable?"

There came a muffled reply, then small sounds and some indistinguishable words. Soft steps approached and Clairice hugged the wall.

Suddenly the barest footfall sounded at hand. She turned and stiffened. Lord Ault came around the corner, his boots making only the slightest noise in his stealthy movements.

She pressed against the stones, praying he would not notice her, but he stopped instantly and whirled to grasp her arms.

"Again! Damme!" His voice was a rasp. "I am beginning to wonder if you are a French spy. Are you following me everywhere I go?" Without waiting for an answer, he shook her lightly. "Why are you doing this?"

"I was running away from someone!" Clairice cried in alarm.

"For God's sake, keep your voice down!" His grip relaxed and his hands dropped away. He took her arm and moved her along toward the house. Clairice followed meekly, too frightened to ask what he was doing. They entered a room and he released her to light a taper. "I will not remain out in the dark and be overheard by anyone else," he muttered grimly. As soon as the light flared he turned to face her. "Sit down, Miss Fairfax."

Clairice sat quickly on the nearest chair. The wind blew gently, causing the flickering light of the taper to throw dancing shadows on Lord Ault's face. His gray eyes flashed in anger. "You eavesdrop, you creep around behind me—"

"I did not creep!"

"Be still!" he commanded. "You crept up behind me at the home of the archchancellor, you have sneaked up behind me tonight. I have had all I can take!"

"Tonight was accidental. I was running away from someone, if you must know."

"Crenshawe, no doubt. At least you have a grain of sense." He stood in front of her and gazed down in anger. "Now—that was extremely vital—what did you overhear?"

"Very little."

"Precisely what, Miss Fairfax?"

"I can keep a secret," she assured him.

Lord Ault reached down swiftly and pulled her to her feet. His eyes bored into hers. "Tell me!" he demanded.

Clairice immediately related all she had overheard. When she was finished, he swore softly and released her. She sank onto the edge of the chair.

He strolled a few paces. "In my whole life I have never known people as infuriating as you and Lady Fairfax." He whirled and looked down at her. "Do you understand what you heard?"

"You are going this night to get the invasion plans," she said, as if those burning gray eyes were drawing the words out of her against her own volition.

"Yes. And now you know all the details." .

"And I have known other secrets and never have betrayed any of them, have I?"

He thought that over. "No, but there must be no indication of this to anyone, not to your grandmother, not another living human being. Do you understand?

"Our lives hang in the balance on this. I was in the hope that absolutely no one would know what we were about tonight except the two of us who will be involved. Now you are the third to know. We are not informing Sir Barthwell, Mr. Crenshawe, Lord Whitworth, or anyone else. Do you understand, Miss Fairfax?"

"Yes, I do," she replied in subdued tones.

"Somebody is revealing everything we do. One of our loyal agents was arrested tonight right after he gave this message to me." He studied her. "You may have placed yourself in a dangerous position."

He watched her narrowly. Clairice lifted her chin. "Do you have to take Mr. Harding with you?"

His gray eyes rested on her, and he regarded her speculatively. Then, he remarked icily, "I cannot believe you would have such impertinence! Perhaps there is a highly justified reason for this question?"

Clairice wrapped her fingers together. "I thought perhaps it would not be necessary to have him along."

"In love, Miss Fairfax?" he inquired abruptly.

Her cheeks flamed, and she raised her eyes to meet his. "Now *you* are being impertinent!"

He lifted his shoulders a fraction. "I find it impossible to apologize if I am."

Clairice leaned forward. "Can you leave him out of it? I mean. . he has such difficulty. . . ."

One black eyebrow raised and his eyes hardened. "And you are fearful he would not return from a dangerous mission with a whole skin. You may well be concerned, because that is highly possible. It would not surprise me in the least!''

A small cry escaped her lips, and her hand flew to her mouth in alarm, but he continued mercilessly, ''How Mr. Harding ever navigated a battlefield as often or as successfully as he did, I shall never understand. It is a hazard for the man to climb into a carriage, and I sincerely and devoutly wish that I had anyone else at my side in this project, but I have no choice in the matter. None at all.'' Lord Ault clasped his hands behind his back and glared angrily into space.

After a moment he looked down at her and continued, ''It would not surprise me in the least to be shot in the back by the stumbling fool, but whether you or I like it or not matters not at all. He is to come along.''

''Are two people necessary to accomplish this?''

He ran his hand across his forehead. ''When they include Mr. Harding—no. I would much prefer to do what is necessary on my own, but my superiors insist that I have him along. If I were to go against their orders then fail, it would be dreadful for our country. So Harding goes.''

''What do you have to do to get these plans?''

His eyes narrowed and he bowed deeply. ''Miss Fairfax, I refuse to continue this conversation further.''

Clairice rose to her feet, lifting her hand in a futile gesture and opening her mouth to protest. Before she could utter a sound, he leaned forward slightly, fixing her with a steely glint.

''Do not, Miss Fairfax, utter another word to me on the subject again. I find it highly irritating that you would discuss such a delicate matter in the same manner you would an afternoon outing. What you fail to realize is that—'' he paused ''—your country's fate may depend on this.'' He studied her intently. ''If I could do so, I would lock you away for the evening to ensure my safety.''

Clairice stepped away from him. ''Do not dare do

such a thing! I promise you can trust me. Do you think I would betray Mr. Harding?'' she cried, then without thought exclaimed, ''I love him!''

Lord Ault laughed aloud. ''Oh, so! And is this burning passion reciprocated?''

Anger washed through her. ''I care not! I cannot help my feelings!'' After revealing her innermost longing, she discovered that Lord Ault's amusement made her tremble with fury. ''I love Mr. Harding!''

''You are a silly young girl. You do not know what love is.''

''I know what I feel toward him.''

His eyes danced. ''Do you want to marry Mr. Harding and spend your days worrying over turnips and potatoes? What would our mild Mr. Harding do with a vixen like you?''

Clairice raised her chin. ''I would not be vixenish with a gentleman who would treat me with respect—as one should a lady!''

He laughed softly at her. ''The man who commands your love, I feel, will never succeed if he treats you in such a delicate manner. You do not know what love is.'' He reached out swiftly and swept her into his arms. His mouth came down on hers.

Clairice struggled against him in vain; he merely tightened his arms until she could not move. His lips moved on hers, parting her lips, kissing her deeply and passionately until the stiffness left her and she leaned against him.

Abruptly he released her. A hot flush of embarrassment swept over Clairice. ''You are dreadful!'' she hissed at him.

He regarded her intently. ''You liked that.''

Clairice jerked her arm free of his grasp. ''I detested it!'' she exclaimed. She reached up with open palm to slap his face.

Like the speed of lightning he caught her wrist and spoke quietly, ''Do not—''

"Release me!" Clairice gritted.

He bowed elaborately and freed her arm. "Come, Miss Fairfax, I shall escort you to the ballroom and your true love. Whatever will you do with Mr. Crenshawe? It'll break his heart when he learns of Harding's success where he has tried so persistently."

"You are abominable!"

He laughed, extinguished the taper and took her arm. Clairice pulled away. "I can get along without your aid, thank you!" She flounced ahead and bumped into a table sending something falling with a light tinkle of glass.

He caught her arm again. "Allow me—we will save the ornaments."

She let him lead her toward the hall. They crossed in darkness with a steady gait that caused her to peer at him. "How can you see? You are like a cat."

They opened the door and Clairice swept into the hall to almost collide with Mr. Crenshawe. He looked over her at Lord Ault and a black scowl formed on his face.

"Miss Fairfax!" he exclaimed.

Her cheeks flamed; Clairice looked at him mortified, and unable to think of any reason for her actions.

Lord Ault spoke easily. "Ah, Crenshawe, we have been searching for you. Or rather, Miss Fairfax said she was looking for you. I accompanied her inside from the garden."

Mr. Crenshawe's dark eyes rested on Clairice in angry speculation. She did not like Lord Ault's statement, but at the moment it was better than anything she could think of. In spite of the excuse, a flush heightened her face at the thought of what had actually taken place a few moments earlier.

"Very well," Mr. Crenshawe said gruffly, "I shall be happy to escort you to the ballroom now."

Lord Ault bowed slightly and they left him behind.

They hurried along the hall with Clairice at a loss for words. After rounding a corner, Mr. Crenshawe suddenly entered an open door to a lighted salon. "Come here, Miss Fairfax."

Lord Ault had been enough to cope with; Clairice did not want to be alone with Mr. Crenshawe. "We'd best return," she urged. "I have been absent for some time now."

"So I know." He pulled her arm and led her farther into the room, then faced her. "Miss Fairfax, I am deeply in love with you. I have asked your grandmother for your hand in marriage."

Clairice wished she were anywhere but with him. "I know. She told me this afternoon."

"Please, my darling, will you do me the honor of becoming my wife?"

"Mr. Crenshawe, I am not in love—"

He interrupted hastily. "You have said so before, but I promise I shall make you fall in love. I shall give you everything you want. I can give you as much as any man. I am not titled, but I have sufficient wealth and power to compensate for it—and I shall not always be without a title."

"Mr. Crenshawe, it has nothing to do with a title. I am not in love!"

"You will be. You would be a perfect English wife. You are exactly what I want for my wife."

"I am sorry, my answer is—"

He pulled her roughly to him. Clairice turned her head, but he caught her chin and forced her to face him. His mouth was on hers, his lips wet and hot as he kissed her as passionately as she had been kissed only moments earlier...but this time she experienced an entirely different reaction.

Lord Ault's kiss had been overpowering, leaving her breathless and faint; Mr. Crenshawe's was cruel and lustful, causing her to be repulsed. She fought herself away from him.

He held her in the circle of his arms and looked down at her. "I will not take no for an answer."

Her patience snapped. "You will have to! I am not in love with you and I intend to marry a man I love."

"Your grandmother has allowed you too much freedom. That is foolishness. I suspect if I were a marquis there would be more love in your heart."

"That is not so!"

"I shall never give up," he said hoarsely.

"That is ridiculous! Mr. Crenshawe, I insist that you release me!"

"Very well. Come, I shall escort you upstairs."

Breathing heavily, Clairice accepted his arm once more, and this time they returned to the ballroom. The minute they walked through the doors, Clairice met her grandmother's hard stare. She smiled and looked away, aware of the time she had been gone and how it appeared to return with Mr. Crenshawe. The evening was ruined. She wanted only to get away to the haven of home and to think about the hours to come.

Adele danced past with Mr. Harding. Clairice gazed at him, envisioning the task ahead and the danger to which he would be exposed. If only something could be done to prevent it! She studied his fair good looks and long-lashed blue eyes with tremulous longing. Mr. Crenshawe turned her to face him to dance. As her gaze shifted, she caught Lord Ault watching her again, a corner of his mouth curled in amusement.

She flushed hotly and turned her back on the man, smiling up at Mr. Crenshawe in a manner she did not feel. They danced and she chatted gaily, hiding her true feelings and hoping in some manner to spite Lord Ault.

Finally they returned home, and once she was in her own room Clairice summoned the maid and sent her on an errand. While she was gone, Clairice unfastened the ties of her dress, flung it off and hurriedly unpinned her hair. The maid returned soon with the items Clairice had requested and Clairice thanked her and sent the girl to bed.

A SHORT TIME LATER Clairice was struggling alone when Adele entered the room. She stopped short at the sight of Clairice, who whirled and whispered urgently, "Come in and close the door, Addie."

Adele did as told, then turned with wide eyes to look at her sister. "Clairice—what are you doing?"

Clairice looked at the contrast of her black men's clothing and Adele's soft pink robe and gown. "Adele, do not breathe a word of this to anyone! Promise me that you will not!"

"I promise. But what are you doing?"

Clairice, having extracted what she wanted from Adele, turned to the task at hand. She tugged long black pantaloons on her legs. "I intend—if I can ever get into these clothes—to go with Mr. Harding and Lord Ault tonight on a mission for England."

"Clairice!" Adele looked stricken. "Impossible! You cannot do such a thing. It is unthinkable!" A frown creased her forehead. "What kind of mission? Is it dangerous?"

Clairice stopped tugging the garments and turned to take Adele's hands. "Adele, swear you will never reveal what I am going to tell you."

"I promise," she replied.

"Lord Ault and Mr. Harding are attempting to steal Bonaparte's plans for the invasion of England."

Adele paled; her hand flew to her mouth. "Oh, no! They can't!"

"You must never, never breathe a word of it to another living soul."

"You must be mistaken, Clairice." Adele studied her sister with worried eyes.

Clairice shook her head. "I am not. I overheard them making plans for it tonight."

"How terrible!" Adele moved to a chair and sank onto the edge as if her knees had grown weak. She looked up at Clairice and said flatly, "That is why they came to Paris."

"Yes."

"Clairice, you cannot go with them. It is impossible! I will tell grandmother."

Clairice whirled to face her again. "You promised!"

"I promised not to tell what you just revealed about Mr. Harding and Lord Ault. I did not promise to keep your own doings a secret."

"Adele, I never will forgive you. I must go with them."

"But it will be so dangerous. Why would they want you to do this?"

"They do not know I am coming along," Clairice said.

Adele fell back in the chair with a small cry. "That is even worse. To go when they have not asked you. It is madness!"

"It isn't!" Clairice placed her hands on her hips. "Addie, suppose I hadn't been along when Mr. Harding attempted to halt the carriage?"

Adele opened her mouth to speak, then closed it.

"Exactly," Clairice declared. "I aided Mr. Harding a great deal then, and I may be able to do so again to-night."

Adele studied her a moment, then asked quietly, "Would you like me to come along, too?"

Clairice smiled. "No, I think one of us will be sufficient."

"But you cannot go alone through the streets of Paris in the dead of night."

"I promise to be extremely careful. I feel I must do this, Addie."

"Suppose grandmother should wake and look for you?"

"Then you shall just have to think up something to tell her to cover for me." Clairice jerked her hand away from her waist with a sharp cry.

"What happened?"

"I have these dreadful things pinned and a pin came out. I pricked my finger."

Adele studied her. "You run a risk, dear sister, of losing your breeches if all the pins come out. Give them to me and I shall sew them up quickly. Where did you get these clothes?"

"I asked the maid to fetch them for me. I told her we were planning a drama to perform for the family entertainment tomorrow."

"Shame on you, Clairice, for being deceitful."

Clairice slipped off the pantaloons and handed them to Adele. "I could hardly tell her to hurry and fetch me dark clothing because I intended to steal the First Consul's invasion plans."

"I suppose not," Adele agreed. "Let me get my needle."

"Here, use mine." Clairice fetched it, then continued dressing, slipping into a black shirt and coat. As soon as the pantaloons were finished, she pulled them on, then knee boots. Quickly she braided her hair and piled it on her head, placing a hat over it and throwing a dark cape around her shoulders.

Adele surveyed her sister worriedly. "Clairice, I know I should stop you. I cannot believe you are actually going to do this. I feel something bad is about to happen."

"Nonsense! I shall be home soon enough."

"I wish you would change your mind, or else let me come along."

"No, you stay to deal with grandmother, should she miss me. Tell her whatever you think, but do not let her know what I am about."

"I won't do that to her, for her own sake."

They looked at each other. Adele rose swiftly and crossed to kiss her sister on the cheek. "Please, take care."

Clairice hugged Adele's shoulder. "I promise." She turned and crossed to the door. "Do you want to go ahead and see if the way is clear?"

"Indeed." Adele ran past and into the hall to motion Clairice to come. She closed the front door quietly behind her sister.

CLAIRICE STOOD IMMOBILIZED by a sudden sweeping fear. The city was quiet, the night overpowering, the moon hidden behind clouds. With a deep breath she plunged ahead. The cold fear did not abate but increased as she neared her destination. She paid for the carriage she had been able to hire a block away from her grandaunt's home, then went the rest of the way on foot.

With each step she had mounting trepidation about coming, recalling Lord Ault's fury earlier. Once again she would be following him when he did not want her along. At the thought of him she wanted to turn back and flee for the haven of the Rollet home, but then the thought of Mr. Harding gave her courage to continue.

She neared the massive church and crept silently along straining for a sound of either man.

She had deliberately come earlier than the time agreed upon by the two men. She stepped into a darkened doorway and waited for either of them to appear.

A short time passed before there was a clatter nearby. Clairice studied the empty night. Within seconds a movement showed; she watched and realized that a man was approaching the church. He drew near; then to her amazement a figure emerged from a doorway close at hand.

She guessed it was Lord Ault, but she had not seen him arrive. The two men moved together, and Clairice hurried to follow them.

She trailed behind, nervous all the time that Lord Ault would once again discover her. Finally they turned into a gate and disappeared behind the high wall of a house. Clairice followed quickly, first around the wall, then around the house itself. She flattened herself in the shadows and watched a figure clad in black scale iron grillwork, climb over a balcony and disappear through a window. Soon another figure followed, swaying precariously before gaining the balcony, and Clairice suspected Mr. Harding had just entered the house.

She waited, hoping they would come out the same place they had entered. A noise from the opposite direction caught her attention.

The steady rhythmic sound of boots against cobblestones was heard. Clairice hurried to the high gate and peered in the direction of the noise. French soldiers were converging on the house. They came from both directions.

Her heart pounding violently, she whirled and ran to the house, then climbed the grillwork. It was a long reach to the balcony, but she was about to attempt it when Lord Ault burst out of the window.

Quickly she cried in a whisper, ''French soldiers are coming in the front!''

''My God! You will haunt me!'' he muttered and turned his head. ''Hurry, Harding! The French!''

CHAPTER NINE

CLAIRICE CLIMBED DOWN as fast as possible, all but falling off the railing. Lord Ault passed her and jumped to the ground, reaching up to catch her about the waist and swing her down. Mr. Harding fell to the ground beside them.

"This way!" Lord Ault called, and the three bolted for the back of the house. They moved through a gate and turned to race down a narrow street when a voice cried, "*Arrêt!*"

"Run!" Lord Ault commanded and veered in another direction, grasping Clairice's hand and pulling her along until Clairice felt as if her feet were not touching the ground.

Loud cries came from behind, then the sound of feet as the soldiers rallied in pursuit.

Clairice's lungs felt as if they would burst. "Go on...without...me," she panted.

No one answered. They ran with Lord Ault holding tightly to her hand.

Suddenly Mr. Harding, a step ahead of Clairice, charged full tilt into a low stone wall.

With a loud cry he went sprawling headfirst over it. Clairice and Lord Ault cleared it at the same moment. Instantly Clairice jerked her hand free to turn back for Mr. Harding.

"Run!" Lord Ault commanded. "You'll be caught."

"No!" she cried and fell to the ground to aid Mr. Harding.

He struggled to his feet. Lord Ault dashed back to

assist, and suddenly they were surrounded by soldiers. Loud cries and commands filled the air.

In the darkness Clairice leaned forward. "The plans!" she whispered in Lord Ault's ear. "Give me the plans!"

In an instant she felt a thick roll of papers thrust into her hand. In haste she swept them inside her boot, then reached up, pulled off her hat and unpinned her hair.

A soldier approached with a lantern, and the enveloping cover of darkness was gone. An officer announced that they were under arrest and ordered them to follow.

"One moment," Lord Ault spoke. "Would you let the *mademoiselle* go free? She is not involved in this."

The officer answered coldly, "That is not for me to decide."

Surrounded by soldiers, they hurried to a waiting carriage. The officer assisted Clairice into the coach, then the men followed. The three prisoners sat facing the officer and another soldier, the doors were closed and the carriage started moving.

Clairice twisted her fingers together and studied the officer who openly returned her look until she dropped her gaze and studied her hands.

All the dreadful stories she had heard when she was a child about the French during the Revolution rose to mind. She shivered and pulled the cape tightly about her shoulders, glancing up at Lord Ault. He looked down with such fierceness that the threat of the French temporarily faded.

The horses' hooves were loud in the still night. While most of the city slept, they were being taken to prison. A fleeting thought of Lady Fairfax and Adele made Clairice's spirits sink lower. Too late, she wished she had listened to Adele. In desperation she glanced at Mr. Harding. He smiled and took her hand to give it a reassuring squeeze.

"We shall see a new side of Paris tonight," he said lightly.

"Where are you taking us?" Lord Ault inquired.

"You shall see soon enough," the officer replied.

"What are we charged with?"

"I am not at liberty to reveal anything. I have my orders."

Lord Ault shrugged and fell silent, but his questions had made Clairice acutely aware of the hard roll of paper pressed against her leg. Napoleon Bonaparte's plans to invade England were squeezed tightly in her boot. The thought of discovery by the French was terrible to contemplate. The carriage ride seemed interminably long, but finally it halted, and they alighted in front of a large stone building.

"Where are we?" Clairice whispered.

"The French version of Newgate," Lord Ault commented dryly.

"This way," the officer commanded, and the three followed him through a thick wooden door into a cold interior.

They were led down a long flight of steps to an underground room. Tapers burned in sconces along stone walls causing shadows to dance in the corners of the room. Two guards were engrossed in a game of cards, another sat by a large barred door, and the fourth was seated behind a wide wooden table.

The officer commanded the guard to unlock the door and motioned Clairice and the men inside. As soon as they passed through the door, it closed behind them with a clang and the bolt was dropped in place. Wide stone steps fell away before them leading down to a cavernous room filled with piles of straw, male prisoners and little else. Most of the inhabitants were asleep, but a few sat together talking.

Without realizing it, Clairice breathed aloud a soft "Oh!"

"It will not be for long," Mr. Harding whispered.

Lord Ault led the way down the stairs with Mr. Harding holding Clairice's arm. The inhabitants of the cell gazed at them in silence; then a man parted from the others and moved forward to extend his hand to Lord Ault.

"*Bonsoir, monsieur,* welcome to The Pit."

Lord Ault shook his hand and made introductions.

"Ah, British!" Two men crossed to join them. The Frenchman introduced the fellow Britons then waved a hand. "Come, make yourself comfortable."

They remained talking about the arrest. Clairice sat down on a pile of straw; she had no inclination to stand and listen to them chat. She was self-conscious about her masculine attire and had a consuming fear of what their future might be. Snatches of the men's conversation penetrated her thoughts as she huddled on the dank floor, and she learned that the prisoners in this area were political, not criminal.

Mr. Harding inquired how long each of them had been there, and she was appalled when one of the Englishmen said thirteen months and he had not yet been brought to trial. She began to shiver and wrapped her arms about her knees, locking her hands tightly together to prevent shaking.

Suddenly Lord Ault removed his coat and dropped it about her shoulders. She looked up in surprise, but he had already turned back to the Frenchman to answer a question.

Grateful, she pulled the heavy material across her shoulders and observed him. His dark linen shirt fit without a wrinkle, tight enough to reveal muscular shoulders and back.

As if aware of her eyes on him, he turned and glanced down. His scowl increased, and he turned his attention to the men again.

Clairice's spirits drooped even more at his obvious displeasure with her. She closed her eyes as if she could shut out her miserable plight.

A hand gently patted her arm, and she opened her eyes to find Mr. Harding sitting beside her. "Cold?" he asked.

She nodded, not trusting herself to speak for fear she might break into tears.

"Here, take my coat and put it over your knees." He handed the garment to her, and she did as he suggested.

"What will they do with us?" she asked.

He smiled. "Don't worry, Miss Fairfax. I am certain they shall release you when we explain that you actually knew little of what we were about."

"I would not get Miss Fairfax's hopes up in vain, Anthony," Lord Ault admonished harshly.

At his severe pronouncement Clairice could no longer control her feelings and broke into tears. Mr. Harding drew her into his arms, and she clung to him. Over her head she heard him speak to Lord Ault.

"See what you have done! There is no need to be so brutal to the girl."

"She had no business getting involved, and now she will have to suffer the consequences for her own actions," Lord Ault replied.

At his accusation Clairice let out a loud wail. Mr. Harding's arms tightened about her, and the Frenchman leaned down to attempt to cheer her, offering encouragement that she would most likely be released soon.

The two Britons turned and seconded the Frenchman's prediction. As the four men offered her encouragement, Clairice dried her eyes and raised her head. She summoned a weak smile of gratitude for their concern. Over Mr. Harding's shoulder she saw Lord Ault standing on tiptoe in order to gaze through a small barred opening at ground level.

"Thank you, gentlemen, you are very comforting," she declared and soon found herself the center of a growing number of prisoners who wished to talk with her. It had been a long time since some of the men had even seen a female, and from the intense scrutiny she was receiving, Clairice was suddenly thankful she had Mr. Harding at her side. And even as unsympathetic as Lord Ault had been, the latter's presence was nonetheless reassuring.

After a time there was a cluster of more than a dozen men around her. Clairice found it a strain to converse about the outside world when she was filled with worry. Lord Ault remained at a distance, and when Clairice looked at him, she noticed him continually studying the ceiling, the door and the cell as if he were searching for some means to escape.

The coats did little to alleviate her chill; she was growing steadily colder. A noise sounded above, the bolt clattered, and all conversation ceased instantly. The prisoners' heads swiveled in the direction of the door.

The barricade lifted, the door swung open, and a guard entered to stand at the top of the steps and call to Clairice to come forward.

A wave of dizziness washed over her, then a hand clasped her arm firmly and pulled her to her feet. She looked up into Lord Ault's eyes. He spoke softly. "They will probably place you with the women prisoners."

"I don't want to go," she said.

"You see what your meddling has got you into."

Clairice clamped her lips together tightly. She snapped, "You are certainly no consolation!" She started to hand him his coat, but he reached out quickly and caught her hand. "Keep it."

She lifted her chin and moved past him up the stairs. Mr. Harding hurried after her and placed his arm about her shoulders until they neared the top. She stopped and Mr. Harding stepped away. She gazed into the black eyes of the guard and asked, "Where are you taking me?"

"This way, *m'amzelle.*" He motioned her to the door.

Clairice preceded him out, then waited until he led the way. They continued upstairs and down another long hall. Finally he opened a door and moved to one side for her to pass.

It was a small bare room with a table and a few wooden chairs. The sole occupant came forward. "Good evening, Miss Fairfax!"

CHAPTER TEN

OVERWHELMING RELIEF flooded Clairice. She ran forward joyously. "Mr. Crenshawe! You have come to get us out of this place!"

She rushed toward him with her hands extended. He took them in his firm grasp and pulled her into his arms. His mouth came down on hers in a passionate kiss.

Clairice's emotions underwent a violent change from elation they would be freed to shock at his passion at such a time and place. She pushed against his chest.

His mouth was hungry, demanding and brutal on hers. She fought with all her strength until he released her.

"What is this? You greet me with a warm welcome, then you turn against me?"

"I never meant...." She flushed and asked quickly, "You have come to get us out, haven't you?"

He nodded in smug satisfaction. "Exactly, my darling."

"How marvelous," she said with feeling. "This is the most dreadful place. Grandmother will be frantic with worry if she finds me gone." She frowned slightly. "When are they going to fetch Lord Ault and Mr. Harding?"

"When I ask them to," he replied quietly.

"Then when shall you do that? What are you waiting for?"

He took hold of her upper arms and moved his hands lightly up to her shoulders, then to her face to hold it in his hands. A sudden deep premonition of calamity surged through Clairice.

"I am waiting for you," he replied in a husky voice.

The feeling increased. She gazed up at him and asked in a level voice while her happiness evaporated like mist, "What are you waiting for me to do?"

He ran a finger under her chin and tilted her face up. "I am madly in love with you, Clairice. Will you marry me?"

She noticed he was no longer addressing her as "Miss Fairfax." She whispered, "You know what my answer is."

"Do you enjoy prison?" he asked in an oily voice. A chill rushed through her.

"You know the answer to that!"

He smiled. "Then accept the alternative—marry me and you may leave immediately."

She stepped back. "How terrible! How could you want a wife who was forced into accepting your offer!"

"I think you would make a superior wife. You are descended from an old and noble family, and you are what I want, Clairice. What is more, I intend to have you."

"The answer will forever remain no!" Clairice snapped, a hot wave of anger overcoming all other thoughts. "I would prefer the most dismal dungeon to such a prospect!"

He laughed softly. "Foolish girl. Do you not realize your situation? You should be honored that I offer you my name...and offer to take you under the conditions of marriage.'

"I find that remark insulting, sir!"

"You are very naive. You have been here only a lit tle more than an hour. Perhaps I should have waited a day and let you suffer the rigors of incarceration, but I wanted to spare you any misery I could."

She narrowed her eyes and studied him. "Why are the French so agreeable for you to free me?"

He shrugged. "They have agreed to do as I ask."

She viewed him and mulled over snatches of conversation and memory of the elegant Paris home. Without thought she blurted, "You are a French spy!"

He did not answer but merely stared calmly at her as she continued, "That is why you have that home and no one in England knows of it. That is why you can free us if you wish!" Another thought occurred to her. "You knew what Lord Ault and Mr. Harding were about. You had them arrested...."

He moved to perch on the edge of the table with one foot on the floor and the other swinging slowly in the air. "Yes, that is correct."

"But why? You are an Englishman. Why would you betray your own country in such a man—"

He interrupted her, stiffening. His foot halted abruptly and he exclaimed, "My country! My British background—bah! I would never inherit according to English law—everything goes to the eldest son. I have had to live by my wits. England has never done anything for me, while France and the First Consul have done everything!"

His voice grew louder. "You have seen my home— here I am a hero. This is my opportunity to serve France and be rewarded beyond my wildest dreams. If I serve England, what shall I have to show for it? A medal and a pension most likely. Here, I am heaped with honors and with wealth! I have all I want bestowed upon me. Bonaparte is very generous with those around him."

"But to betray your country is dreadful! Why would you want an English wife?"

The glazed look disappeared from his face and he relaxed once more. "I told you—I have fallen in love with you. After all, I am still British. You would fit in here as well as I do, and you would be satisfactory in every way. You are of the highest class of English society."

"You are in love with my lineage, I suspect. And you are just British enough to look down your nose at marrying a *nouveau riche* French girl, which is the best you could hope for nere, I would guess."

He gave her a level stare. "Perhaps you are right. It does not really matter. Whatever the reasons, I am going to marry you."

"I find you detestable!"

He shrugged one shoulder. "Perhaps at the moment. You have been shocked by my revelations, but you can adjust, and you will forget the unpleasantness. I am willing to be tolerant."

She studied him. "Didn't you take quite a chance in showing your home to me?"

"It would not have mattered if you had informed Lord Ault or Mr. Harding. From the moment they set foot in France, they have been headed for prison. They could do nothing even if they had guessed my loyalties. I had nothing to lose, and I wanted you to see that you will not be marrying beneath your station."

"My answer is no. You may as well summon the guard to escort me downstairs."

His voice was soft but quite audible. "Are you that willing to sacrifice the lives of Lord Ault and Mr. Harding, also?"

"What are you saying?" she asked, horrified.

He rose and moved leisurely toward her, placing hot hands on her shoulders. He gazed down at her with burning dark eyes. "I mean exactly that. And Lady Fairfax? How would she fare in prison?"

Clairice paled. "You couldn't! You would have no right to do such a thing!"

"Do you realize what you were involved in tonight? Stealing plans of the highest importance to France. You are an enemy of the state, Miss Fairfax, and as such your entire family is subject to arrest and detainment until a trial is held.''

Clairice stared at him in horror. "You would not be so bestial!"

'I would not hesitate in the least!" he snapped, and shut his thin lips together tightly.

She took a step back out of his grasp. "You are an inhuman monster!"

"You will change your mind."

"Never! Don't you see, if I married you under such conditions, I would hate you forever!"

He laughed harshly. "To the young forever is a long time. You would change. I see nothing of the sort. You are too intelligent to be spiteful for long." His eyes moved over her features with undisguised desire. He reached out and once again grasped her arms. "I think I can see to it that you are cooperative. I can be very persuasive, one way or another."

His hands tightened on her shoulders painfully, causing Clairice to exclaim, "You are hurting me!"

He released her with a smile. "What is your answer?"

Clairice bit her lip and studied him. What he offered was abhorrent to her entire being. She loathed the man and feared him, but she could not allow him to throw her family into prison or cause Mr. Harding and Lord Ault to remain prisoners. She sighed. "If I consent, will you free Lord Ault and Mr. Harding and allow them to return to England?"

"Yes."

"My family will be allowed to return also?"

"My darling, if you are to be my wife, your family may remain for as long as they wish. They are free to leave or stay, whichever they choose."

She stared at him. "When would Mr. Harding and Lord Ault be released?"

"As soon as we are wed."

In a cold voice she asked, "When will the marriage take place?"

"This morning if you like."

"No." She shook her head. "I have no intention of being married in these clothes." Her mind raced over the possibilities. "I have some requests." At his nod she continued, "I have just met two Britons here in prison; I would like them released."

His eyes narrowed and he interrupted her. "What do they mean to you?"

"I just met them, but they have been held here for a long time."

"Maudlin sympathy. I cannot do that. I am moving mountains to release Ault. The French could make marvelous use of his capture. He is a valuable man to the prince. Far more than old Barthwell or Harding. You see, you are costing me a great deal, my darling."

"Where is Sir Barthwell?"

"He is still free."

"Very well," Clairice stated. "I want to tell my family and give them the opportunity to depart for England if they so desire."

He nodded. "It can be arranged without difficulty."

"I do not trust you in the least. I want Lord Ault and Mr. Harding released before I leave this prison. They must have time to escape from France. Then I shall marry you."

He sighed. "They shall be released, and eight hours will be ample for their escape. When can you be ready for the ceremony?"

"I would prefer to wait two days."

His voice lowered, and he ran his hand along her slender throat. "I am far too anxious to wait so long. Besides, the longer Lord Ault and Mr. Harding remain in France, the more difficult it is for me to have them freed."

"Then how soon?" Clairice asked.

"It is now shortly past four o'clock in the morning. The civil ceremony shall be performed at four o'clock this afternoon."

"What happens to them after the eight hours are up?"

"Then I no longer am responsible if Ault and Harding are once again apprehended and thrown into prison."

"That is not fair!" she cried.

"My dear girl, that is extremely generous treatment for enemies of France!"

"Very well." She gazed up at him. "I would like to inform them myself."

His eyes narrowed. "You do not trust me, but you will change." He grasped her arm. "Come, my pet, we shall go break the joyful news." He opened the door. A guard waited silently in the hall, and at Mr. Crenshawe's instruction he turned on his heel and led them below.

The men's boots clacked on the stone floor as they hurried along in grim silence, once again descending the stair into the coldness of the underground area.

The door clanked open and the guard stood to one side. Clairice entered and her eyes met Lord Ault's. He stood at the foot the stair. His glance moved past her.

"Crenshawe! Have you been arrested also?"

Mr. Crenshawe stared down at him and his grip tightened on Clairice's arm. His fingers bit into her flesh, and suddenly she longed to tear free and flee down the steps to a haven of safety she felt she would find there in Lord Ault's presence. His imposing stature and absolute calm radiated security.

Mr. Crenshawe spoke with an evil glee. "Good morning, Ault, Harding. Clairice wishes a word with you, gentlemen."

Lord Ault's eyes narrowed. His voice was soft. "So—you are the one! You are the spy, the traitor in our midst!'

"Correct. Regrettably for you, it is a little late to discover the fact—it shall do you no good now."

"How did you manage to convince Sir Barthwell of your trustworthiness?"

Crenshawe replied easily, "I started out quite earnestly working for England, but I found it far more rewarding to change loyalty. Soon it will not matter, for England will belong to Napoleon Bonaparte and to France. Plans are already made for activities when he reaches London as a victorious conqueror."

"That is an impossibility," Lord Ault stated calmly.

"You will soon be proven wrong. That closed English mind, which is so slow to accept change, will be forced into it. But, gentlemen, you are fortunate in another matter—quite fortunate. Miss Fairfax has gained your freedom for you."

Lord Ault's gaze shifted to Clairice and he asked, "In exchange for what, Crenshawe?"

"In exchange for marriage. It is my wedding gift to her."

Mr. Harding rushed toward the steps, his eyes filled with concern. "Miss Fairfax, is this what you want?" He stopped and looked at her.

"Yes," Clairice replied.

Mr. Crenshawe declared, "Bravo, my dear! She has consented to the marriage. In exchange, you will be freed immediately, and I will allow you eight hours in which to escape. After that you are on your own. I suggest that you leave France as hastily as possible."

"We can hardly do that in eight hours!" Lord Ault snapped.

Mr. Crenshawe shrugged. "Eight hours is generous. You should be thankful."

Mr. Harding rushed up and grasped Clairice's hand. "We cannot allow you to make such a sacrifice!"

"Yes, we can!" Lord Ault's voice rang out firmly.

Clairice had been gazing with heartbreaking tenderness at Mr. Harding, fearful if she attempted to thank him that she would burst into tears. At Lord Ault's words she stiffened and gave him an angry look. Ignoring it, he inquired, "And when will her family be allowed to leave?"

Mr. Crenshawe replied, "They are free to remain or go. They are in no danger of imprisonment."

Lord Ault propped a booted foot on a step. "Thank you, Miss Fairfax. I shall inform the prince of your noble sacrifice for His Majesty's loyal subjects."

Clairice looked into his eyes and suddenly felt a weakness at the thought of parting from his company and that of Mr. Harding. She caught her underlip between her teeth and stared at him. His gaze shifted to Crenshawe once again. "Where is the ceremony to take place?"

"You will not be attending, Ault. You will lucky to escape France."

"Our mission was doomed from the outset, was it not?" Lord Ault inquired.

Mr. Crenshawe answered, "Correct! Two more fools to be apprehended, only in this case you will released."

"Why did you let us go this far?"

Mr. Crenshawe shrugged. "To glean as much information as possible before we made our move."

"So all the time we were making plans in London, you knew we would be imprisoned." Mr. Crenshawe nodded in agreement and Lord Ault continued, "What a pity your identity has been revealed. What about your home in England?"

"I have taken care of that. It was growing more dangerous for me all the time, and my discovery was inevitable with your arrest."

"And you were the cause of Henry Tayburn's death, were you not?"

"I may have contributed to it. Actually, if he had surrendered instead of attempting to escape, the fool would be alive today."

Lord Ault spoke in a deadly calm voice. "You are

the fool, Crenshawe, and somewhere, sometime, I shall settle this score with you.''

The dark eyes of the large man beside her narrowed. ''Do not push me, Ault. You make it very difficult for me to keep my part of the bargain. You had better make the most of your eight hours, for I promise you that all of the soldiers I can command will be searching for you after that. You will never get another chance such as this.''

The two looked at each other and Clairice could feel the antagonism between them. Lord Ault snapped, ''You are a traitor.''

Mr. Crenshawe shrugged. ''I told you, soon it will not matter. Bonaparte and France will one day rule the entire world.'' His voice changed. ''One more thing— before you depart this prison, I must have the plans you have gained this evening.''

Lord Ault's expression did not alter. He answered matter-of-factly, ''If we had had a chance to get them. You will find them quite safe—inside the war minister's home. We were on our way in—not coming out—when we heard your soldiers.''

The smile vanished from Mr. Crenshawe's face. ''You are lying!'' he accused.

Lord Ault shrugged. ''You can have us searched.''

''I shall do so immediately! Guard! Take these men upstairs and search them for the documents. Come, Clairice.''

Mr. Harding reached out suddenly and again grasped Clairice's hand. ''Thank you, Miss Fairfax. I cannot say what this means.''

''Goodbye,'' Clairice whispered and turned away. Her knees felt weak and wobbly, and tears blinded her eyes momentarily.

Mr. Crenshawe led her up the stairs. ''Come with me; we will wait until they are searched.''

Clairice was acutely aware of the scroll of papers inside her boot. It was difficult not to glance down. She would have to get the plans sent to England some way. She followed Mr. Crenshawe into his chamber.

He faced her. "Soon you will be mine." He bent and held her tightly as he kissed her in such a manner that Clairice felt sick with revulsion at his touch. He looked down at her. "I want you for the mother of my children. They will be British and of noble birth, yet at the same time we shall be in power here. I expect to return to England with a high post of command after the invasion."

"I do not think France will succeed."

"You know nothing of such matters, Clairice. No woman in England can conceive of military conquest, but it shall come."

A light rap sounded at the door. Clairice moved away from him, and at his order a guard opened the door to announce that the search had revealed no plans.

Mr. Crenshawe mulled aloud, "He said the plans are still at the minister's—"

Clairice spoke quickly. "If the wedding is to take place at four o'clock, please, I have so much to do to be ready. Can you let them free now and allow me to return home?"

He regarded her for a moment as if in indecision, then answered, "Very well. Come and we shall see them go."

Soon Clairice was seated in an open carriage beside the prison door. Mr. Crenshawe sat beside her, then swung lightly down to the ground when a guard led Lord Ault and Mr. Harding outside.

"Eight hours," Mr. Crenshawe reminded them.

"We will meet again, Crenshawe," Lord Ault replied in a cold voice. They turned and hurried out of sight.

"Do they have to go on foot?" Clairice cried as Mr. Crenshawe once again climbed in beside her.

He answered, "What did you expect? A royal send-off? They are fortunate to be free. The rest is up to them.''

She closed her eyes. "I loath and despise you.''

"That attitude will change swiftly. Come here, Clairice. Soon you will be introduced to the important people in France. You have relatives here and you will be happy." He reached out and grasped her wrist to pull her roughly to him.

Clairice jerked violently away and squeezed into a corner. "I do not have to obey you yet, sir!''

"You will soon enough, and I shall see to it that you become an obedient wife. I find you highly entertaining, Clairice, a challenge I welcome.''

She huddled in the corner listening to the steady clop-clop of the horses while her mind was on Lord Ault and Mr. Harding. They had so little time to escape.

She did not want to think ahead to her own fate, so she deliberated how to break the news to Lady Fairfax; but there did not seem to be any good way. She glanced at the dark-eyed man seated next to her; she did not want to be married to him. Unbidden, the memory of Lord Ault's lips on hers returned, and she put it out of mind quickly. Her head ached from the past hour's events.

Clairice tugged the black cape tightly about her shoulders and huddled in the corner until they finally stopped in front of her granduncle's house.

Mr. Crenshawe helped her down, then held her hand. In the flickering light of the carriage lamp his eyes gleamed wickedly, sending shivers along Clairice's spine. "Four o'clock, Clairice," he said. "I shall place guards at the front and back of the house, so do not attempt to escape. You could not get far, and it would be hard on your family. You do not want your grandmother in prison, so you'd best accept what life has handed you. There are many women who would consider themselves fortunate to be in your position.''

"Then I wish you would marry one of them!" Clairice snapped. She tore her hands from his grasp and raced into the house, then fell back against the door as the torrent of tears she had labored to hold back came gushing forth.

"Clairice?" Adele's soft voice came from the darkness in the direction of the library. "Clairice?"

Clairice wiped her eyes. "Here, Addie, I am coming."

A soft blur of pale robe moved in the darkness. Clairice fell into her sister's arms and broke into fresh tears.

Adele's voice was filled with fright. "Clairice, what happened? Please tell me. Is Mr. Harding all right? I heard a carriage drive up—who was it with you?"

Clairice straightened and rubbed her sleeve against her wet cheeks. "Addie, it was disastrous!"

"Shh! Lower your voice. Tell me what happened."

"I will, but we might as well go wake grandmother and tell her at the same time, for she has to know."

"Then hurry!" Adele took Clairice's hand and pulled her along up the stairs to Lady Fairfax's room. She whispered urgently, "I'll light a taper; you wake grandmother."

A loud snore emitted from the inert form in the bed. Clairice hurried to the bedside and reached down to shake Lady Fairfax.

Within seconds the old woman aroused and looked up; her nightcap was awry, revealing white curls standing high in a tangle over her head. "Damme! What is it?"

A light flickered, and Adele brought it to a side table, then sat on the opposite side of the bed from Clairice. Lady Fairfax glanced from one to the other, then sat up quickly.

"Confound it, miss! Of all the bird-witted acts! Clairice, you've been out with Lord Ault and Mr. Harding, haven't you?"

A small shock pierced Clairice's gloom. "How did you guess?"

Lady Fairfax looked disgustedly at her. "Why else would you be dressed like a flash-house urchin? And I see it did not go well." She leaned forward. "Help me, child."

Adele and Clairice piled the pillows behind Lady Fairfax and aided her to be comfortable. Then she said, "Get on with it, Clairice! What happened?"

"It was awful!" Clairice cried. Her voice rose and a fresh wave of crying commenced.

"Stop that confounded wailing, miss, and let us know what happened!"

Clairice rubbed her face and looked at them as she related details of the capture. "Grandmother, when we reached the prison I was taken upstairs. It was Mr. Crenshawe. He is a French spy."

"Damn the man! I never did like the ferret-eyed rascal!"

Adele gasped. "Oh, no! Then he has known everything all this time."

"That is correct." Clairice regarded Lady Fairfax intently. "Grandmother, he wants me to marry him. He desires a British wife, but he has a home here in Paris. He expects France to overpower England soon, and then he will have a high position in government at home. He promised—" her voice dropped "—that if I would marry him, he would free Lord Ault and Mr. Harding."

Instead of the expected outburst, Lady Fairfax merely clamped her lips together tightly while Adele reached across the bed and grasped her sister's hand.

"How dreadful! Small wonder you are tearful. Clairice, I am so sorry. You cannot do such a terrible thing! Grandmother, we have to do something!"

Lady Fairfax waved a hand at Adele. "Let us hear the rest. Go on, Clairice."

Clairice reached down and extricated the roll of

paper from her boots. "Also, grandmother, I have this!" With a flourish she placed the roll in Lady Fairfax's lap.

Lady Fairfax studied it and asked, "The plans?"

"Yes. Lord Ault passed them to me just before we were taken prisoner. They searched the men, but did not search me."

"Excellent!" Lady Fairfax chortled gleefully.

"We must get them off at once for England," Clairice urged.

"We shall have to take them ourselves."

Adele suggested, "You do not think Edgars—"

Lady Fairfax interrupted, "The poor man would collapse of fright." She waved a hand at Adele. "Let us hear the rest. Go on, Clairice."

"There is not much more to tell. They released Lord Ault and Mr. Harding. Mr. Crenshawe told them they will be allowed eight hours in which to escape from France; after that he will attempt to find them and put them in prison again."

"How awful!" Adele whispered.

"What are the wedding plans?" Lady Fairfax inquired.

Clairice closed her eyes in repugnance at the mere thought. "It will take place at four o'clock this afternoon. That is all the time I have."

"What about us?" Lady Fairfax persisted.

"You are free to stay or go, whichever you choose, since you are my family. Grandmother, I think you should take Adele and Aunt Lavinia and the servants and return home."

"Let me be the judge of that." She sat in silence for a moment while Adele sympathized with Clairice.

Their conversation was cut short by Lady Fairfax. "Clairice, summon Betsy. Adele, get Lavinia in here. Then you get ready for the wedding, Clairice, but also prepare to return to England."

Both girls cried out in wonder at how they could

hope for such an event. Lady Fairfax hushed them quickly. "We shall all get ready, have the carriages loaded to travel, and take everything along to the wedding. We will inform Mr. Crenshawe that the family is returning to England, and he will think nothing of the trunks."

"I still do not see how I can plan on leaving," Clairice remarked.

"I am not finished," Lady Fairfax declared archly. "I shall take my pistol, concealed, of course, and kill the man. Then we shall make our escape."

Adele shrieked and Clairice's hopes sank. "Grandmother, you cannot do that, and we would never get out of Paris if you succeeded," Clairice stated wearily.

"I most certainly can. Would you rather be married to the man or take a chance?"

Clairice gazed into Lady Fairfax's dark eyes and answered quietly, "I would rather take a chance, but I do not want you in such danger."

"If we get caught, I shall tell them that you knew nothing of my intentions. It would give me the greatest pleasure to put a shot through that traitorous charlatan's heart! Now hurry! Both of you pack quickly; we have a great deal to do in a short time."

Both rushed to do as instructed. Clairice hurried to the bellpull to summon Betsy while Adele left to wake her aunt. Clairice's hand shook with eagerness at the sudden hope of escaping from the fate she dreaded. She dashed for her room to bathe and pack, but as she completed her tasks, the relief disappeared and cold reality set in.

Even if Lady Fairfax succeeded in killing Mr. Crenshawe, which was doubtful, escape would be a miracle. The servants would be nothing but a hindrance, Lady Fairfax moved slowly, and Clairice felt that neither she, Adele nor Aunt Lavinia were capable of getting everyone safely away.

Two hours later Clairice was packed and dressed.

She studied her reflection and smoothed the sleeves of the white silk dress. Her hair fell in soft waves about her shoulders; the red curls gleamed with cleanliness and smelled freshly of soap. She took up a silk pelisse that matched the dress and left the room to go to her grandmother.

The house was transformed into activity, with servants hurrying to and fro while a pile of baggage grew in the center of the downstairs hall. The pale light of dawn revealed dark overcast heavens with large clouds rolling. Soon a light drizzle began to fall. It brought a chill to the house even though it was the first of May. Fires were lighted and wraps readied for the journey.

As soon as Clairice entered Lady Fairfax's room, she hurried to ask, "Grandmother, what about Uncle Marcel? After all, he is a Frenchman."

"And loyal to France. But that does not necessarily mean loyal to the First Consul. He will not betray us. He does not approve of all that is taking place. This talk of invasion of England is souring to many French. Don't worry about your uncle, Clairice."

"I hope so," she replied doubtfully. "We all felt that way about Mr. Crenshawe only a week ago."

"You look lovely, my child, but you will need your cape with this rain. We are progressing well from—"

Her words were cut short as the door flew open and an ashen-faced Lavinia flung herself into the room. She was clad in a robe that she threw open in a wide sweep of her arms to reveal a chemise-clad body.

"Look what he has done to me!" she shrieked.

"Damme!" Lady Fairfax exploded. "What has happened, Lavinia? You look the same as ever!"

Clairice could not help but concur; the thin body under the chemise had not changed that she could perceive.

Lavinia hurriedly wrapped the robe around herself once more and glared hotly at her aunt. "Uncle Marcel has done it!"

Clairice gasped. Lady Fairfax snapped, "Done what, Lavinia?"

Miss Milsap closed her eyes in horror, and her voice was filled with agony as she replied, "I have the itch!"

"Oh, for God's sake!" Lady Fairfax exclaimed. "That is the least of our problems!"

Lavinia scratched her shoulder. "It is dreadful—I itch all over!" She scratched her knee vigorously.

"Then have some tea, Lavinia. It has done wonders for Marcel."

Lavinia closed her eyes and murmured, "I might have known." She opened them and declared staunchly, "I prefer the itch!" She headed for the door.

"Lavinia," Lady Fairfax called, "are you ready to leave?"

"I do not know what I am about!" She scratched her neck and hand.

"Be ready, or you will be left—"

"It will not be such a light matter, Aunt Cornelia, when you have contracted it also," she uttered darkly and left the room in haste.

"Poor Aunt Lavinia," Clairice said sympathetically.

"Bosh! She will recover. Marcel has."

Clairice promptly forgot her aunt's dilemma in the face of the more pressing problem ahead of them all. "Grandmother, I beg you once more not to do this. It is too dangerous. Why don't you take the family and return to England now?"

"Be still, Clairice. I am doing exactly what I most want to do. I would guess that Lord Ault is suffering because he cannot commit this act himself. Wait until Sir Barthwell learns the news of this traitor."

"Sir Barthwell!" Clairice's hand flew to her mouth. "I had completely forgotten him!"

"We shall not concern ourselves with him. Mr. Crenshawe was his aide, and Sir Barthwell shall have to deal with the consequences of his poor choice." Lady Fairfax sat down heavily in a chintz chair. "I think I am ready." She smoothed the skirt of her bright blue wool dress and said emphatically, "That Crenshawe—a low man!"

"He was thoroughly convinced," Clairice said, "that I would not marry him because of his lack of a title."

"The fool sounds power hungry; he has sold out to the highest bidder for his own personal gain. Well, I shall give him his just deserts soon enough!"

Clairice crossed to sit at her grandmother's knee and hold her hand. "Do be careful. I would rather marry Mr. Crenshawe than have you hurt."

Lady Fairfax ran her hand lightly over Clairice's red tresses. "You are a good child and very courageous. You have freed Lord Ault and Mr. Harding. I am doing just what I want to do, and I shall be very careful."

They gazed into each other's eyes and the rapport was close. Clairice lifted her grandmother's hand and kissed the back of it lightly, then smiled and rose to stand by the window to hide the tears that had come to her eyes. After a moment she glanced over her shoulder

Lady Fairfax was examining reticules. In a burst of impatience she exclaimed, "Gammon! A dueling pistol will not fit into a reticule!"

"That settles it then, grandmother. You will have to leave the pistol behind."

Lady Fairfax ignored Clairice's comment. "Get my muffs down, please."

Clairice looked at her in exasperation, then turned to do as ordered. She opened the wardrobe and stared at the collection on the shelf. She lifted two large muffs and laid them in her grandmother's lap.

"Excellent!" Lady Fairfax lifted a muff of soft ostrich feathers. The heavy black pistol slipped inside and was gone from sight. "This is perfect!" She turned the muff and gazed at it with satisfaction.

"Grandmother, I cannot bear to watch you! The very thought is dreadful!" Clairice returned to the window to gaze at the street below. She wrapped her arms tightly across her waist and shivered against a chill not caused by the dank weather. In a small voice she said, "I think I would prefer to be Mr. Crenshawe's wife than to have you commit this act!"

"Bosh! The devil deserves such a fate. He is a traitor, a spy and a rogue to take advantage of you in such a manner. He would do the same to Lord Ault and Mr. Harding. Do not be fainthearted, miss!"

Clairice leaned her forehead against the cool pane and stared at the street below. The drizzle had continued sufficiently long that the cobbles gleamed wetly and the window glass was streaked with water.

A vendor rounded the corner and pushed his cart along with a noisy thump of the large wooden wheels passing over the stones. He cried aloud, hawking his wares. A shabby brown hat was pulled low over his forehead and his clothes hung about his large frame. Clairice ran a finger along the pane leaving a streak against the glass. Her heart was filled with an ache as gloomy as the day. She did not see any hope for the coming events to conclude satisfactorily. Visions of Mr. Harding and Lord Ault riding for the coast rose in her mind. Without realizing it, she spoke aloud. "I hope they escape."

"If I know Lord Ault, they shall," Lady Fairfax replied.

"How far do you suppose they could be by now?" Clairice asked.

"'Twould be difficult to say. Depends if they found mounts or not, or if Lord Ault took his carriage."

"I hope so. Oh, I pray they did!" Clairice breathed intensely. Her breath made a hazy circle on the glass. The vendor had paused in the street directly below and cried loudly, selling eels. Clairice raised her forehead from the window so he would not think she was signaling him to wait.

"How simple his life must be. And, most likely, he looks at these houses and thinks how uncomplicated our lives must be. We each have to face our own problems."

"Clairice, whom could be you discussing?"

"There is a vendor on the street, grandmother." She changed the subject abruptly. "How can we get away—afterward?"

"The carriages will be ready and waiting and we shall simply make a run for the coast. As many smugglers go back and forth across the Channel, I am certain we shall be able to manage to be taken to England. Marcel has already informed me that we may take his carriage."

Clairice shook her head slightly; her spirits drooped even lower at the prospects. "We shall not get away," she whispered. Visions of their capture and the terrible prison came to mind with chilling clarity.

The vendor pushed his cart on with his back to Clairice. As he neared the corner two priests appeared. They moved in slow step with the dark cassocks swirling about their ankles and their round-brimmed hats pulled down low over their faces, shielding them from the rain.

The vendor paused at the corner and called again to the uninterested neighbors. No door opened and no one appeared to purchase his goods.

The priests halted when they drew abreast and conversed with the man. He gazed about, then pointed toward Clairice.

"It is unfortunate," Lady Fairfax commented, "that Lord Ault did not know of our plans. If they do not get away, they could have waited off the coast and picked us up."

Clairice's attention was on the men below, her curiosity aroused since they were obviously concerned with the Rollet house. The priests nodded at the vendor and moved around the cart in her direction. The distance between the peddler's cart and the priests widened as the vendor started to push in the opposite direction. Suddenly the hem of one of the priest's cassock caught in a wheel.

The priest tugged at the garment; all three men halted. The priest pulled again while the peddler talked and waved his hands. Behind Clairice Lady Fairfax grumbled, "Goodness knows, we need all the help we can get in this endeavor. We must think of the best route to the Channel."

"Grandmother . . ." Clairice said softly, watching the vendor jiggle his cart while the priest worked at the caught material. The other priest returned to help.

"Once again," Lady Fairfax continued, "we will have to travel unaccompanied by any male protection."

"Perhaps not," Clairice said quite clearly, her eyes riveted on the scene below.

"Eh? Oh, Edgars! He will be little help. Betsy usually has to take care of him."

"Grandmother—" Clairice's voice rose "—grandmother! I think we shall have Lord Ault and Mr. Harding with us!"

CHAPTER ELEVEN

"WHAT WOULD CAUSE YOU to think that?" Lady Fairfax asked.

"Come look! There are two priests below in the street. I think they are Lord Ault and Mr. Harding. Hurry!"

"What on earth would make you think that two priests are—"

Clairice interrupted, "Because, grandmother, one of them has the hem of his robe caught in a peddler's push-cart."

"Great God in heaven!" Lady Fairfax pushed herself up from the chair with sudden agility and hobbled to the window to stand beside Clairice. She held tightly to Clairice's arm.

Clairice pointed at the tableau. "See!"

"Damme! It is! I would recognize those broad shoulders anywhere. That is Lord Ault, and it is not difficult to determine who is caught in the wheel."

"But why are they coming here?"

Lady Fairfax cackled gleefully and squeezed Clairice's arm. "To take us along!"

Clairice looked down in surprise. "Oh, grandmother," she breathed, "you don't suppose—come with me!" She took Lady Fairfax's arm and together they hurried out of the room toward the stairs to meet the men. By the time they approached the door, the knocker sounded loudly against the plate.

The butler opened the door. Clairice stepped forward, but Lady Fairfax pulled her and gave a faint shake of her head. Clairice glanced again in the direction of the door and heard low masculine voices in discussion, then the butler appeared.

"*Madame,* two priests are at the door to speak with Miss Fairfax concerning the nuptials. If you wish, I can show them into the blue salon."

"*Merci,*" Lady Fairfax accepted gratefully, and they went to the salon. As soon as they closed the door, Clairice asked, "Why the formality?"

"Clairice, this is not our household and we are in a precarious position. How do we know which servants can be trusted?"

Clairice's eyes widened. "I did not give one thought to such a possibility!"

She ceased talking as the door opened and the butler announced the men of the cloth. Lord Ault was in the lead; his black clothes were even darker across his shoulders where the cloth was wet from the rain. He removed the round hat from his head.

Clairice could not contain herself. With joy she rushed forward and grasped both men's hands. "I am so thankful to see you! I expected you to be on your way to the coast by now, not still here in Paris."

"We would have been here sooner if we had not had unexpected difficulties." He glanced briefly at Mr. Harding.

"Where did you get the clothing?" she asked in wonder.

Lord Ault said, "Mr. Harding must get the credit." He added dryly, "We have found his long suit—he has a very agile and capable mind."

"Thank you, sir," Mr. Harding replied cheerily.

Suddenly conscious of clinging to both Lord Ault and Mr. Harding, Clairice turned away to sit in a chair. Mr. Harding crossed to stand before the hearth and warm his wet hands, while Lord Ault got to the business at hand by asking Clairice, "What time are you to be married?"

"Four o'clock. Mr. Crenshawe will come for me."

Lady Fairfax sat down quietly in a wing chair as Clairice answered.

Lord Ault said, "Tell me the plans."

"We are to go at four o'clock. Grandmother has already had a meeting of the family to inform them of the situation. . . ." She paused and glanced at Lady Fairfax.

"And. . .?" Lord Ault urged.

"And—" the words were difficult for her to say "—and grandmother plans to kill Mr. Crenshawe during the ceremony!" Clairice's voice was low. "Our carriage is being readied now for the journey home."

Lord Ault swept across the room in long strides and bowed low, lifting the gnarled hand that rested on the arm of the chair. "Lady Fairfax, you have my deepest admiration." He raised her hand to his lips and kissed it lightly.

She smiled and her eyes twinkled. "I am deeply flattered, Lord Ault."

"Magnificent!" Mr. Harding exclaimed.

Lord Ault crossed to the windows. After a moment he faced them again. "You will not have to go through with it, I hope. Instead we will make a run for the coast."

"The house is being guarded," Clairice informed them.

"We saw them," Mr. Harding announced. "Two French soldiers each entrance, I presume?"

"We shall manage the guards. How many are going along?" Lord Ault inquired.

Lady Fairfax replied, "My sister and her husband will not leave with us."

Lord Ault was emphatic. "We must go quickly. Not only will Crenshawe be after Clairice, as well as soldiers after us, but also as of today all Englishmen on French soil are to be placed under arrest!"

"Gammon!" Lady Fairfax exploded. "Surely you are mistaken!"

"How would it be possible?" Clairice cried. "Perhaps your information is incorrect."

"Not in the least," Lord Ault assured them and produced a torn piece of paper from the folds of his sleeve. He glanced at each of them, then said, "This morning Governor Junot received an order from the First Consul." He raised the paper and read, " 'All Englishmen from the age of eighteen to sixty or holding any commission from His Britannic Majesty, who are at present in France, shall immediately be constituted prisoners of war.' "

"Incredible!" Lady Fairfax exclaimed and Clairice cried, "How awful—all Englishmen from eighteen! What will children do? What will happen to them if their parents are cast into prison? The monster! Why would he do such a vile act?"

Lord Ault replied tersely, "It is to be carried out by seven this evening!"

"Can we possibly escape?" Clairice cried. "How can we travel?"

Lord Ault answered calmly, "They cannot carry out such an order efficiently by seven, but we are in danger until we are off French soil."

A light rap at the door interrupted them. All three stared a moment before Clairice called, "Enter," and Betsy appeared looking distraught.

"Begging pardon, ma'am, but Miss Lavinia sent me to fetch you."

Lady Fairfax swore under her breath and rose. "I shall return," she declared, slowly crossing the room.

Once again Clairice asked, "Why would Bonaparte do such a dreadful thing?"

Lord Ault replied, "We have heard the rumor that the British Navy has captured two French ships. It would be sufficient to infuriate the First Consul. Only yesterday Lord Whitworth made Talleyrand an offer concerning Malta—that we would give it up after ten years and the French are to evacuate Holland immediately. This was received with little welcome, and no reply was given at the time." Lord Ault shrugged. "I heard nothing further about it."

"But how do we know they will not come for us any second now?"

"We don't," Lord Ault stated grimly. "But we have little else we can do except use whatever time we are given. I suspect you are not on the list yet because of your French relative and the fact that Crenshawe plans to marry you. He could manage it."

"This is the most dreadful news." Clairice wrung her hands. "Think of all the Britons we have met while we have been here—the Stanhopes, the Westridge family...."

"Britons are fleeing Paris like animals from a fire, and soldiers are scurrying everywhere." Lord Ault ran a hand across his forehead. "It does not make our task any easier."

"We must locate Sir Barthwell," Mr. Harding stated.

Lord Ault looked down at Clairice and his eyes clouded. "Miss Fairfax, I do not know if we can get your grandmother out of the country. We shall have to let her ride in a carriage, and the chances of escape are slim. The roads will be congested, and covered by French troops. All we can do is try. A French prison would be her funeral."

Clairice shivered. "You are right."

He looked over her head at Harding. "We will get mounts, and Harding can take all those who can ride. I will go with Lady Fairfax and the others in the carriage." He frowned. "I can give you little hope. The sheer numbers—seven of you plus nine with Harding and me, then ten if we find Sir Barthwell—nearly make escape impossible." He shook his head. "We shall try and perhaps those of you who can ride will get through. The yacht is waiting off the coast."

Clairice saw the hopelessness of the situation. She looked up at him. "Thank you, but I want to go with grandmother. You should take Adele and go with Mr. Harding.''

He shook his head at her. ''Lady Fairfax would want you to go, and I swear to do everything in my power to get us out of France.''

''I trust you, Lord Ault. It is not your place actually. You are the one who should ride with Adele and the others and let me take my chances with grandmother and Aunt Lavinia.''

He sighed. ''Miss Fairfax, we are forever at loggerheads, and there isn't time for argument now. Your grandmother will want you to go with Adele.''

''My lord,'' Mr. Harding said, ''you mentioned that a French prison would be Lady Fairfax's funeral.''

Lord Ault looked at Mr. Harding. ''Yes?''

''Perhaps we could find a funeral coach and use it for a disguise.''

Clairice turned in her chair to look at Mr. Harding. Lord Ault contemplated the suggestion and after a moment replied thoughtfully, ''Perhaps you have something, Harding. It is worth a try.''

''But how could you get a funeral coach?'' Clairice cried.

Lord Ault brightened. ''Let's go, Harding.'' He looked down at Clairice to answer her question. ''I told you—Mr. Harding's long suit is his agile brain. We shall get that coach, and Barthwell, too. Be ready any time we come.''

He started for the door with Mr. Harding behind him. Clairice rose and hurried after them. She asked quickly, ''Suppose...suppose the soldiers arrest us while you are gone?''

Lord Ault paused and answered quietly, ''There is nothing we can do. We shall be back as quickly as possible.'' Before he could reach the door, it opened and Lady Fairfax entered, then closed it behind her.

''Leaving, my lord?'' she asked.

''Clairice can explain,'' Lord Ault replied quickly.

"Before you go—" Lady Fairfax raised her hand and extended a roll of white paper "—here are the plans."

"Excellent!" Lord Ault exclaimed. He looked at Clairice. "I was quite fearful that you would be caught with them," he said quietly.

She met his gaze and found it curiously disturbing. She dropped her glance to the papers in his hand. He continued, "Let me see if we have been hoaxed here. It would not surprise me in the least."

She recalled something and asked, "Lord Ault, you informed Mr. Crenshawe that the plans were still at the war minister's house. Suppose he had sent soldiers to look."

"That was also a chance I was willing to take." He unrolled the sheaf of papers. They curled in his strong fingers, but he straightened them and read, "Let me see. *La Grande Armée* assembling...Boulogne, Calais, Dunkirk, Ostend...." He turned a page and intoned grimly, "a list of frigates, flat-bottomed boats, 20,000 cartridges supplied with cases carried on sloops and prams. This looks quite authentic. Thank heavens we can get it to England." He raised his head. "Come, Harding."

With one last look at Clairice, Lord Ault urged, "Be ready!" The two men strode toward the door.

Clairice did not wait to see them leave but took Lady Fairfax's arm. "Come upstairs, grandmother. Let us find Adele and Aunt Lavinia, and I shall tell all of you the plans."

They mounted the stairs and Lady Fairfax snapped, "Do not push, Clairice!"

"I am so anxious to be away! We'd better summon our servants, also."

"I have sent Edgars and Betsy on errands."

Clairice stopped. "Grandmother! They may be arrested! What a dreadful time to send them out! Suppose Lord Ault and Mr. Harding return for us before they get back?"

"They will be here. Calm yourself, Clairice. You sound like Lavinia."

Clairice was silent, but her thoughts ran on with the possibilities that lay ahead. As soon as she had assembled the others, she related the plans made by Lord Ault and Mr. Harding to get a funeral coach.

"How can they do that?" Adele asked with worry. "They will be arrested because they are English."

"I think they shall succeed," Clairice replied, not knowing if she truly felt they would or if it was merely that she wanted them to so badly. "Mr. Harding's French is excellent; he could pass anywhere for a Frenchman. Lord Ault's isn't quite as good, but it's passable."

"I have no intention of riding in a funeral coach!" Lavinia exclaimed and scratched both knees.

"You had better ride in it before you are carried in one!" Lady Fairfax snapped. She rose. "Enough of this. I want all of you to be ready and waiting. We must not delay one second when they arrive. Come, Clairice, help me down again."

At the head of the stairs Clairice paused. "Grandmother, I am going to change to my green riding habit. I do not care to even pretend about this wedding."

"Suppose Mr. Crenshawe arrives first?"

"I shall tell him I did not care what I wore." She looked at Lady Fairfax. "I will fetch your velvet pelisse. You will need to keep warm, too."

"Hurry up about it, child!"

Clairice ran to do as instructed. Within a short time she was ready; she started for the bedroom door when it opened and an ashen-faced Betsy peered into the room. "He's here, ma'am."

Clairice's heart leaped to her throat. "Who is here, Betsy?"

CHAPTER TWELVE

NEVER IN HER LIFE had she heard more welcome words than Betsy's "Lord Ault, ma'am."

"Hurry, Betsy, fetch the rest of the family! The time has come."

Clairice gathered her things and rushed downstairs. Voices came from the library and she hurried inside, then halted with a gasp.

With a grim countenance Lord Ault turned to face her. Beside him stood Sir Barthwell and Mr. Harding. Both Mr. Harding and Lord Ault were in the bright blue-and-white uniforms of the French guards.

"The uniforms?" Clairice looked at them in astonishment.

Lord Ault replied, "The guards—from the rear of the house."

At that moment both Rollets appeared and joined Lady Fairfax, Adele and Lavinia. While they said their farewells, Lord Ault told Clairice, "Summon the servants who will go and do so quickly. Any moment a guard could come from the front of the house, and we will be discovered."

"They are waiting in the hallway," she informed him, then inquired, "How are we to go?"

"We have the Rollets's carriage and a funeral coach waiting behind the house." He raised his voice slightly so all in the room could hear him. "We must go now; a second's delay could prove fatal."

The family followed him out; at the exit to the back he placed his fingers on his lips and cautioned, "We must have absolute silence."

Clairice hugged first Aunt Hyacinth, then Uncle Marcel, before she followed Lord Ault into the rain. The Rollet traveling coach was directly in front of the open doorway. Behind it was the long funeral coach. The black vehicle added the final note of grimness to the proceedings. Lord Ault gave orders and Mr. Harding aided everyone, helping Lady Fairfax, Lavinia and the servants into the traveling coach for the journey.

As Mr. Harding climbed up to sit beside the driver, Adele and Clairice entered the gloomy interior of the funeral coach. Lord Ault followed to speak with them. A wooden casket rested in the center of the coach, and both girls looked questioningly at Lord Ault.

"It is empty," he said. "I shall ride behind it on horseback. Pray we make it out of Paris." He turned and was gone. The doors closed softly, and Adele clasped Clairice's hand as they sat together on a narrow wooden seat. "This is horrible," she said tearfully.

Clairice peered at her through the gloom. "No, Adele. It is freedom." She thought of Mr. Crenshawe. "I am grateful for it beyond words."

Adele shivered. "I wish we would start." Her voice died as the coach began to roll slowly over the cobblestones in a jolting uncomfortable ride. Both girls held hands tightly and rode in silence.

"It is terrible to sit in here and not know what is going on around us," Clairice declared and attempted to peer out the tiny oval window beside them. "At least we keep moving."

She became as silent as Adele, listening to the continual clatter of the wheels over bricks. Occasionally a carriage passed, going in the opposite direction. Once the sound of hooves grew loud, then receded.

A voice rang out. "That's grandmother!" Clairice cried. The coach halted.

"What can be happening?" Adele whispered.

"I don't know, but I intend to see. I do not care to sit here and wonder." Clairice rose and moved in a crouch to the rear of the coach. She opened a door and jumped down.

Lady Fairfax's voice called clearly, "Lord Ault!"

Lord Ault cantered past Clairice with a dark scowl on his face.

They had halted on a narrow street lined with rows of tall old houses. Ahead there were two carriages also halted on the opposite side of the street. The drizzle had changed to a heavier rain that fell against Clairice's face. She pulled the collar of her riding habit up about her neck and moved in the direction of Lady Fairfax's carriage.

Lady Fairfax's head was thrust out of the carriage window. Lord Ault reined his prancing black horse and looked down at her. "What is the meaning of stopping?"

Lady Fairfax waved a hand toward the other carriages. "I have informed friends of the intentions of Boney. We are being joined by fellow Englishmen."

Clairice's eyes widened. She looked at the two carriages, each with more than the usual number of lackeys clinging to the top and rear seats. "Gammon!" she whispered.

For once Lord Ault was completely nonplussed. He whirled in the saddle to look at the two carriages.

Clairice hurried toward her grandmother. Lady Fairfax said calmly, "You cannot abandon them to a French prison."

"This is unbelievable!" Lord Ault exclaimed. "We cannot do such a thing!" He looked down at Lady Fairfax. "I have been worrying how we can escape with such a number as we have now—twelve, to be exact—and you want to add two more carriages?" As he spoke his voice rose incredulously.

"I have the ultimate faith in your ability," Lady Fairfax declared.

"The admiration is not mutual!" He bit off the words. "You have gone too far this time!"

"My lord—"

"Madam—" his voice was icy "—I am attempting to sweep twelve people out of the grasp of the French. We are as conspicuous now as a three-legged horse. You cannot have the temerity to ask that I add two additional carriages. It is absolutely unthinkable!"

Mr. Harding climbed down the far side of the carriage and moved quietly around to stand facing Clairice and Lord Ault. Lady Fairfax replied, "Lord Ault, you cannot send these people, your own countrymen, to prison. You stated yourself that we are as conspicuous as a three-legged horse. A five-legged one will attract very little more attention than a three-legged one. These people shall merely become part of the mourners. It will look quite natural."

"Impossible! I refuse to do it."

"Your Lordship, please. By our sheer numbers the effrontery of so daring an escape shall give us an advantage."

Lord Ault closed his eyes and his lips moved. Suddenly he opened his eyes and wheeled his horse toward the carriages. He swung down and opened a door to peer inside.

A string of oaths erupted, and he straightened with a glance over his shoulder at Lady Fairfax before he moved to the next carriage to repeat the procedure.

Clairice had reached a close-enough vantage point to be able to see partially into the carriage. It was crammed with humanity. She clutched the side of the Rollet carriage in shock. "Grandmother, what have you done?"

Lady Fairfax glanced at her. "We must get everyone out we can," she answered quietly. "Here he comes."

Lord Ault wheeled his horse and returned. His face was dark as he snapped, "You have guaranteed we will all rot in prison. I have worried for hours over how I could possibly get twelve people out—" his voice rose in crescendo "—so how the hell do you think I can get out forty!"

"You can do it," Lady Fairfax declared.

He pulled the reins and moved to the center of the street, halted and contemplated the carriages, then looked back at Lady Fairfax. "By God, I'm not going to do it. I am leaving you."

A wave of fright ran through Clairice. Without thought she dashed to grasp his mount's bridle. "You cannot!" she cried.

He looked down, his gray eyes flashing fire. "Miss Fairfax, your meddlesome grandmother has pushed me beyond the limits of my endurance! I am through with all of you! Get away from this horse!"

"Lord Ault, please. We do not have time to waste. We need you...."

"You and your grandmother do not need one shred of anything more or anyone else's help. God help anybody who gets involved with either of you! I shall not extricate you from this. I have not had a moment's peace or order in my life since you two have come into it!"

His attitude banished Clairice's fright. She exclaimed, "And you would sacrifice all these people for order? Or for peace? How terrible!" She stamped her foot angrily and shouted at him, "You are selfish, self-centered, bullheaded and...and unadaptable!" Her cheeks flushed angrily. "You are only half-alive with your orderly life and your unfeeling heart. We shall manage quite well without you!"

Lord Ault stared at Clairice. The rain fell against her upturned face as she looked into his gray eyes, and her anger drained away into disbelief over what she had just said to him.

He leaned down and ordered, "Release this horse at once!" in such a tone of voice that Clairice jumped back and did as he asked.

He turned his horse and stopped next to a carriage. "Get out!" he commanded.

Clairice stared as person after person piled out into

the street. She turned and walked back to Lady Fairfax. Mr. Harding said, "I will assist," and hurried toward Lord Ault.

"I said some terrible things to him, grandmother."

"Yes, you did," Lady Fairfax replied. "But he is going to remain and take everybody, and that is important."

Clairice gazed in wonder at the people pouring out of both carriages. A few faces were familiar, but many were strangers. "Grandmother, where did you find all these people?"

"I got a list of Britons from Hyacinth. She put down all she knew, any staying at her friends' homes, whoever could be trusted. Then we sent Edgars, Betsy and two of Hyacinth's loyal servants to inform them of the departure."

"Grandmother, I do not want to leave anyone behind, but I am beginning to think Lord Ault is right, that this is madness. How can we hide? There are so many of us now. Here they come."

Clairice hurried to the funeral coach and climbed inside, her spirits ebbing.

"What is going on, Clairice?" Adele asked. "I heard you shouting at Lord Ault. Who are all those people?"

Suddenly Clairice was engulfed with regret for her treatment of Lord Ault. She burst into tears. "Oh, Addie! I have been so terrible! I called him the worst names... and he is not... he is good...."

"Heavens, Clairice! Whom are you talking about? Tell me what has happened."

Clairice looked at her sister, then shut her eyes. "I...I never should have been so mean to him!"

"To whom, Clairice?"

She sobbed, "To L—Lord Ault!"

"Do I understand right? All of this crying is because you said something unkind to Lord Ault?"

A commotion sounded outside the coach and Adele said, "I think I hear someone coming."

Clairice raised her head quickly. "If it's Lord Ault I mustn't let him find me this way." She wiped her eyes, then turned to Adele. "Do I look—" She stopped abruptly. "Adele, you look extremely happy. Have you been listening to me?"

Adele laughed and squeezed Clairice's hand. "Of course I've been paying attention to you." Before she could say more, Lord Ault stepped into the coach and reached down to assist others inside. Lord and Lady Stanhope, their three young children, a governess, butler and three maids entered, to be followed by Mrs. Whitney and Mrs. Pritchett. Everyone crowded together on the hard wooden planks that formed seats around three sides of the coach. When it was filled, the others sat on the floor.

Cautioning them to be quiet, Lord Ault jumped to the ground and closed the doors. Introductions were made, then Clairice warned, "We must keep our voices down. It would not do to have our English carry to outside ears."

Everyone followed her prompting, speaking quietly and finally lapsing into silence when the coach once more started its ponderous journey.

The roads were rough, once they left the city behind. In the most comfortable carriage, traveling conditions were not good; French roads were inferior to England's. In the funeral carriage it was intolerable, but the passengers traveled without murmur or complaint, being far more concerned with detection by French soldiers.

They were occasionally stopped, and sometimes Mr. Harding's fluent French was clearly heard, but each time they were allowed to pass.

Clairice was dozing with her head against Adele's shoulder when the coach halted one more time. She roused instantly and the sisters looked at each other. "Do you think it is soldiers?" Adele whispered.

Before Clairice could speak, the doors were flung

open and Mr. Harding announced, "Everyone can get out and stretch a moment while we make our plans. After this we will not stop until we reach Calais."

"Thank God!" Lord Stanhope exclaimed. He looked at the others. "I am proud of all of us; this has been a long hard journey without rest. You have ridden remarkably well." He looked down and patted the tousled head of his youngest boy. "Let's get out and stretch."

He alighted and turned to lift each child down, then help the ladies. Clairice climbed out with relief and turned with Adele to go to Lady Fairfax.

The late afternoon sky was cloudy and overcast, with a cool breeze that felt refreshing after the crowded, stuffy coach. Lady Fairfax leaned heavily against her cane, chatting with Lavinia and Sir Barthwell. Clairice and Adele joined them to hear complaints of stiffness, itch and gout until Mr. Harding was at their side to usher everyone inside the carriages once again for the last part of the journey.

The ride grew tedious; the patch of gray daylight seen through the small oval windows changed to black. Finally the coach halted, the doors at the rear opened, and Lord Ault climbed inside, then shut them carefully.

"We are at a hotel in Calais," he whispered. "Mr. Harding will get us registered. Do not speak any English where you will be overheard." He paused and looked at each of them. "Let us hope they will accept us as what we say we are," he continued. "We have sympathizers we can contact here to find out what the situation is concerning my ship. This is the last of the journey on French soil, and we have little time before the soldiers from Paris catch up with us. Be ready to move quickly when the word is given and pray that the way is clear. Any questions?" Once again his gaze circled the silent group. When no one responded, he opened the doors and dropped lightly to the ground.

One by one, they rose and filed out into a chill foggy night. When Clairice reached the door, Lord Ault took her arm firmly and aided her down. She paused before the simple structure of dark stones and narrow casement windows. The rain and mist had changed to fog, which swirled about them and blurred the outlines of other buildings. Noise from a neighboring tavern carried through the foggy quiet.

Lord Ault continued to hold Clairice's arm in a warm firm grasp, and he steered her into the hotel in grim silence. She walked beside him, aware of his large-ness and of the terrible things she had said to him earlier.

She hurried to keep up with his long stride until they fell in step behind Lady Fairfax, who climbed the nar-row stairs assisted by Mr. Harding and Adele.

They entered a small, plainly furnished sitting room. Lady Fairfax struggled into a chair near the window. Lavinia and Sir Barthwell had preceded them and were already seated. In the privacy of the room Clairice final-ly felt free to speak. She turned to Lord Ault quickly. "How long do you think we'll have to wait?"

"Only a brief time, I hope. I sent a man ahead to find one of our French friends and bring him to the hotel. Every minute we are here decreases our chances of escape, but I want to make certain the way is clear before we attempt to board ship."

As he finished speaking, a knock sounded lightly on the door. Mr. Harding opened it, and a slender, dark-haired man in plain black clothes entered. At the sight of Lord Ault he hurried forward.

"Ahh—a soldier of *La Grande Armée*! *Bonsoir,* m'lord," the new arrival said. "Welcome to Calais."

Lord Ault grasped his hand and shook it vigorously as the Frenchman added, "We have been expecting you for several days now."

Lord Ault clapped him on the shoulder and intro-duced Etienne Coudmont to the others, then faced him. "We have little time for pleasantries. I don't know if Napoleon's edict has reached Calais yet, but we are in a state of war and all Britons on French soil are to be imprisoned by seven o'clock tonight.''

Etienne's eyes swept the group. "I see he has missed a few.''

"Indeed,'' Lord Ault answered grimly, "but just barely. The soldiers will be here for us before long, I'm certain. Mr. Harding and I were released from prison this morning. Miss Fairfax was being forced to wed a French spy and traitor, Crenshawe, so she will be missed.''

"*Sacrebleu!* Crenshawe, eh?''

"Yes. He succeeded in tricking all of us.''

"And you think he expects you to come to Calais?''

"I can't say for certain. He knows this is where I left my yacht. We've brought a large number of people with us, and it wouldn't be difficult to follow our trail, I'm afraid. I think this is one of the first places he would look.''

Etienne surveyed them all again. "We did know about the arrest order. Calais has been chaos all day. You are not the only ones attempting to flee from France tonight. There are six of you—quite a number as you say—but not so many that we cannot conceal you.''

Lord Ault's jaw tightened and Clairice experienced a sinking sensation as she heard Lord Ault's gruff, "Etienne, this is not all of our entourage.'' He spoke softly and looked down at the slender Frenchman's upturned face. "There are forty-one of us.''

"*Quarante et un!* Impossible!''

"Unfortunately, no, not impossible. We have made it this far as a funeral procession.''

Etienne stared at Lord Ault in wonder. "You mean you brought forty-one people out of Paris today?'' The Frenchman clapped him on the shoulder. "*Magnifique!*'' His hand dropped away and his eyes clouded. "This changes the picture.'' He shook his head soberly. "We cannot hide forty-one Britons in Calais tonight. There are too many homes already taken.''

Lord Ault inquired, "Etienne, what about my yacht? Can we get to it?"

"No." The word fell like a sentence of doom and Lord Ault's jaw tightened. "It was taken over, m'lord, more than a week ago," Etienne explained. "I was afraid that what had occurred in Paris might cause them to make such a move. There was nothing we could do to prevent it."

"I understand," Lord Ault assured him. "And the crew?"

"Your crew has been taken prisoner by the military, and a guard placed on the ship."

Lord Ault swore under his breath and turned away to cross to the window. He lifted the lace curtain a fraction and peered in the direction of the road that led to Paris. Near him sat Lady Fairfax, the flickering tapers giving a soft glow to her white hair. Lord Ault looked over his shoulder at Etienne, who said, "We have already checked—there are two French soldiers on board and two stationed on shore."

Lord Ault studied Etienne while Mr. Harding exclaimed, "We should be able to overpower four guards! That won't be a problem!"

"What is it, Etienne?" Lord Ault asked, discerning the look of defeat in the Frenchman's face.

"It would not be that simple. They have soldiers from headquarters here who check on those men continually. With any kind of alert, or with the time you would need to overpower the four and get forty-one people on board, you would be discovered."

"There is no way," Mr. Harding inquired, "to dispose of the soldiers sent from camp to check on the guards?"

Before Etienne could answer, Lord Ault spoke. "Even if we succeeded, my crew is under arrest. I cannot leave my own crew here." He turned from Mr. Harding to Etienne. "How heavy is the guard where the crew is quartered?"

Etienne waved a hand in the air. "They are the camp at headquarters. The number of men stationed here grows each day, and accommodations are not adequate for them. They have commandeered a large old farmhouse at the edge of town. There are tents and other houses commandeered, but they are scattered and not yet concentrated in one area. Your crew is on the top floor of the old farmhouse, and the rest of the place is filled with soldiers. There are three floors to the house. Offices are on the first, Frenchmen are quartered on the second and the prisoners are on the third."

Lord Ault swore again and turned to gaze out the window. "Our time is running out, but I cannot leave that crew. They have risked their lives for me and other Britons time and time again. They wouldn't be under arrest now if they had not waited for me to return. I cannot desert them."

"I still suggest, m'lord, that for now, while you can still get away, you go into hiding. Difficult as it may be for some, it may be the only alternative to a long French imprisonment. Take these people along the coast into isolated areas. We'll see to it that you have food and blankets."

Lord Ault shook his head and hit his fist lightly against the table beside him. "We cannot! Gammon! It was nigh impossible to get them all this far. I know we cannot flee as you suggest. It would have to be on foot to get over that type of land."

Etienne nodded. "That's correct."

Lord Ault's jaw tightened. "Well, many of these people cannot undertake such a feat."

Lady Fairfax said, "Perhaps you should leave us behind, then."

All heads turned in her direction. "I am one of those who cannot navigate up and down hills. Leave us here, Lord Ault, and take all who are physically able to go."

He stared at her a moment in silence. Clairice watched him with mounting apprehension. She would never leave her grandmother under any conditions, even if prison lay ahead. Suddenly Lord Ault's answer was of paramount importance to her. She wanted him to decline the offer, and it mattered terribly whether he did or not. She waited while he deliberated, then finally spoke.

"You've made a gracious offer, Lady Fairfax, but my answer is no. We are all going—or we all are staying. We have come this far together, and I intend to get us to England." There was steely determination in his voice.

Clairice's eyes misted and she looked down quickly, thankful for his answer. After a moment she raised her head and regarded him, while Lord Ault once again looked out the window. He murmured, "We may have to make our stand right here in the hotel."

Etienne replied quickly, "Then, m'lord, you'll never succeed. There are hundreds of soldiers in Calais, and the number grows steadily. The First Consul is reinforcing towns all along the coast."

Mr. Harding stared at Lord Ault. "I think, my lord, for the sake of those here, that you'll have to leave your crew behind."

"Even if you should get the ship under your control," Etienne stated flatly, "there is a line of French ships just outside the harbor. You could not get your yacht past their guns."

"How many ships?"

Etienne shrugged. "I'm not certain, but you have no way to fight them. You would be absolutely helpless."

Lord Ault gazed out the window again and spoke slowly. "If we could only get that far; there is a light fog—on the water it might be heavier. I'd be willing to attempt to slip past the French."

"Impossible!" Etienne was emphatic.

"Lord Ault—" Lady Fairfax spoke firmly and all eyes turned toward her "—Lord Ault, I think I might be able to help."

For an instant he appeared amused, then the strain of the dilemma was back on his face. "Yes?"

With a struggle she rose from her seat and looked at all of them. "I shall need Clairice and Adele, as well as either you, Lord Ault, or Mr. Harding, to accompany us. Can you manage the guards at the ship?"

"Yes," he said in a puzzled voice.

"We can help," Etienne added grimly, "but you'd still have all the soldiers garrisoned here to overcome."

"*Monsieur,*" Lady Fairfax asked, "tell me, if the soldiers in the headquarters were incapacitated, the crew freed and the guards at the ship eliminated, would it be possible for us to escape?"

Lord Ault's eyes narrowed slightly while Etienne considered. "But that is impossible."

Lady Fairfax persisted. "You do not answer my question."

Etienne studied her and replied slowly, "Perhaps. . . at night, in a fog. . . who knows?" He shrugged eloquently. "There are tents, men quartered in that area, but if all in the headquarters were unable to stop you and you could slip away quietly without discovery, then you might have a chance to reach the ship unmolested."

"Excellent!" Lady Fairfax replied. She waved her cane slightly. "Lavinia, you and Sir Barthwell go join the others. Clairice, you and Adele summon Edgars to fetch your trunk, and Betsy to help you change quickly. Clairice, wear your green silk, and Adele, you must wear the blue silk. Now hurry, girls!"

Lady Fairfax turned. "Lord Ault, you send the others on the way to the ship. Have them ready to board, merely waiting for the signal. Give me half an hour—yes, half an hour should do. Then, eliminate the guards at the ship and get everyone on board. I shall get that crew of yours free."

Adele rushed from the room to summon the servants as instructed, but Clairice merely closed the door and waited as Lord Ault looked down at Lady Fairfax with curious eyes and inquired, "How?"

She gazed up at him, a small white-haired woman bundled in a deep blue pelisse that made her appear even smaller standing beside the tall powerful man in a French uniform. He repeated his question, "How can you free my crew, my lady?"

She smiled and answered forcefully, "The Fairfax brew, Lord Ault—the Fairfax brew."

CHAPTER THIRTEEN

HE NARROWED HIS EYES. "What do you intend?"

She leaned on her cane. "If you will make the arrangements, my lord, I will take the girls and pay a visit to the French headquarters. I shall inform them that I am an old woman, suffering terrible grief at the loss of my grandson, a French soldier who died fighting valiantly for the First Consul and the glory of France. I would like to make arrangements for a military burial in the morning. Then, after satisfactory arrangements are concluded—because I love France, the glory of France and the soldiers of France—I shall share the Fairfax brew with the entire staff and officers!"

"Gammon!" Clairice whispered.

Lord Ault looked over Lady Fairfax's head in a silent glance exchanged with Mr. Harding.

Etienne spoke. "I do not understand. You have a French grandson, m'lady, killed in our wars, yet you are a Briton."

"A bamboozle, sir!" Mr. Harding stated.

Clairice spoke hastily. "Grandmother does not actually have a grandson—that is a mere ruse—and she certainly is not French."

Lady Fairfax drew herself up, adding a quarter of an inch to her stature, and looked at the curious Frenchman. *"Cette nuit, monsieur, je suis une citoyenne de France!"*

Clairice cried, "Grandmother, you cannot do this! You don't know that they will even touch it; they might not like it."

"Bosh! No man ever lived who didn't like my brew!"

"What do you think you would do?" Lord Ault asked. "Serve tea to an army headquarters—utterly impossible!"

"The bottled brew I am carrying has no tea added. We can pass it off as wine," Lady Fairfax declared with a glance at Mr. Harding. She looked Lord Ault directly in the eye. "It is sufficiently tasty, and both of you gentlemen are aware of its potency even when diluted, much less full strength."

Clairice gasped at her grandmother's indelicacy in bringing up such matters.

Lord Ault's countenance darkened, but he merely stated, "An entire headquarters—impossible. Thank you, anyway, Lady Fairfax."

"Do you have a better idea?" she snapped.

Clairice stepped forward and cried, "Grandmother, if it didn't work, we would be in the French quarters and never get away. They would imprison us on the spot!"

"That's enough from you, young lady! You have no better solution, either." She looked steadfastly at them all. "None of you does."

"Pardon," Etienne broke in, looking from one to another. "I do not understand any of this. What is this brew? It seems you will attempt to intoxicate these men."

Lord Ault answered, "That's correct, Etienne, but we cannot do it. It is absolutely impossible. You couldn't succeed, Lady Fairfax, and you don't have that much brew anyway."

Lady Fairfax interrupted. "I am traveling with sufficient brew to paralyze the entire town of Calais!"

"Those trunks!" Lord Ault exclaimed, momentarily sidetracked from the issue at hand as he recalled the job of loading the carriages. "That is what you are carrying in all those damnable trunks!"

"Do not swear, Lord Ault, over what may well save your life," Lady Fairfax answered with a sniff.

The thin Frenchman asked in disbelief, "Am I to understand that you plan to intoxicate the entire headquarters?"

Lady Fairfax turned to face Etienne, and Clairice recognized the thrust of her jaw as a definite danger signal that the Fairfax temper was about to be unleashed. Unaware of impending doom, Etienne continued, "Lady Fairfax, you may not realize it, but these are French soldiers, experienced and hardened men. They could consume any intoxicating beverage all night long and you would not render them helpless."

"Give me half an hour!" Lady Fairfax repeated.

"With all due respect, this is impossible!" Etienne muttered.

"You have no choice!" Lady Fairfax snapped. "Gammon! I give you a chance and no one takes it!" She looked at all of them. "You can come up with nothing better, and every moment we stand here and argue is hurting our chances of escape. Confound it! There is nothing else to do!" She prodded Lord Ault lightly on the boot top with her cane. At the touch he glanced down. For a fleeting instant a shocked look crossed his face as well as the faces of the other members of the group, then his mouth curled slightly. "Very well."

"Lord Ault!" Clairice exclaimed, "You cannot allow this! It is insanity."

Lady Fairfax thumped her cane on the floor. "Clairice, stop shrieking! If you do not want to do this, then go along with Lavinia and the others."

Clairice's jaw thrust out in much the same manner as Lady Fairfax's. She looked at Lord Ault. "Are you going to allow this?"

His face was impassive. "I fear I have little control over your grandmother's actions." He sobered and added, "Desperate circumstances call for desperate actions. We must take the risk!"

Etienne came forward a step. "I am interrupting

where I have no place to speak, but I agree with the girl.'' He looked at Lord Ault and continued. ''If you persuaded them to drink all night, m'lord, you could not get them drunk enough to enable you to free your own men.''

''We are wasting precious time,'' Lady Fairfax stated emphatically.

Lord Ault replied with a sigh, ''I see no choice, Etienne. This is the most hopeful proposition put forth.'' He turned to Lady Fairfax. ''Where is the brew?''

She smiled faintly. ''Edgars knows which trunks.'' Her gaze moved to Clairice. ''Hurry, child, and get your dress changed.''

Lord Ault spoke quickly. ''Lady Fairfax, can we leave Clairice and Adele out of this?''

Lady Fairfax observed him. ''No. They shall serve well as distractions, and I need Adele's command of French. It is much better than my own.''

Clairice looked at Lord Ault, then realized he had to include her in his concern for Adele. He was far too much the gentleman to ask for Adele to be excused from such a mission and not include Clairice, also, when she was standing only a few feet away. Unaware of it, a small sigh escaped her lips. She regarded Lady Fairfax and asked, ''How can you convince anyone you're French, grandmother? Your French is not that good.''

''Impertinent chit!'' Lady Fairfax answered haughtily. ''I shall say that I've been living in southern Italy for many years, but am a loyal Frenchwoman.''

Clairice shook her head hopelessly and left the room. She hurried into the bedchamber and closed the door softly. Adele had already changed into the blue silk dress and was attempting to shake the wrinkles from its folds.

Clairice rushed to change into the green silk, which was laid out on the high bed. As she struggled with the fastenings, Adele hurried to her side to assist.

"Hold still, Clairice, or we'll never get through." She finished one hook and reached for the next. "I pray this hoax of grandmother's works. Just think, by this time tomorrow night we could be home!"

Clairice studied their reflection in the mirror. "I suspect," she said slowly, "that Lord Ault shall ask for your hand when we return to England, Addie."

Adele glanced at the reflection in the mirror. "I think not, Clairice, but even if he does, I shall refuse."

Clairice whirled to look at her. "Why?" she cried.

Adele looked up with a smile and placed her hands lightly on Clairice's shoulders. "You love him very much, don't you?"

Clairice blinked. "Yes, how did you know?" she whispered. "I only realized it. . . ."

"You were crying over the things you said to him, remember? Why else would you care that much?"

A small frown creased Clairice's brow. "Addie, do you love him?"

Adele smiled and shook her head, returning to fastening the dress. "No, but I'm glad you do."

Clairice spun about and hugged her sister. "Thank goodness you don't!" She pulled away, the worry back. "I don't think it will matter, though, Addie. You are the one he cares for, not me."

Before Adele could reply, the door flew open and Betsy appeared, wringing her hands. Her skin was unusually pale and stray gray hairs were flying in all directions from under the edge of her cap.

"Oh, misses, your grandmother is ready and waiting for you. She expects you down now."

"We're coming, Betsy. Adele, this is an impossible venture. I don't think grandmother realizes what she is undertaking."

"We shall have to pray that we succeed, Clairice. Come on, you are fastened."

Clairice paused to study her reflection in the oval pier glass. Her cheeks were flushed from excitement, her red hair tumbled in curls about her shoulders. The emerald dress set off her white skin vividly, contrasting with the flaming tresses and highlighting the green of her eyes. She scooped up her pelisse and threw it around her shoulders as she rushed after Adele.

Once she neared the ground floor, she descended the stairs and crossed the room at a sedate pace, aware of heads turning in her direction.

THE MIST HAD CHANGED to fog, which shrouded the carriage and the dark corners of the block. Lord Ault stood beside a waiting carriage. Clairice met his eyes and could not look away. His handsomeness was etched in her mind, the firm mouth and shock of black hair curling over his forehead. He extended a hand to assist her into the carriage. Clairice held back a moment and spoke softly.

"You are not...self-centered and unadaptable. I am sorry for what I said to you in Paris."

He regarded her intently and said, "We'll discuss it later."

Clairice felt swallowed up in the depth of his eyes; she could not turn away. Something passed between them. She leaned slightly toward him and glanced at his mouth, remembering his burning kiss. A voice called from the carriage.

"Clairice! Get in this carriage, miss!"

Reluctantly she turned and climbed inside. Lord Ault followed, closed the door and sat beside her. His broad shoulders and long legs seemed to fill the interior. The carriage began to move slowly and Clairice inquired, "Where is Mr. Harding?"

Lord Ault looked down at her. "I suspected you would be concerned. He is in charge of the ship. Etienne is sending men to help, and we have the men who traveled with us from Paris. Etienne will join us at the headquarters."

"Join us?" Clairice asked.

Lord Ault spoke grimly. "He will be outside, with others nearby, to lend whatever aid they can." He turned to Lady Fairfax. "Does this bottled brew have tea mixed with it yet?"

"No, indeed. It should be quite effective if we can just get everyone to partake of it." She looked at her granddaughters. "Pull your dresses a little lower, girls. I want their attention to be distracted."

"Grandmother!" Adele whispered in shocked horror, turning a deep pink at the same time. Lord Ault's lips twitched, but he remained solemn.

Clairice wriggled and did as instructed, poking Adele with her toe. "For goodness' sakes, Addie! Just lower it a little!"

"Clairice!"

Lady Fairfax ignored the girls and tilted her head to one side to look askance at Lord Ault. "How much time do you think we have before Crenshawe arrives—if he does?"

"I'd guess a little more than an hour now. He may come in all haste and leave the soldiers to follow."

Clairice turned to face him, acutely aware of his presence. "What makes you so certain he will come to Calais?"

He gazed down at her, and Clairice longed to reach for his hand and declare what she felt for him. With an effort she pulled her thoughts to what he was saying.

"He knows this is where I always land and embark, so most likely he is the one who had the yacht placed under guard, and I am certain he'll be determined to catch us himself. I presume he'll send others searching for us at different places, but I suspect he'll travel to Calais himself with all possible speed."

"What will we do if he comes while we are at this place?" Adele asked.

"I don't know," Lord Ault replied honestly. "Etienne promised to bring men to help, but there's no way of guessing if Crenshawe will come alone or with a detachment of soldiers. We shall just hope that we can be gone in time.''

The carriage slowed and stopped. Clairice looked up to find Lord Ault watching her. "Here we are," he said softly. He looked around at all of them. "Ready?"

Lady Fairfax nodded, and Lord Ault stepped down and turned to assist them. Mist swirled around the high thatched roof of the old farmhouse. Breaking the dismal gloom, lights burned at the multipaned windows, throwing squares of yellow patterns on the ground.

The horses were tethered to a rail nearby, and the small group moved from the damp yard into a sparsely furnished house with bare floors scuffed by boot marks. Soldiers moved about in a long hallway, turning to look at the newcomers briefly, then continuing about their business. The Fairfax party was ushered into a large chamber with wooden chairs and a long narrow bench along one wall. Two sturdy desks were in the room.

Their guard brought them before one desk behind which a dark-eyed French lieutenant was seated. Lord Ault saluted smartly and remained at attention. The lieutenant spoke briefly to Lord Ault and asked their business.

In passable French, Lord Ault explained that he had been sent to accompany the Belvoir family to bury their slain relative, Lieutenant Philippe Belvoir.

He further explained that they would like a military burial in Calais. He introduced Lady Fairfax as Madame Belvoir and her two granddaughters, Delphine and Gabrielle Belvoir. Every male eye in the room was on either Adele or Clairice. They stood out in the obviously male domain like exotic birds in a desert.

The lieutenant rose, raised Lady Fairfax's hand to his lips perfunctorily and informed her, "*Madame,* my pleasure. I am Lieutenant Florac." He turned next to raise Clairice's hand to his lips, and his eyes rested hungrily on her. His voice was soft as he murmured, "*Mademoiselle, bonsoir.*" He reached for a chair to pull it near his own and motioned Clairice to it, moving deftly to lift Adele's hand and plant a lingering kiss, then seated her next to Clairice.

Lady Fairfax sank into a chair facing him across the desk, and Lord Ault stepped back a discreet distance to stand near the guard at the door. All work in the room had ceased as the sergeant behind the other desk and two soldiers seated at narrow wooden tables covertly or openly admired the two young ladies.

With difficulty the lieutenant pulled his attention toward Lady Fairfax. He contemplated her a moment, then spoke. "Now, Madame Belvoir, how can I be of assistance?"

Lady Fairfax produced a handkerchief from her reticule and dabbed at her eyes. "We have come on a sad mission. My grandson—I am bringing him home to Calais to be buried."

"Ah, my sympathies. I am truly sorry, *madame*. You have family here in Calais?"

Lady Fairfax shook her head. "No. But this is where Philippe was born; his parents are buried here."

"I see," Lieutenant Florac replied. His eyes swept over Adele and Clairice. "And these are the unfortunate Philippe's sisters?"

"Yes, lieutenant. He was the only boy in my late son's family." Lady Fairfax pressed the handkerchief to her eyes; Adele took over in soft fluent French. "*Grand-mère* has lost both her son and grandson and daughter-in-law. We are all the family that is left."

The lieutenant smiled, first at one girl, then the other. "What a comfort you must be to your grandmother."

"Can you assist us in a fitting service?" Adele asked. "Our brother was a loyal soldier and *grand-mère* wants the military to take care of everything. She will spare no expense. Philippe would have wanted it this way."

"Certainly," the lieutenant readily promised, torn between a choice of gazing at Adele or Clairice. He studied Clairice and asked, "When would you like the service held?"

Lady Fairfax interrupted. "Lieutenant, you will never know how much your cooperation pleases me."

His smile broadened. "Indeed, *madame*, I am happy to be of service to your enchanting family."

"We have traveled a long sad journey to accomplish this." She leaned forward. "I must show my gratitude to you. While we conduct our business, I'll have a bottle of wine fetched from my carriage."

The officer paused a moment, a small frown knitting his brow. "*Madame,* that is kind, but—"

Clairice laid her hand on the lieutenant's arm and leaned against him. "I am so glad you accept *grand-mère*'s offer." She looked up into his eyes. "A little wine is a comfort at such a tragic time."

He gazed at Clairice, then his shoulders moved in a faint shrug. "Very well. A small glass should not hurt. The hour is late and it should not matter." The moment he consented, Lord Ault left the room.

"Ah, lieutenant, I know about boys away from home," Lady Fairfax remarked. "You have a hard lonely life with little joy." She dabbed at her eyes again. "My poor, dear Philippe. I hope some kind soul shared a bottle of wine with him."

With a sweeping motion Clairice rose and let the pelisse drop from her shoulders. "I will assist with serving so that you can go on with your discussion, if you will tell me where to find some glasses."

Every eye in the room was riveted on the slender girl with cascading red hair and the deep green dress that nipped in at a tiny waist, then swelled into an expanse of creamy skin.

Lord Ault reappeared and placed two bottles on the edge of the desk. He opened one, and Clairice reached to take it from his hands. Their fingers brushed lightly. For a fraction of a second he paused in releasing his hold on the bottle, and she glanced up, receiving a small shock at the displeasure that shone clearly in his eyes. It was gone so quickly she turned away, uncertain if it was what she had actually seen. She smiled at Lieutenant Florac and asked sweetly, "Are there any glasses?"

"Indeed," he said, rising. "Come, Mademoiselle Belvoir, and I shall show you where to find them."

He opened a door at the rear of the room, then stood to one side to allow her to pass into a storeroom. He followed, and Clairice could feel the warmth of his presence as he stood close beside her; the rough material of his uniform brushed lightly against her bare arm. He reached around her and closed the door, then gazed into her upturned face. "Are you staying in Calais long, *mademoiselle*?"

"I'm not certain, lieutenant. It is up to *grand-mère*." Aware of his nearness, of his dark eyes alight with interest, Clairice smiled and leaned closer against him. "I hope so," she whispered. "Perhaps if *grand-mère* likes the people of Calais, she will stay for a time."

For a second his glance flicked to the closed door, then returned to her. "We must go," he breathed. "Where are you staying?"

"At the Hotel Port de Mer."

Once more his glance went from her to the door, then he looked intently at her. "You are very beautiful, *mademoiselle*."

Clairice tilted her head and regarded him through long lashes. "Lieutenant, you are teasing...." Her voice trailed away, and she leaned against him a fraction harder.

His voice was hoarse as he thrust glasses into her hands. "Take these and come back for more."

With a dimpling smile she whirled and opened the door. Instantly her eyes met slate-gray ones that unmistakably flashed fire. Lord Ault stood stiffly at the door, looking as though his patience had reached breaking point. Adele came forward to accept the glasses.

"Ah, gentlemen, now we can pour the wine." Under

her breath she accepted the glasses and whispered to Clairice, "Really, Clairice! You are overdoing it!"

Clairice smiled and whispered savagely under her breath, "If it gets us free—"

Adele moved to the desk, and Lord Ault started forward to assist her, but was immediately stopped by the sergeant. "I'll do that," he said firmly and stepped to Adele's side to take the bottle from her hands and pour the brown liquid. Adele lifted the first glass and handed it to Lady Fairfax.

Lady Fairfax thumped the desk with the end of her cane. *"Merci."* The ebony stick made a dull whack, which gained the attention of everybody in the room. "I want everyone in here to share this. Pour all of these wonderful young boys a glass, Delphine."

"Bien entendu, grand-mère." Adele hurried to do as instructed, while Clairice returned to the storeroom and the waiting lieutenant. The minute she entered the room, the door swung shut behind her and an arm slid around her waist. Clairice turned, placing both hands against a hard chest, and smiled up at him. Her voice was a coy protest. "Lieutenant, you mustn't!"

"Mademoiselle, you are the most enchanting creature I have ever seen. You have come out of the night like some fantasy of my imagination, and I cannot let you go. Do not allow your *grand-mère* to depart from Calais too soon." His voice had deepened and he leaned down, tilting her face up to his to brush his lips against hers.

For one brief instant Clairice entwined her arms about his neck and yielded to his embrace, then abruptly she pushed with sudden force and wriggled free.

"Lieutenant Florac! *Grand-mère* will whisk me away immediately if we do not stop. There will be another time and another place." She gathered up all the glasses she could carry and hurried out of the room.

She did not want to face Lord Ault, but in spite of her intentions to refrain from doing so, her eyes went to his immediately and met the same icy stare that seemed to go right through her.

Clairice felt as if he had been able to see through the solid wooden door of the storeroom. She experienced a hot blush and knew her guilty embarrassment was as evident as a verbal proclamation of what had just taken place. She turned and placed the glasses on the desk, looking down and straightening them unnecessarily as the sergeant poured.

Handing out drinks, she felt those burning gray eyes on her every second. Lieutenant Florac emerged from the storeroom with his arms full of glasses, far too many to be needed. He hastened to the desk, set them down and looked at Lady Fairfax.

"*Madame,* you are quite generous. You know the life of soldiers well, I see—what will please them and what will not."

She smiled at him. "It is a chill foul night and we are on a sad mission. It is difficult for an old lady to take charge of two healthy young girls. Our hearts are heavy in this dire time, and a little wine will ease the strain. I am more than happy to share it with all you brave lads."

"A soldier's life is a lonely one," the lieutenant said softly, with his eyes on Clairice. She looked demurely at him as she handed a glass to a soldier. Then she reached Lord Ault and extended a glass to him without looking up.

His hand closed over hers tightly, forcing her to raise her face and look at him. There was no mistaking his displeasure, and it stirred a mixture of curiosity and guilt in Clairice.

She attempted to extricate her fingers, only to have the pressure on them tighten. She flushed hotly and tugged again. This time he released her, and she moved away from him, circling the desk to hitch her chair nearer the lieutenant's. Lady Fairfax turned to Lord Ault and asked him to fetch more wine.

Lord Ault left the room, his boots making a clatter as he hurried to the carriage.

Edgars, hovering inside, jumped violently when the door was yanked open. The man's eyes rolled. "Cor—scared the livin' daylights out of me, ye did, m'lord."

"More wine, Edgars. So far, it goes well."

Edgars raised the lid to a trunk and handed over three more bottles with a grin, "I'll be glad to see the last of this place."

"No more than I will," Lord Ault answered with feeling. "Stay out of sight, Edgars."

"On your life, I will, m'lord." Edgars settled into a corner.

Lord Ault closed the door, crossed to the entrance, then extended a bottle to one of the guards.

"Lieutenant Florac said to share this with everyone. It's a celebration."

"The lieutenant?" came an incredulous question, and one guard leaned around to look in the lighted window. "*Merde!*" He turned back to Lord Ault. "We are on duty." He shook his head, his eyes on the tempting bottle.

Lord Ault said derisively, "On duty against what—invasion by Britons?"

Both guards laughed and Lord Ault shrugged. "Whatever you say." He passed them casually and re-entered the room.

Lady Fairfax and Lieutenant Florac were making arrangements for the service. "I would prefer this shortly after dawn," she informed the lieutenant.

"Ah, *madame*," he replied. "I am afraid it will be impossible. We have been so occupied today; these are not ordinary times. With the arrest order, tomorrow may be quite busy. I think the earliest we will be able to manage would be afternoon."

"I did have my heart set on dawn," Lady Fairfax said sadly.

"I am truly sorry." He waved his hands expansively.

Lady Fairfax lifted her glass. "A toast, my friend—to the soldiers of France!"

Every glass in the room was raised. Clairice merely touched hers to her lips and lowered it.

Lady Fairfax drank, then lowered her glass. "Very well—afternoon it will be."

"I hope you do not plan to leave Calais soon," Lieutenant Florac said.

"I've not made any decision on the matter. It is of no consequence as we are in no hurry."

"Where is your home, *madame*?" he inquired.

"Paris, but I lived in southern Italy for a number of years."

Lieutenant Florac smiled at Clairice. "And where was your brother stationed?"

"He fought in Egypt, at Abukir."

Lady Fairfax lifted her glass hastily. "To the glory of France—all over the world!"

The officers echoed the toast, lifting high their glasses, then drinking. Adele slipped quietly around the room, refilling each man's glass while Clairice pressed Lieutenant Florac's arm with her fingers.

"Were you in Egypt at any time? Perhaps you served with Philippe."

He covered her hand lightly with his own, sipping his drink. "Philippe Belvoir?" He shook his head. "No, I cannot recall."

Lord Ault looked at the pale slender hand resting lightly on the officer's arm and fought down a desire to reach across the desk and yank the man out of his chair. And just as clearly he realized with a shock what his anger signified.

His gaze shifted to Clairice. Although she didn't turn her head, a faint pink rose in her cheeks under his unwavering observation. With great clarity Lord Ault recalled the steady admiration of Mr. Harding that she had shown. For an instant the menace of danger faded in the face of the threat to his own personal desires. He turned and left the room to step outside. Before he reached the carriage, horses appeared. Two soldiers approached with two bound civilians riding between them.

Lord Ault met them as they slowed and halted. "Aah...Britons—arrested in Calais?" he asked, giving the men a quick curious perusal to make certain it was not someone he knew.

"We need to return quickly," one soldier remarked. "A companion of theirs escaped, but we had to bring in these two."

"I'll see that they are locked up." Lord Ault reached out to lead the horses after him; the two soldiers uttered a brief thanks, then turned to ride back into the mist out of sight.

Lord Ault tethered the horses and motioned to the men to dismount. "This way," he directed in flat French and motioned them ahead.

They passed the guards and entered the lighted hall. "Up the stairs," he ordered and followed silently as the men climbed. The large room downstairs was quiet; no sound of voices carried when they passed. At the second floor he met one French soldier in the hallway. The man paused and regarded the sullen prisoners. "More?"

Lord Ault merely nodded and continued the final flight of stairs. At the top a guard was seated behind a narrow desk; a long hallway stretched ahead with barred rooms opening off it.

"Argh...enough's enough. We are full." The guard pushed a sheet of paper across the desk and motioned to them, speaking in broken English, "Sign your name, why you are here, and who to contact."

Lord Ault produced a knife and cut the men free, then waited while they did as instructed. Finally the guard rose with a scrape of his chair. "This way," he ordered and motioned to them with a jerk of his head.

They moved down the hallway. Lord Ault stepped to the open door and gazed at the rooms, each with iron bars securing the doorways. Men were standing beside the grills, staring at the newcomers. At the first barred door a man stood clutching the iron.

At the sight of Lord Ault he stiffened, then relaxed once more. Only the look in his eyes had changed in the brief encounter. Lord Ault smiled faintly, then turned on his heel and descended the stairs to hurry outside to Edgars and replenishment. He jerked open the carriage door, startling Edgars once again.

"How long has it been?" Lord Ault asked quickly.

"Little over 'alf an 'our, m'lord. A lifetime...." He shook his head.

"The devil!" Lord Ault looked about him. The fog was heavy, dripping off the tips of branches where moisture had clustered and become sufficient to fall to earth. Across the yard, divided by a fence, on the other side of the carriage a field sloped gently away. Near the fence dim shapes of soldiers' quarters showed. Lord Ault peered through the gloom and could not detect any stirring of life.

He leaned into the carriage once again. "How much movement have you seen over there, Edgars?" He jerked his head to one side to indicate the direction.

" 'Tis grown quiet while I've waited, m'lord."

Lord Ault shook his head grimly. "The hour grows late, which helps us, but our time is running out."

"Aye, m'lord. To be away from this place will be a blessed thing."

Lord Ault lifted bottles with a swift decisive movement. "Edgars, signal Etienne as we planned after I am inside. He can approach the other side of the carriage without being seen by the guards. Ask his help in removing the guards. They will not touch a drop of the brew while they are on duty."

Edgars clutched his side and replied in a quivering voice, "Aye, m'lord."

"Tell him to wait another quarter of an hour."

"Oh merciful saints!" Edgars interrupted.

Lord Ault continued. "A quarter of an hour should

give me time in the house. I will take care of inside, but I need their help out here.''

Lord Ault gathered the bottles, kicked the carriage door closed and headed for the house. He entered the main room with a stealthy tread. His spirits rose a fraction at the glassy-eyed stare on the face of the men. He placed two bottles on the desk, stating, ''Here is another round.''

Lieutenant Florac grinned happily. *''Mer—merci!''*

The sergeant was sprawled in his chair with a dazed look on his face. One of the soldiers was slumped over a table and the other looked blankly into space. The guard at the door was seated on the hard bench ignoring all.

Lord Ault left quickly and placed the bottles of brew outside the door, retaining one. He crossed the hall and began methodically opening door after door to see if anyone else occupied any of the rooms. One held supplies, high piles of containers, sealed barrels and blankets. The next room had a long table and chairs, but was empty of life.

With a stealthy tread Lord Ault opened the last unexplored room. A soldier in shirt-sleeves worked over a desk with his back to the door.

Lord Ault cleared his throat and saluted when the man turned. ''Lieutenant Florac wants the report now,'' he stated and crossed the room.

''Report?'' The man looked up quizzically.

Lord Ault shifted the bottle behind his back from his left hand to his right. He gripped the neck tightly and pointed at the desk with his free hand. ''There... ''

The soldier turned to look, a frown furrowing his brow.

Swiftly Lord Ault raised the bottle and brought it swinging down.

The Frenchman saw the movement and leaped to his feet, a sharp outcry coming from his throat. He swung to block the blow, but too late to succeed.

The bottle slammed against him and he slumped over the desk. Instantly Lord Ault ripped free the man's shirt and lowered him to the floor. He knelt and bound the shirt tightly over the man's mouth, then got up and looked around.

Faded curtains covered the narrow window. Lord Ault yanked them down swiftly and tied the soldier's hands and feet to the desk.

He retrieved the bottle, extinguished the light and left the room. The hall was empty with little sound coming from the large room. Lord Ault gathered the bottles and hurried to the second floor, then knocked lightly at the door nearest the stairs.

He entered to find two soldiers lounging on iron beds. They came quickly to attention, but Lord Ault put them at ease and passed out a bottle of brew to each.

"Lieutenant Florac wants a celebration for all the Britons arrested today. Help yourself."

"*Sacrebleu!* I shall arrest ten more tomorrow!" One of them laughed and accepted the bottles with little apparent thought for Lord Ault.

Lord Ault hurried on his mission along the second floor until he had distributed all but one bottle.

With grim determination he climbed the third flight of stairs and faced the guard once again. Lord Ault sat down across from him.

IT WAS STUFFY on the third floor with the acrid smell of mold, decay, and a cloying stench of too many bodies and too much fear.

The guard's thick hands rested on the table, black hairs covering the coarse-grained skin, grime under each nail. With a thump, Lord Ault produced the bottle and placed it on the desk before the man. He declared bluntly, "We are celebrating."

The man's eyes narrowed and he stared at Lord Ault. "Celebrating what?"

Lord Ault waved a hand casually. "This hard day's work. All these arrests."

A scowl covered the heavy face. "Bah! I cannot. I am on duty."

"No, the lieutenant sent me up here with this. It was his order." Lord Ault uncorked the long-necked container.

The soldier eyed him skeptically, then rose without a word. He stomped to the stairwell and called down, "Aubert!"

Immediately a voice answered from below. Lord Ault leaned forward enough to see a dark head come into view at the foot of the flight of steps. The man called, "*Oui?*"

"What is this celebration?" the guard growled.

The man below had been one of the occupants of the first room on the second floor. He waved an open bottle and shouted, "*Vive la France!*"

With a surly look the guard turned and studied Lord Ault. "Who are you? I have not seen you before."

"No. I am new. You will have many new soldiers arrive in the next few days." Lord Ault leaned back in the chair, relaxed, with his long legs stretched before him. "The First Consul has ambitious plans for us."

The dull eyes of the guard moved from Lord Ault to the bottle in speculation. He returned to sit heavily behind the desk again. "I cannot believe the lieutenant would do such a thing."

Lord Ault shrugged. "Go down and ask him, then." He rose casually. "You do not have to drink." His fingers closed around the neck of the bottle.

The man looked up and stared hard at Lord Ault who looked him in the eye. Suddenly a large hand shot out and grasped the bottle, jerking it free of Lord Ault's fingers. "Good enough." The guard popped it open, lifted it to his mouth and drank deeply, his bearded throat working as he gulped the fiery liquid. Lord Ault's breath went out slowly in satisfaction. He sat down once more in the chair.

The guard lowered the bottle and wiped the back of his mouth with his hand. After a moment he grinned at Lord Ault, who merely grumbled, "I get my share."

"What the hell is this?" the guard asked and squinted at the bottle.

"Isn't it cognac?" Lord Ault asked and reached for the bottle.

"Doesn't matter," the guard mumbled, raising the bottle and drinking greedily.

"I said, I get my share," Lord Ault stated.

"You will." The guard drank again.

Lord Ault rose and looked down at him contemptuously. "I'll be back. Do not consume the entire bottle!" He turned on his heel and descended the stairs. The noise of revelry from the second floor was reassuring. Men were talking and singing noisily, paying no heed to him as he passed.

Lord Ault descended the last flight and walked outside. No guards stood at the door. There was no evidence of French soldiers anywhere—nor of anyone else. The carriage waited. An eerie quietness enveloped the house, broken by singing from above. Lord Ault turned in for the main room.

Lieutenant Florac was engaged in conversation with Clairice, his words slurring. Lord Ault regarded Lady Fairfax and said softly, "Just a few more minutes upstairs and we'll be ready."

The others in the room were long past being of any concern. With a crash the lieutenant suddenly flung himself backward in his chair and toppled to the floor. Clairice slid to her knees beside him quickly, then looked up at Lord Ault.

"He's passed out."

Lord Ault surveyed the room and its occupants, then stepped around the desk and withdrew the lieutenant's pistol. While he primed it, he commanded, "Get into the carriage quietly. I shall tend to matters upstairs.

Etienne will lead you to the ship. Don't wait for me; I'll catch up with everyone.''

He turned and took the stairs two at a time until he neared the top, then slowed to a normal gait and shoved the pistol into the waistband of his breeches under his coat. At the head of the stairs on the second floor he reached out and closed the door to the hall, which shut off all view of the stairs. Then he hurried up the last flight.

At the top of the stairs he slowed and faced the guard.

"Lef' you a little," the guard murmured and extended the bottle.

Both of the man's hands were on the table. With a deft movement Lord Ault withdrew the pistol and held it, pointing steadily at the guard's face. His voice was ominous. "Don't make a sound and don't move."

"*Mon Dieu!*" the guard breathed; his eyes widened, then narrowed. "It was a ruse," he snarled.

Lord Ault ordered, "Stand up and turn around, hands high."

When the guard obeyed without question, Lord Ault continued. "Unbuckle your belt and drop it on the desk. Don't reach for a weapon."

Quickly the man did as told. The heavy belt with innumerable keys to the barred doors fell to the desk with a clatter.

"*Merci.* Now turn around slowly."

The two faced each other, the guard's countenance clearly mirroring his hatred. Lord Ault stated flatly, "Don't move or you'll lose a face. Take that bottle and finish it off."

For the first time a flash of pure fear crossed the man's features. His skin paled; he glanced at the bottle then at Lord Ault. "What is it?" he whispered.

"Drink it—it's not deadly, merely intoxicating." Lord Ault declared harshly. "Hurry up!"

The man complied, lifting the bottle, swallowing loudly, letting some of the liquid spill and run into his beard.

"Now turn around again, hands high."

The moment the man turned, Lord Ault moved with lightning speed. He turned the pistol and brought the side of it down in a hard blow on the back of the guard's head. Weapon met flesh with a dull smack; the man toppled heavily in the corner between the desk and the wall.

Lord Ault jerked up the man's belt and grasped the keys, then rushed to the first barred door. Men and women stood at the doors watching him. He tried each key, struggling to locate the right one.

"Quiet," he commanded. "We have to slip past the troops on the second floor."

Captain Barrow moved forward. "Well done, my lord! How did you manage?"

"Later, Barrow." He thrust the pistol into Barrow's hands. "Take this; you may need it."

The men of his crew surged forward with murmurs of gratitude and praise. Lord Ault silenced them quickly. A key finally fitted, the lock squeaked and the door swung open. Lord Ault was already moving to the next barred doorway. He regarded the released men. "Some of you wait to assist the women. The rest of you go now, but quietly. There is a carriage waiting and horses. Someone will lead you to the ship, but remember—not a sound."

All waited in a strained silence as Lord Ault's fingers fumbled hurriedly with the keys, unlocking the next door, then moving to a room filled with women—all Britons—who had been imprisoned that very day, captured because of the First Consul's declaration. Lord Ault glanced around him in dismay at the number of people, realizing that the forty he had hoped to slip safely away from France were doubled at the least. For an instant he paused, then continued his work until all were free.

Lord Ault was the last to leave. He noted with satisfaction that the guard had not moved; the man's broad back rose and fell in deep steady breathing. Lord Ault felt that between the blow and the brew consumed, he need not expect any difficulty in that direction. A drawer was pulled open on the left side of the desk, revealing the guard's pistol. Lord Ault reached over the inert form and lifted the long black weapon from the drawer, then turned to descend the stairs.

Even the second floor of the house had grown quiet, with one male voice giving a poor rendition of a marching song.

His own stealthy tread sounded loud in his ears; the old wooden stairs creaked in protest of his weight. He crossed the long hall to the door of the large office and started to enter when he heard a scrape. He lifted the pistol and moved ahead.

CHAPTER FOURTEEN

CLAIRICE HEARD A FOOTFALL in the hallway. She rose and moved around the desk. Lord Ault filled the doorway, a large pistol primed and ready in his hand.

His breath went out in a rush. "You!" His eyes narrowed and he asked, "Why hadn't you gone?"

"I sent them ahead. Everyone has left. I heard the carriage and the horses go. You and I are the only ones here."

"Why are you here, Clairice?" he demanded.

A hot pink rose in her cheeks. "I didn't want to leave until... you did."

Lord Ault started to reply, but he merely lowered the pistol and motioned to her. "Come, we have to away quickly. We could be discovered at any second."

She gathered the pelisse tighter about her shoulders and rushed to him. They turned down the long hall to the front door and stopped abruptly.

Clearly there came the sound of a galloping horse.

"Get back!" Lord Ault hissed as the thudding hooves came to the very door and stopped. The clack of boots on stone was heard for a second, then the door burst open.

Framed in the doorway was Austin Crenshawe. With pistol drawn and a black cloak swirling about his boot tops, he halted in shock. For an instant the two men faced each other.

A small cry escaped Clairice's lips at the sight of the man she detested. She could only watch helplessly as the two antagonists faced each other.

"At last!" Crenshawe snarled as he jerked the pistol up and fired.

The volley was deafening. Clairice screamed in horror as Lord Ault reeled backward, stumbling into the stair railing as Crenshawe sprawled forward on his face, his pistol dropping uselessly from his hand.

Clairice ran to Lord Ault. "Are you hurt?" she cried.

Something rattled overhead. "Quick!" Lord Ault grasped her across the shoulders and propelled her through the back of the house and outside. Two horses were tethered at a rail, but Lord Ault swung up on one and lifted her to sit sidesaddle in front of him. He turned the animal, and they thundered away from the building for the haven of darkness and fog.

Clairice clung to him, her arms wrapped tightly about his chest underneath his opened coat. Her head was against him; in her ear his heart hammered beneath the thin shirt.

She looked up at him. "Are you hurt?"

The wind tore away the words as they galloped over rough land, skirting the edge of town and heading in the direction of the sea. Occasionally the lights of a house would show through the gloom, but Lord Ault avoided drawing closer. Finally Clairice raised her head and asked again about his condition.

He slowed and gazed down at her, his chin against her hair. "I'm all right."

"Where is your ship?"

"It's outside the harbor, farther away from town. We'll have to go with speed to have privacy enough to board, if they have taken care of the French guards properly. Etienne gave me directions, and I hope I can locate it without difficulty."

He urged the horse to a gallop again, and Clairice clung tightly, all chance for conversation gone in the race into the wind. She wanted to hold him always like this, feeling his warmth, keenly aware of his broad shoulders and firm muscles. One arm was locked tightly about her waist, holding her steadily against him.

Finally he slowed the horse and murmured softly,

"Now comes the worst part. We must go through a section of Calais."

Clairice looked about. They were on a lane with houses that gradually changed to narrow shops and taverns. He spoke against her hair. "There is no way we can avoid Calais without going far out of the right direction and losing a great deal of time. Pray no one stops us."

Clairice was suddenly aware of how tightly she was holding him. Her arms slipped lower and her hand touched a sticky wetness. She jerked it away and stared down at the dark smear against her white flesh. She gasped and looked up at him. "You were shot!"

He shook his head. "Clairice, lower your voice! I'm all right, just as I told you. I merely have been grazed in the arm. It's nothing."

"Are you certain?"

He looked down at her upturned face. His voice was low. "Would you care?"

Her eyes widened. "Of course I'd care," she whispered.

Just then a door opened and a drunken reveler staggered into the lane. Lord Ault tugged the reins and they crossed to the shadows on the opposite side. He tightened his legs and the horse gained speed, breaking into a trot. They moved along at a brisker clip, silent until they left Calais in the fog behind them.

THEY MOVED OUT OF A GROVE OF TREES along a rough path. The fog swirled and rolled about them, hiding the world and whatever menace lay around them. Its thick blanket appeared danger-filled, and it made Clairice want to cling tighter to the haven of the strong man who appeared the one tangible thing in a world of writhing gray mist. She felt the vibration of his voice deep in his chest as he said, "We are near the water now."

She turned and peered through the gloom. "How can you tell anything? I don't hear a sound except the horse and our own voices. This fog is terrible."

"Be thankful for it—it may be our salvation yet."

The path grew rougher and the horse slowed, picking its way. Suddenly there was a burst of noise behind them. Lord Ault's head whipped about, then he kicked the horse and leaned forward as they surged ahead. "The French!" he snarled under his breath.

"Are you certain?" Clairice gasped, but any answer was whipped away by the wind. Horses pounded behind them. Clairice's heart lunged at the noise. She clung tighter to Lord Ault and looked over her shoulder for any sign of water or a ship.

The mist rolled away and they were on the bank, the dark water glistening in the fog like black oil and lapping in a steady slap at the sloping land. Two men and a wide flat-bottomed boat waited at the water's edge.

"'Urry, there! They be comin'! This way and be quick!" they cried, pushing off without waiting.

Riding the horse into the water, Lord Ault leaped into the waves and swung Clairice from the saddle into the boat. He bent over to help push off the craft. "Away with it!" he shouted.

They moved into deeper water and he climbed into the boat. He produced a pistol from his belt and worked to prime it while the two men rowed for all they were worth.

The noise ashore was growing louder. The mist still hid any sight of the enemy, but the sound carried across the stillness of the water.

"Row heartier, lads, or we are done for!" Lord Ault cried.

Then the mists no longer hid the menace as rider upon rider broke into view and pounded into the water, firing a volley of shots at the slowly retreating target.

Lord Ault knelt to fire at the adversary. He glanced over his shoulder and commanded, "Clairice, get in the bottom. Get down!"

One of the seamen spoke. "'Ere, m'lord, 'ere's a pistol in me belt if ye can use it."

Instantly Clairice sat up and, to the astonishment of the man, pulled the pistol from the waistband of his breeches. Lord Ault was too occupied to notice her action.

Some of the French soldiers had ridden into the water, but the boat was slowly widening the distance between them. A shot hit the boat near Clairice with a sharp thunk and splintering of wood. She blinked in surprise, flinching away from the noise, then continued readying the pistol. She thrust it into Lord Ault's hands and lowered herself to the bottom of the boat. "Here, and get down yourself!"

"Clairice!" After a split second of stunned surprise he snatched it and fired.

A long scrape of wood against wood caused Clairice to sit up again. Shouts were heard at hand. She looked up and saw that they had reached the haven of the yacht. Shots still rang out and the ship was in line of fire, but far less exposed than the little boat had been.

"Get aboard!"

Lord Ault swung Clairice up to waiting hands, then scaled the side quickly and ordered, "Cast off!"

He then commanded, "Clairice, get to a cabin!" He passed her and hurried forward.

Chains rattled and timbers creaked as men hurried to and fro. Clairice knew she should do as she had been told and go to a cabin, but she could not bear to think of sitting with a group of people in a cabin away from the deck, away from all the action that meant escape or capture. She could not bear not to know what was happening to Lord Ault.

A longing for him swept through her. If only she had realized long ago her feeling for him! She hugged her arms about her, chilled now without his warmth close at hand. Spray from the water, together with the fog, was gradually causing the silk dress to cling with a cold thinness to her skin.

The shots from shore were coming as steadily as ever,

returned by a constant barrage from the men on ship. Lord Ault's voice rang out clearly, shouting commands.

The deck shifted and changed motion; they were seabound, the long wait over.

Flashes of fire showed from the gun bursts on shore. Even though a greater danger might lurk ahead, Clairice wanted away from that steady onslaught—away from France.

The gap slowly widened and the shots grew fainter. Then the fog closed in, hiding the shoreline and those along it. An occasional shot echoed and carried across the water.

Suddenly someone moved within a foot in front of her. Clairice gasped with surprise.

"Clairice!" Lord Ault whirled to discover her.

"I had to see—"

"You little fool. I told you to get to a cabin!"

She stared at him through the gloom, hardly aware of his words. "Are we safely away?"

"Aye," his voice was filled with concern, "but the biggest threat lies ahead. It's those damnable French ships."

"Won't we be able to get through in this fog?"

"I do not know," he replied truthfully. "We could sail right into a ship in this. But 'tis a better chance than no fog, so pray it doesn't lift."

For an instant they looked at each other in silence. Then Lord Ault took her arm. "Come with me."

He turned and lifted a lantern off a hook. He carried it to a small cabin filled with charts and maps, placed the lantern on a ledge and closed the door.

Clairice felt as though she could not get her breath. In the tiny cabin he appeared overpowering. He reached out and caught her arms and gently pulled her to him.

"Clairice, I must talk to you before we encounter the French. I do not know what lies ahead."

She gazed up at him and listened, afraid he would hear the wild thudding of her heart. His eyes held hers; a steely grimness made small lines about his mouth. He spoke harshly. "Clairice, when we return to England I intend to offer for you." Then his voice softened. "Clairice, I love you."

Her lips parted, her gaze was held by his as she replied, "I love you also."

His eyes changed, something flickered in the gray depths. He looked at her quizzically. "And what of those tender feelings you had for Mr. Harding?"

She laughed shakily. "Who is Mr. Harding?"

She had no chance to say more. He crushed her in his arms and his lips moved on hers, murmuring words of passion, of love. as he kissed her. He raised his head and looked into her eyes. "We will get through this. I shall not be thwarted this time!"

Clairice felt as though nothing on earth could harm her while his strong arms held her in their embrace. "I love you," she murmured.

He swept her up again in another crushing kiss. When he released her this time, he looked down at her sternly. "And no more outrageous flirting such as you did tonight!"

Clairice looked up, startled momentarily as she had forgotten about the French or anything else except the man before her. Then she smiled at him. "Jealous?"

"Terribly. I was ready to charge into that storeroom and throttle that damnable Frenchman for kissing you."

Clairice blushed in spite of his teasing voice. "How did you know?" she blurted.

He ignored the question, the mocking tone leaving his voice. "Also, if you pull your dress lower henceforth, it will be for me only!" He leaned down, and his warm lips lightly brushed her skin along the neckline of the green silk.

With a deep blush Clairice caught his head and raised it, feeling the thick soft curls against her fingers. He groaned in sudden intensity and folded her in a tighter embrace, his mouth a searing promise that made her senses reel.

Suddenly he released her. "I must go. Every second we are in mounting danger." He lifted the lantern off the ledge and paused, the mocking tone back in his voice. "If we ram a ship, I cannot be shut away in a cabin tumbling a maid!"

Clairice gasped, "How awful of you—"

He laughed and lightly brushed her lips, silencing her protests, then opened the door and stepped out on the deck. "Now, the cabins are that way." He pointed and asked sternly, "Can I trust you to get to one on your own and not hide out where you are in danger?"

She reached out and clutched his arm. "Please—I cannot wait in a cabin and wonder about you."

She heard the laughter in his voice. "What have I done—chosen a wife who'll forever follow me wherever I go?"

"I pray you are not in this much danger every day!" she exclaimed.

He grasped her shoulders and sobered quickly. "The French sloops could be around us even now. You should go inside, Clairice." He moved his hands slightly on her shoulders and peered at her. "Are you cold?"

"No, my lord."

"Clairice—" the amusement was back in his voice "—please call me Jonathan. I do not intend to be addressed by my wife as 'my lord'!"

"Jonathan," she murmured softly.

He looked down at her and sighed. "I am an utter fool to allow this, but come with me."

Without question Clairice followed him into the wheelhouse. Captain Barrow, Mr. Harding and two seamen were there. Lanterns swayed with the motion of the ship. The mingled odors of seawater and fish filled the small space.

At their entrance Captain Barrow turned and said, "We should be drawing close to the French by now."

Lord Ault had seemingly lost all awareness of her presence, and Clairice moved to a high seat to be out of the way.

"There must not be anything," Lord Ault emphasized, "to reveal our presence—no sound, no lights, nothing." He reached out and extinguished the nearest light.

Mr. Harding spoke quickly. "I'll see to the lights."

Lord Ault said softly, "I'll take the wheel, captain."

Darkness descended as Mr. Harding took the remaining lantern and left; everyone lapsed into silence with the exception of an occasional low-pitched exchange between the captain and Lord Ault. The motion of the ship was steady, rising and falling with a soft splash of waves. Other than a squeak of the wheel or grating of timbers, there was an utter silence that seemed as thick as the fog. Clairice locked her fingers together and peered hard out the high window at the gray swirling mist.

And as the yacht moved slowly forward, her tenseness grew until it was almost a tangible thing enveloping her.

The image of the prison came to her mind, and she shuddered. They must not be captured. Her sentiments on that concurred fully with Jonathan's. She realized how easily she had slipped into using his Christian name when, until a few moments ago, she had not even known it.

The mist boiled against the glass, opaque and menacing, hiding the French navy. Somewhere close by, the big sloops moved. She watched Jonathan turn the wheel slightly and wondered how he knew where to steer. The captain spoke in a low monotone to him. The fog seemed to thicken, and Clairice realized they might ram one of the French ships inadvertently any minute; it was absolutely impossible to see.

They were completely enclosed in a gray shroud. It looked as though she could reach out and grasp it in her hand...but then it would float away in streamers against the glass.

No progress was visible; nothing changed about the grayness on the other side of the panes. Her eyes had adjusted and she looked at Jonathan. He stood behind the wheel, slowly turning it, moving it slightly in his hands. She could not see his features clearly, and within a moment she turned her attention again to the window. Captain Barrow shifted and she turned.

The captain stepped closer to Lord Ault and declared softly, "Perhaps we have passed through their line."

Clairice strained to hear. "I don't think so," Lord Ault replied. "If there is a concentration of ships—a line of them off the coast around Calais—then I don't think we'll get through without encountering them."

She shivered and rubbed her hands over her arms; her eyes ached from the effort to detect anything through the fog. Nothing changed. The same grayness whipped past.

Then suddenly a shape emerged, more startling for its silence. It moved in a rush that was like a physical blow.

"Look!" Captain Barrow exclaimed in a hoarse whisper.

There was no need for his warning. All eyes were riveted to the glass. Clairice stiffened. The mists parted and the bulk of a large ship loomed over them.

Instead of the mist, they were now staring at a high wooden hull. Clairice wanted to scream. It looked as if they would crash into it, like hitting a solid mountain.

She turned to observe Jonathan. He spun the wheel rapidly, completely absorbed in what he was doing.

The ship seemed to fly at them, the planks of its hull clearly visible. The hull rushed past them like some predatory monster, giant and deadly, moving in quick silence.

And then it was gone. The fog closed in once more.

"We are past!" Clairice murmured softly, feeling weak. Instantly Jonathan answered in a quiet voice, "Perhaps, but there may be more."

"Pray God not," Captain Barrow said fervently.

Clairice remained silent, her fingers clasped tightly together while she stared through the glass and waited for another giant ship to bear down on them.

Finally Lord Ault broke the silence. "Get all the speed you can, captain. I want away from France."

"We are in a calm," Captain Barrow declared.

"Yes, but it is changing," Lord Ault remarked.

The captain seemed filled with concern. He faced Lord Ault and asked, "And if we meet another ship?"

"We will take that chance. We have drifted long enough."

Orders were given and men hurried to carry them out. The ship remained in darkness, but after a few moments Lord Ault said, "Captain, take the wheel." He stepped away. "No lights yet, not for a while. This fog could roll away and we would be exposed. For all we know, the entire French fleet may be within range of our own guns. I want away from France, as quickly as we can manage to do so."

"Aye, my lord."

"Clairice," Lord Ault said softly at her side and she felt his warm fingers close over hers. "Come with me."

They stepped out into the damp air and moved to the bow. Lines creaked as yards were hauled into place. Fog still rolled about them, and Clairice asked, "Do you think it is safe now?"

"No; at least we cannot be certain. I hope the French ships were in a line and we have passed through it."

He peered through the gloom, and Clairice realized he was not as certain as he sounded about not meeting another French ship. She started to ask, "What happens if another—"

He turned and placed his finger on her lips. "Shh. . . we shall not consider the possibility." His attention reverted to the fog. He placed his arm around her shoulders and pulled her to his side. Both stood and peered into the night; she felt the warmth of his body through the thin silk of her pelisse and dress. She laid her head lightly against his shoulder and his arm tightened, but he continued his vigil.

The rolling mist parted and a shiny black expanse of water was dark against the gray white fog.

"Damme!" he murmured.

She looked ahead in alarm, but could see nothing "What is it?"

"The fog is lifting. Pray that we have passed the French navy, for I think we are losing our protection."

As if to demonstrate his statement, another patch of water showed. Then fog closed over it and once again they were enveloped in gray, but in seconds they sailed into another open stretch of water.

Lord Ault stood quietly watching the sea. They moved through the water undisturbed but still he did not move. A chill began to penetrate Clairice; the damp air was cold against her skin. As though he could read her thoughts, Jonathan looked down and asked softly, "Cold?"

"Yes."

He pulled her close in front of him and wrapped his arms around her. "Now, is this better?"

"Yes," she murmured, feeling as she had earlier, that there could be no danger anywhere as long as she was in the circle of his arms.

They sailed on; the fog thinned to streamers of gray floating over a black sea. Lord Ault's attention remained fixed on the horizon.

He stiffened suddenly, and Clairice strained to see what had caused it.

A great hulking ship loomed in view off starboard bow, and a wave of coldness washed through her.

Then, to her shock, Lord Ault whooped loudly and lifted her high in exultation. "It is the Royal Navy! Never did a ship look so beautiful! Hurrah! Clairice, my darling love—we have made it safely home!" He put her down gently as his cries were echoed all over the ship.

Within seconds, lights began flickering on. Lord Ault

swept Clairice to him again in a long hard kiss, then released her and breathed, "Home!" He looked down at her. "We have done it!" He ripped off the coat of the French uniform and flung it over the rail into the sea, then pulled her to him once more in a crushing embrace.

Tears of joy and relief filled Clairice's eyes. Passengers began to stream onto the deck. "I must find grandmother," Clairice said. Before she had taken two steps a couple lurched into view. Their arms were entwined and their voices raised in song to "His Majesty the King."

"Jonathan, look!" Clairice exclaimed and tugged at his sleeve in disbelief at the sight of Aunt Lavinia and Sir Barthwell!

"Gammon," Lord Ault whispered, then broke into a peal of hearty laughter. "Old Barthwell. . . that silly old maid!"

"She is, at that," Clairice murmured.

He laughed. "I was not speaking of Miss Milsap."

They continued on, leaving the pair to themselves, and found Adele and Lady Fairfax standing at the rail. Lady Fairfax turned to gaze up at Lord Ault.

"Well, young man, you succeeded in getting us safely home."

He smiled down at her. "I had a little help along the way."

CHAPTER FIFTEEN

Clairice studied herself critically in the hall mirror. She straightened a blue ribbon on the soft white muslin dress. Its classic skirt clung to her slender figure, and the round neck flattered her face, which was framed by the shining red hair that curled across her shoulders.

Adele stood to one side watching; she laughed and clapped her hands together. "Do quit fretting, Clairice. You look beautiful!"

"But what could they be doing so long?" Clairice whispered and looked at the closed library door.

Adele's eyes twinkled. "It is not every day that grandmother gets to consent to a granddaughter's wedding; do not rush them. I do think it's exciting!"

Clairice looked at her sister, and all concern left her face. She dimpled. "I suspect it shall not be long before she will be consenting to another."

Adele's eyes softened. "Perhaps."

Clairice's attention returned to the library door, then she looked once again in the mirror to search for any imperfection.

The door opened a fraction and Lord Ault called her name. When she rushed to him, he grasped her hand and looked down at her in such a manner that a thrill ran swiftly through her. She gazed up questioningly. His eyes danced, but he remained silent as he led her inside, then closed the door.

Across the library, Lady Fairfax, dressed in blue silk, was ensconced in a large wing chair with her feet propped up and her cane in hand. Her white hair glowed about her face and she looked supremely happy.

The tall windows to the terrace were thrown open and sunlight poured into the room. The fragrance from a large bouquet of May roses filled the air, but Clairice was unaware of it or anything else except the tall man at her side and her grandmother.

Lord Ault turned to Clairice and smiled; then spoke in a tone she had rarely heard. "Your grandmother has given her consent to our marriage." He leaned forward and kissed her lightly on the forehead.

Clairice smiled up at him for an instant, then turned and rushed to Lady Fairfax. "Grandmother! I am so happy!"

Before she could say more, the door opened and Betsy appeared with an enormous silver tray laden with an ornate oversized silver teapot, creamer and sugar, fine porcelain cups, an elegant cake knife and sugar tongs. Crumpets swam in butter; there were sandwiches of cucumber and watercress, strawberry jam and thin strips of celery. Betsy placed the tray before Lady Fairfax and withdrew quietly. Clairice sat across from her grandmother on a small love seat, and Lord Ault sank down beside her.

He regarded the tray and raised an eyebrow. "The last time I did this, it changed my life."

Lady Fairfax smiled. "All for the best, you must add."

He met her eyes and smiled. "I suspect that you prefer to hear me admit it in so many words."

She laughed and raised a cup to pour the tea.

Lord Ault said with a note of wry amusement, "I suspect this is the granddaughter you wanted me to wed all along."

Lady Fairfax handed Clairice a cup of tea and replied, "You are well suited."

Lord Ault smiled. "I agree with you fully."

The tea was served and Lady Fairfax sat back in her chair. "What does Prinny think of the invasion plans?"

Lord Ault's brow raised. "That is quite a confidential matter."

"Bosh! I am to be your grandmother-in-law, and I would think by now you know you can trust me."

His lips twitched slightly as he exchanged a look with Clairice, then remarked dryly, "I have a suspicion my orderly life is gone forever."

Lady Fairfax waited in silence and Lord Ault's smile faded. "He was pleased to get the plans. All along the coast we are readying for such an event. I pray it never comes, and there is hope that it won't."

Lady Fairfax cocked her head to one side. "What would prevent it? Boney has the men to commit such an act."

A hard note came into Lord Ault's voice. "True. But we have Lord Nelson and the Royal Navy. If we can keep the French ships blockaded—" he shook his head, his eyes grave "—then perhaps such a dreadful event can be circumvented."

"Pray that it is," Lady Fairfax said fervently. With an abrupt change of subject she inquired, "When is the wedding to be?"

"As soon as possible," Lord Ault replied. "I should like for it to be in May."

"You are in quite a rush. You are getting a child bride, Lord Ault."

He looked at Clairice. She flushed hotly at his glance, and as she smiled up at him he said dryly, "I suspect that she is sufficiently like a certain relative to be quite a woman."

Lady Fairfax chuckled. "Whatever you both plan will be fine with me."

Lord Ault sipped his tea, then looked up in surprise. "This is ordinary tea...."

"Yes," Clairice laughed. "Grandmother took such a large quantity of her brew to Paris, and so much was lost or consumed, that she is without any."

"All that is left is at Fairfax Hall now," her grandmother informed him. "I have asked to have some fetched to London. It will be here in time for the wedding."

"Heaven forbid!" Lord Ault leaned forward. "We shall have none of that brew at our wedding! It has done enough to all of us now."

"Calm yourself, Lord Ault. If you do not want my brew at the wedding, then none will be present."

He regarded Clairice and smiled. "I think that is best."

Lady Fairfax said, "Be off with both of you! You look too lovesick to stay and chat with me."

"Grandmother!" Clairice blushed, but Lord Ault rose and took her hands. "Come, Clairice, out to the garden." She moved ahead of him to the terrace. Lord Ault turned to Lady Fairfax and gazed down at her.

"You were right; I do thank you for forcing me to accompany you to Paris. I am delighted to have you for a relative. It will do my family a world of good!" He leaned down and kissed her cheek, then said sternly, but with a twinkle in his gray eyes, "But never, never foist that damnable tea on any of my children!"

She chuckled and gazed fondly at him. "Clairice is waiting."

He turned and hurried outside. Clairice, standing in the doorway, moved easily beside him. They descended the stone steps into a garden filled with a riot of color. There were roses in every shade of yellow, red and pink, as well as forget-me-nots and daisies. Behind a high clipped hedge Lord Ault stopped and pulled her into his arms.

He kissed her passionately, then released her slightly to smile down at her. "My darling Clairice, how I love you! I have loved you forever and I always will."

She laughed with joy. "You have not known me always—and you certainly did not love me at first!"

The corner of his mouth curled. "Oh, yes, I did! I simply was too stuffy to recognize my own feelings."

Clairice blushed. "I will never listen at a keyhole again."

He laughed. "You took my staid, orderly bachelor life and wrecked it, my darling—and thank heaven you did! I will spend a lifetime showing you my gratitude and how much I love you."

She gazed up into his eyes, her whole being swept with longing for him. "I love you, Jonathan, with all my heart."

His lips came down on hers, warm and gentle, touching her tenderly with love. His kiss changed as he crushed her against him. Burning with passion, his mouth awakened responses from Clairice that she had never experienced. She clung to him with rapture, and joy filled her entire being at the thought of the love that would be theirs forever.

Harlequin reaches
into the hearts and minds
of women across America
to bring you

Harlequin American Romance ™

Harlequin American Romance

Twice in a Lifetime
REBECCA FLANDERS

YOURS FREE!

Enter a uniquely exciting new world with

Harlequin American Romance™

Harlequin American Romances are the first romances to explore today's love relationships. These compelling novels reach into the hearts and minds of women across America... probing the most intimate moments of romance, love and desire.

You'll follow romantic heroines and irresistible men as they boldly face confusing choices. Career first, love later? Love without marriage? Long-distance relationships? All the experiences that make love real are captured in the tender, loving pages of **Harlequin American Romances**.

What makes American women so different when it comes to love? Find out with **Harlequin American Romance!**

Send for your introductory FREE book now!

Get this book FREE!

Mail to:
Harlequin Reader Service

In the U.S.
2504 West Southern Avenue
Tempe, AZ 85282

In Canada
649 Ontario Street
Stratford, Ontario N5A 6W2

YES! I want to be one of the first to discover **Harlequin American Romance**. Send me FREE and without obligation *Twice in a Lifetime*. If you do not hear from me after I have examined my FREE book, please send me the 4 new **Harlequin American Romances** each month as soon as they come off the presses. I understand that I will be billed only $2.25 for each book (total $9.00). There are no shipping or handling charges. There is no minimum number of books that I have to purchase. In fact, I may cancel this arrangement at any time. *Twice in a Lifetime* is mine to keep as a FREE gift, even if I do not buy any additional books.

Name	(please print)	

Address		Apt. no.

City	State/Prov.	Zip/Postal Code

Signature (If under 18, parent or guardian must sign.)

154-BPA-NADZ

AR-SUB-300